Praise fo

"Porn legend Aiden Shaw's comm ... big gay party of the 90s is so sharp it will draw blood. Shaw's wry take on those drugged-out weekends that go on forever is never less than brilliant." *GI*

"Aiden Shaw's descriptions of tripping must now rank among the finest in literature – roll over Bill Burroughs – and the sex scenes are brilliant. This is an affectionate account of lost souls meandering in a doomed world. He has clearly been there, done it, survived and sent us the postcard. Recommended." *G-News*

"There's loads of pill-popping, hands-in-the-air club moments and of course plenty of sex, but at the same time there are many tender moments to keep you romantics happy." *Boyz*

"Engrossing, highly readable fiction... It would be difficult for an open-hearted reader to put down this book without having been enriched, a little stunned and somewhat educated." *Gay Times*

"A saucy, drug-addled tale of fast living and shifting alliances in modern gay England." *Gay People's Chronicle*

"If you want a few hundred pages of witty banter about love lives worked out in every possible combination, and fuelled by every imaginable drug, *Wasted* does nicely." Amazon.co.uk

"Following on from his uncompromising novels *Brutal* and *Boundaries*, sexual outlaw, renowned porn star and now exceptional author Aiden Shaw presents a harsh and gritty view of a world broken down... in his honest, intelligent prose." *AXM*

"Intense." *MAN* magazine

"Shaw sensitively evokes a sad, pressurised world, demonstrating that no matter how beautiful and sexualised you are, loneliness and death are still part of the equation." *The List*

"A roller-coaster of a good read." *Positive Nation*

Aiden Shaw has been a photographer and a director of pop promos, a model and an actor. He has an international reputation as a star of American-made hardcore films and is probably Britain's best-known male sex star. His first novel, *Brutal,* was published in 1996 and has been reprinted several times since, as well as being translated into German and French. His second novel, *Boundaries,* appeared in 1999; *Wasted* is his third. He is also the author of *If Language at the Same Time Shapes and Distorts Our Ideas and Emotions, How Do We Communicate Love?* (1996), a volume of poetry.

Wasted

AIDEN SHAW

First published 2001 by GMP (Gay Men's Press),
PO Box 3220, Brighton BN2 5AU

Reprinted 2003

GMP is an imprint of Millivres Prowler Limited,
part of the Millivres Prowler Group,
Spectrum House, 32–34 Gordon House Road, London NW5 1LP

www.gaymenspress.co.uk

World Copyright © 2001, 2003 Aiden Shaw

Aiden Shaw has asserted his right to be identified as the author of
this work in accordance with the Copyright, Designs and Patents Act 1988

A CIP catalogue record for this book is available from the British Library

ISBN 1-902852-34-6

Distributed in the UK and Europe by Airlift Book Company,
8 The Arena, Mollison Avenue,
Enfield, Middlesex EN3 7NJ
Telephone: 020 8804 0400

Distributed in North America by Consortium,
1045 Westgate Drive, St Paul, MN 55114-1065
Telephone: 1 800 283 3572

Distributed in Australia by Bulldog Books,
PO Box 300, Beaconsfield, NSW 2014

Printed and bound in Finland by WS Bookwell

Limited by the world, which I oppose, jagged by it,
I shall be all the more handsome and sparkling as the angles
which wound me and give me shape are more acute and the
jagging more cruel

(Jean Genet, *The Thief's Journal*)

1

The door opened, and David stood grinning.

'Had enough, hey?' he said.

Ryan slid a large rucksack off his shoulder.

'So enough.'

'What happened exactly?'

'She found some pot in my jacket.'

'And?'

'Big deal, right?'

'She's a different generation.'

'She's only a year older than you.'

'Yeah, but she's a parent. They're a different species.'

'From Planet Freaky.'

'I don't need to tell you she loves you, do I?'

Ryan shifted his weight from one leg to the other, sighed and said, 'Are you going to make me stand out here all day?'

'Cheeky!'

'You love it.'

'Well, I love you,' said David. 'So I guess I love it.'

'That's why I'm here.' Ryan took hold of David's arm. 'Listen, I appreciate this.'

'Shut up, you soft bugger. I couldn't have you sleeping on the street.'

The house smelled of fresh paint. It had, as long as Ryan could remember. He had been visiting David for years. Ryan was taken into the living room. It was empty apart from a wooden bench, which faced a huge tv monitor. On the floor were some beer cans and what looked like a paper wrap from some drug. Knowing David and Joe, he guessed it was cocaine.

'I see you're a beer drinker,' said Ryan.

'Love it.'

'Me too.'

'You drink?'

'I *am* sixteen.'

'Woo! A proper person finally.'

'Not so proper.'

'Make yourself comfortable,' said David leaving the room and heading towards the kitchen.

Ryan sat on the bench. 'Yeah, sixteen, so don't mess.'

'I wouldn't,' said David as he returned. 'I don't want to have to deal with the NSPCC.'

'Hey, less of the C. If you don't mind.'

'Oh that's right, you're sixteen.' David handed Ryan a can of beer.

'You read my mind.'

'No, your expression.'

'Whatever. Cheers.'

Ryan opened his can, tipped it to toast David and took several swigs. David was surprised how old Ryan seemed. Since Ryan was eight, David had seen him nearly every year. Still, it surprised him that his nephew was turning into a man. Not just any man, but one of the most beautiful David had ever seen. As Ryan drank, he lifted his head back, and his baby-blond hair scrunched on his neck. Relaxing, he lay back on the bench revealing his hairless tummy. For a moment David watched Ryan's Adam's apple moving up and down as he swallowed.

'Do you feel different now you're a man?'

'Don't patronise me, please.'

'Sorry, puppy.'

'I said, don't patronise me.'

'I didn't.'

'Puppy?'

'It's a term of affection. Please let me call you that. I call everybody I like puppy.'

'Okay,' said Ryan and looked about his new home. 'Where's Joe?'

'He's gone to the West End with some kid.'

'Bitter?'

'No. I just don't know his name.'

'I saw the Levi's ad he did,' said Ryan. 'That was so cool.'

'Yeah, Joe's cool all right.'

'There's that tone in your voice again.'

'I'm just a bit down. I could do with a holiday.'

'So why don't you have one?'

'The first reason's money, the second's work. Saying that, I guess they'd be okay about it.'

'So go.'

'And you won't have a party when I'm away?'

'Of course not.'

'Of course you would. You act as if I was never young.'

'You were young?'

'In the Eighties. Or Seventies.'

'Keep going.'

'The Sixties?'

'Try Fifties.'

'Give me a break,' said David. 'I'm only thirty. How old did you think I was?' He saw Ryan smile. 'Stop, don't you dare.'

'You know I dare.'

'That's what I hate about you.' He paused. 'And love. Did you have any problem with the tube?'

'No, but it took ages.'

'That's the Northern Line for you.'

'You think there'd be a special service for their Hampstead clientele. A high-speed train.'

'Get recent. London Underground, spend money?'

'Sorry,' said Ryan, thinking David was trying to sound hip.

'I'm not up with your big city ways.'

'You country kids are so adorable.'

'I hardly think Manchester's classed as country.'

'Where is that place, anyway?'

'What place?'

'That Manfester place you mentioned. I have heard of it.'

'It's Manch*ester*. And it's a little place in between here and San Francisco.'

'I thought that was New York.'

'It's near New York.'

'You must take me sometime. While I'm there I'll visit Judy.'

'It's funny hearing her called that.'

'What should I call her?'

'Mum.'

'It would be a bit twisted calling my sister mum. Don't you think?'

'That would suit you.'

'Enough,' said David. 'You're too quick for your own good.'

'That's what my girlfriend says.'

'You've got a girlfriend?'

'Yeah! Not everyone's gay.'

'In that case, where do babies come from?'

'What?'

'Just kidding!'

'You're a funny one, David.'

'Thank you. Anyway, what's she called?'

'Her name's Leila, but she answers to baby, foxy, or slut, depending on her mood.'

Ryan thought Leila was beautiful. She was six feet tall. Her lips, eyes and general face shape verged on average. This worked to her advantage. Make-up artists could make her look any way they chose. Once, when modelling for Vivienne Westwood, she went on drinking whisky from a bottle. Then she showed her cunt to the photographers at the front of the catwalk. She wasn't allowed back on.

Leila was infatuated with Ryan, so when he dyed his hair green, she did too, and when he shaved his head, so did she. They looked stunning together. They had been seeing each other a little over a year. Leila often tried to impress Ryan. She knew he liked unusual behaviour, so played up to this. One of her favourite tricks was to shock strangers. When entering a busy café, she would stand in the middle of it and lift her skirt over her head. Leila generally didn't wear underwear. Usually nobody complained. Women tended to pull a sympathetic expression, or look away. Men simply stared; embarrassed, confused, and excited.

Another of her favourites might follow immediately afterwards. She'd sit next to somebody, sometimes at a table full of people. Putting her head in her hand, and resting on one elbow, she'd stare at the food they were eating. She'd lick her lips, not taking her eyes off the plate in front of them. After a short time, the people who were eating would often give her their food. Other times, she'd wait until they were finished eating, then ask if she could have what was left. If they said yes, she'd slide the plate in front of her, and using their fork, would finish their meal. Predictably, she was banned from several cafés. Still, Ryan encouraged her behaviour, thinking it was funny.

Ryan painted Leila's car. It was gaudy and unusual. He used regular household paints. Five colours. Orange, lime-green (which Ryan's father once used on a backdrop for a school play), red, blue, and yellow (originally used to brighten up the cellar, where Ryan's mother liked to go to read her Bible, or just get away from the rest of the family). Using a large brush, Ryan painted squares randomly, all over the car, then stuck plastic flowers on with superglue. As they drove around Manchester, people always stared. More annoyingly, the police stopped them too often.

When Leila's head was shaved, she took to wearing a long red curly wig. On close inspection, it was obviously not real hair, but from a few feet away it was surprisingly deceptive. When stopped at a red light, other drivers would always look to see who was driving. This is when Ryan took hold of the wig, from the bottom, out of sight. Slowly, he'd pull at the wig so it slid back, off Leila's head. Sometimes, she would pretend nothing had happened, simply turn towards those watching and smile. Other times, she would face the other drivers, put both her hands to her head and scream.

Leila had a scar in the middle of her chest, two inches under the base of her neck. She liked to wear V-necks, so it showed clearly. No matter how glamorous a dress she was wearing, it was never covered. The way it was displayed seemed to say, "So what!" She lived off a large allowance given her by her parents, so had enough money to have it removed, but preferred to keep it.

'I like her,' said Ryan.

'Sounds serious.'

'I didn't use the L word.'

'Everyone knows like is a euphemism.'

'Give me a break.'

'Sorry! Don't straight guys do love?'

'No, it's so Victorian. Why? Do gay guys?'

'Of course not. We're famous for our fickle relationships, and proud.'

'Oh, yeah! I saw the movie Cruising.'

'It's all we do, you know.'

'That, and decorate.' Ryan looked around.

'Yeah, but you have to admit, we do it well.'

'What, decorate or cruise?'

Now David looked around at the décor, gesturing subtly with his eyes. 'Cruise, of course.'

'Of course.'

'So. What's going to happen with Leila now?'

'She said she'd move down here as well. Manfester's too small for her, anyway.'

'We'll have to meet her first, but she could always stay here until you both get settled.'

'Cool!'

'Don't mention anything to her yet. First, let me have a word with Joe.'

'God that would be so great.'

'Room, we've got,' said David, using a caricature of a Jewish accent.

'What rooms they are.' As Ryan spoke he got up and walked over to one of the walls. It was covered in A-four pieces of paper, with writing on. They'd been pasted on, like wallpaper.

'What's this?'

'A fairytale.'

'I won't make the obvious joke.'

'You'd be the first not to.'

'Who wrote it?'

'Joe did. You might recognise it. I read it to you when you were a kid.'

'No, I don't remember,' said Ryan, and paused. He read a little. 'Nice idea.'

'Thanks. It was Christmas, the first time you visited. I read it to you in bed.'

'Ah! Heart-warming.'

'You loved it at the time.'

'I bet I did. It looks sweet, but I really can't remember.'

'Really?'

'Sorry, I'll read it sometime, see if it jolts my memory. But, why on the wall?'

'I haven't a clue. It was Joe's idea.' David paused, seemingly distracted. 'He likes how it looks, I guess.'

'He's an even funnier one.'

'He's so creative.'

'That sounds like you're referring to his sexuality, or what he likes to do in bed.'

'He is creative in bed.'

'Spare me the details.'

'You're the one who brought it up.'

'Actually, I'd love to know what you get up to.'

'Really?'

'It's interesting for me. I haven't a clue, you know. What's the weirdest thing you've ever done?'

'Joe's not weird,' said David. Then, almost wistfully, 'He's quite vanilla actually.'

'Ah! Give me something juicier than that.'

'Well, it would have to be somebody else then. I used to see this man called Rob.'

'Yeah.'

'He used to like to take Rohypnol, that's a sleeping tablet.'

'I know. Do you think I was born yesterday?'

'Almost. I don't know what you get up to. Anyway, it's hard to get hold of now.'

'You've just got to know the right people.'

'And do you?'

'My man can get me any shit I want,' said Ryan with an admirable Brooklyn accent. David was a little surprised. Ryan dropped it seamlessly and continued, 'Anyway, what about Rob?'

'Oh yeah. Rob. He used to like us to take enough to knock us out. It usually took three or four to do the trick properly.'

'So what's so fun about sleeping?'

'Only one of us would sleep. The other would do whatever he wanted.'

'I get you.'

'I *mean* whatever.'

'Did you do it to him?'

'Oh yes.'

'What did you do?'

'I'd usually play with him for a while. Then I'd usually end up fucking him.'

'Jesus!'

'I used to love it.'

'You let him do it to you.'

'Of course.'

'But he could have done anything.'

'Exactly. Sexy, huh?'

'I guess so.'

'The thought of it still turns me on.'

'I'll have to try it sometime.' Ryan blushed. 'With Leila, I mean.'

David smiled. 'Of course.'

2

'My place. Eight o'clock.'

'Sure.'

'Okay. See you later.'

'Flora?'

'Yes.'

'I'm really looking forward to it.'

'Good.'

Flora put the receiver down. For a moment she stared into space, her eyes squinting. She was lost in thought.

The phone rang again, bringing her back to the present.

'Flora?' It was the same voice as before.

'This better be good.'

'Do you like me?'

'I'll show you tonight, eight o'clock. Bye.' Flora hung up.

She finished work, went to the gym, popped round to see her drug dealer. By the time she got home it was seven o'clock, so she just had time to eat, and quickly get ready.

The doorbell rang. Flora walked to the door as she reached back under her blouse to fasten her bra. She was having trouble.

'Fuck!' she said, gave up, reached for the door handle and pulled it open aggressively.

A man stood leaning against the door surround. He had a large bottle of vodka in one hand and a bottle of Dom Perignon in the other.

'Madame,' he said, with an exaggerated French accent.

'Hey cutie,' said Flora.

'Have I caught you at a bad time?'

'No, it's just this fucking bra.'

'Let me help.'

'I want to do it up, not take it off.'

'Would I?'

'Err. Yes!'

'No really! Let me help.'

'Is there any point? It will be coming off soon.'

'That's the kind of talk I like.'

'That's if you're horny.' Flora paused for a reaction, and she got one. It was positive, and excited. 'Would you like that?'

'Sir, yes sir!'

Flora smiled and said, 'I think I like that.'

'Sir, yes sir!'

'Yes, let's keep it.'

'Sir . . .'

Flora cut him off. 'Okay! I'm over it already.'

The man didn't reply, only put his head down and looked hurt. Seeing this, Flora softened, 'Oh, come on, you,' she said. 'Do you want a coffee, a drink, a line of crystal?'

'Ugh! I don't know how you can do that stuff. Caffeine keeps me up all night. Just some crystal, please.'

'That's my boy.'

Flora went to a nearby table. There was a mirror on it, with two big lines already prepared.

'After you,' said Flora.

The man picked up a gold tube beside the mirror, bent down, and snorted hard. Flora stood behind, looking at his arse.

'Nice view,' she said, and got hold of his hips.

He turned round and pulled her close. 'This way's okay, as well. I hope.'

'I rather like the other, but I've got plans for that later.'

'What plans?'

'You'll see.'

'What are you up to?'

Flora bent down to do her line. 'I said, you'll see.' As she came up she held a finger against each nostril. 'God, that stuff burns.'

'You're telling me.'

'So how about some champagne?'

'Oui, Madame.'

Flora poured a drink, knocked back the first, and then immediately poured another. She handed one to the man, then took hold of his hand and led him across the room. She pushed him onto the sofa, unbuttoned her blouse and opened it.

'Shit!'

She wore a sheer blue bra, but it was still undone.

'You look fuck . . .'

Flora cut the man off in mid-sentence. 'You can stop there.'

'Okay, you look fuck.'

'Do I really? You're so sweet.'

'Or should I add, able.'

'Not necessary. Fuck's fine. I think I get your gist.'

Flora put her wrists together, lowered her hands, and her bra slid off. In the same movement, she unzipped her skirt, and let it drop. Now she stood in a pair of black high-heeled shoes, and a pair of seamless tights, exactly the same colour as the bra that had dangled from her neck moments before. The man looked at her without her clothes on. His eyes darted over her body, but at the same time they lingered, enjoying the view. He caught Flora's eye, and for a split second, he thought he saw indecision, even vulnerability. This was something he never expected to see there. It made his groin ache with desire. Within the same second he smiled.

'You're so goddamn fuck.'

'Keep your mouth shut, unless you want it filled.'

Flora knelt over him, and kissed him for a few seconds. Then she straightened up, took hold of one of her breasts and aimed its nipple towards the man's lips. Then she let the whole weight of her body squash against him. The nipple was dead on target.

'Mm!'

'Suck on mama's nipple.'

'Mm, mm, mm!'

'Yeah. There's a good boy.'

Flora pulled away. 'You're hungry for that nipple, hey? Crystal will make my baby so piggy.' Flora held his face in between her hands and looked at him. She squashed his cheeks together, making his lips pucker. Unable to resist them she leant forward and opened her mouth around them. This turned into a passionate kiss. Her tongue went deep into his mouth. She groaned, pulled away abruptly, then got off his lap.

'Let's do another line.'

'Whatever mama wants.'

'That's my boy!'

Again she swigged back a glass of champagne and poured another. When the man bent over, Flora reached round from behind, undid the button and unzipped his fly. She pulled his jeans down over his solid thighs and knelt, taking them to his ankles.

'Off with these.'

The man stepped out of his jeans. Flora came back up and did the same to his underpants. When she came up, she leant over his back and took hold of one of his arse cheeks. Then she straightened up, leant back and looked down. The man's arse was small, round and very pale.

'Jesus! Your arse is good enough to eat.'

'So eat it.'

'So, bend over.'

The man bent over the table again. He used the back of his hands to support his chin. Flora knelt down and kissed his arse.

'You're fucking hot,' he said.

'You ain't seen nothing yet.'

Flora ran her tongue down the crack of his arse.

'My God,' said the man.

'Let's go into the bedroom,' said Flora, and passed him his glass.

'Actually,' he said, 'I fancy a vodka.'

'Good idea,' said Flora.

She poured and drank two large shots then headed towards the bedroom, taking the champagne with her. She pushed open the door with her hip, kicked off her shoes, and put the champagne on the bedside cabinet.

'Where do you want me?' said the man.

'On the bed. Face down.'

The man pulled off his sweatshirt, and despite the swirls of dark hair, his frame still looked wel-defined.

'So what's in store?'

'Do you trust me?' said Flora.

'Sure.'

'Okay. Lie down. Relax, and I'll be back in a second.'

Flora darted out of the room, leaving the man lying naked, with his face in the pillow. She was gone a good five minutes.

'Flora!' the man shouted.

'I'm coming. Close your eyes.'

She stood just outside the door. 'Are they closed?'

'Yeah,' said the man, wondering what was going on. He heard Flora come back into the room. She must have stood at the end of the bed. He felt her lift one of his legs, and move it away from the other. He now lay with his legs wide open.

'What are you up to?'

'You'll see.'

She knelt on the bed in between his legs. The man felt Flora lift one his arse cheeks, and push something against the hole. It felt slippery.

'What's that?'

'Patience!'

Flora massaged the man's arsehole, until it began to relax. She started to prod it a little. He moaned and arched his back, his arse pushing against her finger.

'Slow down, greedy,' she said.

Flora took her hand away. Next the man felt something odd, hard and scratchy against his sphincter.

'What the fuck?'

Something spurted inside, warm and tingling. He'd never felt anything like it. 'What the hell's that?'

'It's a booty bump.'

'I hate to sound naïve, but what's a booty bump?'

'Crystal.'

'What?'

'Crystal in water.'

The man tried to look around at Flora. 'How?'

'With a syringe.'

'Jesus. You're a crazy bitch.'

'I'll take that as a compliment. It's how everyone does crystal these days. It's less hard on the sinuses and it's a smoother ride.'

'Smoother ride?'

'The high kind of comes from within, and it feels less twitchy too.'

'Since when have you been such an expert?'

'I first read about it on the Net.'

'Hang on,' said the man. Then he paused and squirmed. 'Ooh!'

'You feel it?'

The man didn't answer at first. Then he said, 'Woo, woo, woo.'

'You feel it.'

'Woo.'

'You're very eloquent all of a sudden.'

'You can hardly complain. You did this to me.'

'And aren't you grateful?'

'Fucking yeah.'

'I know what will help that.' With this she rammed her face into his arse and pushed her tongue into his hole.

'Jesus!' he said loudly. Then his voice got even louder. 'Woo!'

Flora slapped his arse. 'That's right cowboy. Fucking squirm.'

'I love that.'

'Of course you do. I've never met a man who didn't.'

'I'm not surprised.'

'You've never had it done before?'

'No.'

'In that case, this night might be one you never forget.' Flora reached over and picked up the champagne. 'Let's drink to that.'

'But I don't know what I'm drinking to.'

'Let's just say, new experiences.' Flora took a swig and passed it on.

'To letting go,' said the man twisting his torso just enough to take a swig.

'To beautiful arses,' said Flora and swigged.

The man pulled it away from her mouth. 'Hey, don't finish it.' Champagne ran down her throat. 'To mama's juicy . . .'

Flora leant forward and pressed her breasts into the side of his face, muffling the end of his sentence.

'What, these? To baby's juicy dick.' As she said this she slid her hand under his abdomen and got hold of it.

'You haven't given it much attention.'

'I'll get round to that. I'm going to ask you again. Do you trust me?'

'Sure. What more can I say?'

'Will you let me do whatever I want?'

'Yeah.'

'Can I tie you up?'

'I guess so.' It's not that this man trusted Flora particularly, but if what he'd experienced so far was anything to go by, he didn't care. The crystal was already affecting his decision-making. This was exactly what Flora had hoped for.

'Okay, stud.' Flora reached to the side of the bed, and felt under the mattress. 'There!' she said. The man had his arms above him, with his face in the pillow, so couldn't see what was going on. Flora clicked a pair of handcuffs around his wrists.

He looked up at them. 'Hey! What's this shit?' He got up onto his elbows.

'Calm down, cowboy. Are you scared of little old me?'

'No.'

'So behave. Come on, be nice to mama.' The man lay back down. 'This is where the fun begins. Close your eyes, baby.'

He did as he was asked and heard shuffling, a cupboard door squeak on its hinge, a drawer open and close, then an odd sound. It was almost familiar. Flora's breathing seemed to change. It was held, released, then stammered. Possibly it sounded like somebody was trying to put on something that didn't quite fit. He was confused. 'Here comes the good bit.' Flora knelt on the bed again, between his legs. Again, he felt the slippery sensation on his arsehole. A finger slipped into his arse. It eased in and out, at the edge of his sphincter. Gradually, it went in deeper. She began to use two fingers. The man squirmed more than ever, thrusting his balls into the bed, then pushing his arse back towards her hand. Each time her fingers went in deeper. And each time he groaned a little more. His breathing became heavy, his grinding deeper.

'Fucking hell, Flora. That feels amazing.'

'I've only just started.'

'You do what the fuck you want.'

'That's exactly what I was going to do.'

'Please. Do what ever you want,' said the man, his voice muffled by the pillow.

'Don't you worry, baby. I'm going to take good care of you.'

The sensation in his arse got better, then better. It felt like she was climbing inside. He'd never felt anything like it. Flora continued to prod his arse, but she no longer used her fingers. A thick rubber shaft now pushed in deeper and deeper. Flora pulled back her hips and the shaft came with her. She pushed forward and it disappeared inside.

'Fucking hell. What are you doing?'

'I'm fucking you, baby.'

'What?'

'I'm fucking your hard arse, my sweet baby.' Again, she thrust forward. He cried, 'Fucking hell!'

'This isn't hell, baby. It's the nearest thing to heaven you'll ever feel.'

'I believe you mama.'

Flora pounded the arse beneath her, giving him no time to react. With each thrust came a cry. Then before he had voiced it, another came. Simply pounding, and pounding, fucking and fucking.

'Do you like my dick up your arse?'

'I love it.'

'Beg for it, baby.'

'Please, please, please.'

'Beg me to fuck you with my big dick.'

'Please fuck me. Please don't stop!'

Flora looked down and could see the shiny rod sliding in and out. Like a mirror image, another went inside, into her cunt. There was even a little bit that prodded her clitoris. So each time she thrust, it tickled her, making her wet. It was such a clever contraption; so handsome, and so useful. So this was what it was like to fuck. No wonder men went crazy for it; the competence, control, and intrusion. Such a beautiful arse, to honour and defile. She wanted to bite it, but kept fucking it instead.

Flora fell forward onto the man's back. Her face was at the nape of his neck. She could smell the odour oozing from within him, and could feel his body heat.

'Fucking hell!' cried the man. Flora's pace increased. Her dick hovered at the edge of his hole, then plunged all the way in. The man's body seemed to spasm. 'Oh God!' Flora did the same thing again. 'You're going to have to stop!' His voice gravelled, and he didn't use proper words. He almost couldn't. The sensation was too intense. He was all physicality now, with no logic, or reason, or clear strands of thoughts. 'Jesus, fucking Jesus!' he cried. There was only sensation, followed by ecstatic pleasure. It surged through his body. 'I can't take much more. Please, please, please!'

'Please more?'

'No. I don't know.' He started to sob. 'I don't know!' As though it were an after-thought, the man took hold of his dick. After just a couple of strokes, he said, 'I'm going to cum.'

Flora felt the same thing stirring within. First it was deep. It began to grow. Her clitoris became electric. 'Fuck, I'm going to cum,' she said. Something started to stream from within, yet flicked on her clitoris too. Some prickling, itching, almost stinging sensation rushed around her cunt. It was painfully right, and hyper-beautiful, vibrating then seeming to grind, until all she could feel was bliss. 'I'm cumming!'

This sent the man over the edge. Some power ran along his prostate gland, twisted and swung around the walls of his arse. A spark shot towards his sphincter, yet to each of his balls as well. It smashed to the head of his dick, beat, pulsed and punched as though more than alive. Now nothing could stop this force.

'I'm cumming too. Fucking hell, fucking hell, fucking hell!'

'Me too. I'm cumming too.' Still she kept on pounding.

'Jesus!' was his final spoken word.

The man shook, his whole body trembling. His tears began to drown out his speech. Flora now saw things with a more physical self. It made her feel, rather than think.

'Baby!' she said.

There was now this thing beneath her. It was soft and weak. It needed babying; not wanted, but *needed* holding, and loving, and kissing. Anything she had to give. Her dick was still deep inside him, exactly where she wanted it. She imagined it felt secure, reassuring, and very real. Especially when things weren't making sense.

Flora watched the crying man, the baby lost and confused. The desire to be tender overpowered any other. Now she had no choice but to protect, to look after and hold. She had no choice but to care.

3

Killing time, Joe flicked through CDs on the living room floor. Ryan sat watching him, waiting. The doorbell rang.

'That'll be her,' said Ryan, getting up, darting towards the front door, and opening it.

'Baby!' he said. 'Hair do.' This was his response to Leila having dyed her hair lilac. 'It's grown so much.'

'I did it last night. Sorry I'm so late. The train stopped at Milton Keynes for about half an hour. Do you like it? My hair, I mean?'

'Sure!' He tousled it with his hand, and stroked her face. 'No doubt they were checking passports. They probably knew you were trying to escape.'

'I applied for my visa months ago.' Leila stepped into the hall. 'Nice place.'

'It's just my summer pad, you know.'

Ryan led her into the living room.

'Joe, this is Leila. Leila, Joe.'

'Nice to meet you, Leila. I've heard a lot about you.'

'Hope you don't mind if I fast-forward past the formalities for a second,' said David. 'Is pasta okay?'

'Sounds great,' said Leila.

'Good. In that case. Hello! All we've been hearing is "Leila this, Leila that."'

'Vice versa,' said Leila.

'I wouldn't worry what the food is,' said Ryan. 'He's a great cook.'

'Stop,' said David. 'Now I've got to live up to it.'

'That's why I said it, stupid.'

'It looks like you've settled in okay,' said Leila.

'Yeah,' said Ryan. 'I just can't wait for these two dudes to move out, though.'

'We'll be gone as soon as we find somewhere proper,' said Joe.

'This looks proper to me,' said Leila.

'That's Joe's doing,' said David. 'If it were left to me, it would be white walls throughout.'

'Ryan told me it was cool, but it's something else.'

'A paint showroom?' said David.

'I was thinking, more an art gallery,' said Leila.

'People have said that,' said David. 'It must be what Joe finds comfortable these days.'

'Home,' said Joe.

'This bag's my home for a while,' said Leila.

'That's what youth's all about,' said David.

'You're only thirty,' said Joe.

'I imagine these two think that's retiring age.'

'Of course,' said Ryan. Then, 'Give us a break!'

'Yeah,' said Leila. 'I once knew somebody who was thirty-two.'

'There you go,' said David.

'Who was that?' said Ryan.

'I don't know. Some woman I read about in the paper. She lived in Japan, or somewhere, and she lived off potatoes.'

'Enough, already! I'm obviously going to have to watch you, young lady.'

'That's *my* job,' said Ryan. He looked at Leila, and she looked back. It lasted for seconds. Then, they both looked away a little embarrassed.

'How cute,' said Joe.

'You used to look at me like that,' said David.

'I don't think that was ever in my vocabulary,' said Joe.

'You used to love me.'

'I still love you, retard. But I hate you for making me say it.' Now it was their turn to look at each other.

'How cute,' said Ryan.

'Watch it,' said David. 'If you're hungry, that is. That reminds me.' He left the room, smiling.

Joe followed him with his eyes, but quickly turned his attention to Leila. 'Take a seat.' He paused for a moment for her to sit and get comfortable, then crouching beside her, he said, 'Can I get you anything?'

'Do you have any whisky?'

'I think so. What would you like with it?'

She took a few seconds to decide. 'Milk?' she said finally.

'I've never heard of that,' said Joe with a look of surprise.

'Me neither,' she said.

Ryan burst out laughing.

'Leila, you're one hell of a crazy cow. Joe, can I have the same?'

'Sure. That's two whisky and milks coming up. If you two get sick, I'm not cleaning up.'

'It's a deal,' said Ryan.

'That's if I can choose a CD,' said Leila.

'Okay,' said Joe, slightly amused.

When Joe left the room, Leila went over to the CD player, pulled a CD out of her bag and put it on.

Ryan waited for the track to start. He knew Leila well enough to expect a surprise. It started.

'What is this?' said Ryan.

'TV jingles,' said Leila.

'From?'

'Hong Kong.'

'Where did you find it?'

'A thrift store just off Sixth Avenue.'

'That's New York, I presume.'

'Aha.'

Joe returned looking confused. 'This wasn't in our collection?'

'No,' said Ryan. 'Leila brought it.'

'How,' Joe paused trying to find the right word, 'resourceful,' he said, a little confused.

'That's my Leila.'

After much repetition, seemingly endless samples and synthesisers that barely sounded like glockenspiels, the CD ended.

'Got anything else, Leila?' said Joe, a little sarcastically.

'I do have one more. If you're sure you don't mind.'

'No,' said Joe. 'Why would I?'

'You might once you hear it,' said Ryan.

'Shut up, you,' said Leila, and handed Joe another CD.

There was nothing on the outside cover, no clue as to what might be inside.

'Here goes,' said Joe, putting the CD on.

He and Ryan both lifted their heads to listen carefully.

'I like this one the best,' said Leila.

A dog started barking. It kept on barking. A couple of minutes into the track, Joe said, 'Does it do anything else?'

'No,' said Leila. 'Isn't it great?'

'Yeah,' said Joe absentmindedly. 'It's...' He stopped. 'Actually, it is great. It would be perfect for my exhibition.'

'Fill us in,' said Ryan.

'Can I borrow it?' said Joe, ignoring Ryan.

'Definitely,' said Leila, pleased that Joe liked it. 'But you won't lose it?'

'It's too late,' said Joe carefully putting the CD into its case. 'I lost it years ago.'

David walked into the room just in time to hear the tail end of laughter.

'What have I missed?'

'Us, I hope,' said Ryan.

'You're getting too cute for your own good, sonny.'

'I wish I was your son.'

'Ryan, don't say that. If your mother heard, she'd be so upset. She's already phoned.'

'Like I care,' said Ryan, pouting.

'Don't act so hard. It doesn't become you. I called her back.'

'You did what?'

'Did you think I wouldn't?'

'I did run away.'

'She *is* my sister,' said David.

'That's not my problem.'

'Be reasonable. I can't have her worrying about you.'

'So what did she say?'

'She was just glad you were okay. She wants to come and visit.'

'Jesus!'

'She only wants to see you. You don't have to go back with her. Anyway, dinner's ready. You lot must be starving. You sounded like a pack of dogs from the kitchen.'

'That wasn't us,' said Leila.

'I know,' said David. 'I was just kidding.' He watched Leila's face for a couple of seconds as she caught up, surprised at how naïve she seemed. 'Anyway, if you'd all like to follow me.'

They were led into the kitchen where a huge wooden table was set for dinner. The walls were completely covered in fluorescent blocks in different colours. It had a Fifties feel to it.

'Wow!' said Leila.

'Thank you,' said David. 'Well, thank Joe, again.'

'It's beautiful,' said Leila.

'It's not too much, is it?'

'No,' said Leila.

'Damn!' said David. 'I knew it wasn't enough.'

'Don't worry honey,' said Joe. 'I'll get somebody in to sort it out next week.'

'He will. Just you wait and see,' said Ryan.

'It wouldn't surprise me,' said Leila looking at Joe and David as though they were naughty children. Then she made an expression as though she'd just had a good idea, and said to Ryan, 'Why don't you do it? You could do with some extra money.'

'Good thinking,' said David. 'We could actually do with some help.'

Ryan made a face, which merged surprise with resignation.

'Are you interested?' said David.

'Sure,' said Ryan.

'You don't sound that sure,' said Joe.

'Well, who actually likes working?' said Ryan.

'I do,' said David.

'It depends on the job,' said Leila.

'Excuse me! Miss Never-done-a-day's-work-in-her-life,' said Ryan.

Leila didn't bother answering.

In an attempt to change the direction of the conversation, David said, 'Eight pounds an hour sound okay?'

'More than okay,' said Ryan. 'Cash in hand?'

'Of course. I wouldn't miss a chance to screw the taxman.'

'So it's true,' said Ryan. 'You would screw anything.'

'When did you get so cheeky?' said David.

'You leave my cheeks alone,' said Ryan.

'You wish,' said David. 'How's Monday sound?'

'I'll be there, cheeks and all.'

'Can't wait,' said David.

They sat down to dinner. Joe opened wine, which they all drank quickly. Two bottles later, they were all getting a bit drunk, whilst laughing and stuffing themselves with the delicious food David had prepared.

Without warning Leila stood up and lifted her skirt. David looked at Joe, who looked at Ryan, who simply shrugged and smiled.

'Leila,' said David. At first she didn't respond. 'Leila.'

Hesitantly, she lowered her skirt a little, enough for her head just to appear over the top. She looked puzzled. 'Leila, be a dear and pass the pepper.'

She did as she was asked. In doing so she had to put her skirt down. She handed David the pepper. 'I can't eat spinach without it. How about you?'

'I like butter on spinach,' she said. Then she sat down and continued, as though nothing had happened. 'I'm having trouble believing the sauce on this pasta is low fat.'

'You don't have to believe,' said David. 'As long as you eat it.'

'Why do you care about fat?' said Leila.

'You may not believe this, but I used to model.'

'I believe it,' said Leila. 'You're fucking beautiful.'

'That's very sweet. The agency liked my stomach really ribbed, so I usually watched what I ate. Now, I guess, it's just habit really.'

'Why did you stop modelling?' said Leila. Joe frowned. Ryan winced. 'What?' Joe raised his eyebrows. 'I guess I've said something wrong.'

'Don't worry,' said David. 'It's okay.'

'Somebody may as well tell me now.'

David's manner changed quite dramatically. 'You may have noticed this scar on my forehead, and this one just under my nose.'

'No,' said Leila.

'You can bring her again,' said David.

'You do know they're sexy, don't you?' she said.

'I'm beginning to like you a lot.'

'I knew you would,' said Ryan.

'Fill me in,' said Leila, curious, but not sure if she should really go any further.

'Okay,' said David.

'David,' said Joe. ' Are you sure?'

'If it's a big deal,' said Leila, definitely beginning to feel uneasy, 'we can skip it.'

'No. It's okay.' David paused. Leila's head came forward, ear first, waiting to hear what he said. 'I was attacked.'

'You were almost killed,' said Joe.

'Okay!'

Leila put her head down. 'I'm sorry. It's so unfair.'

'That's life,' said David. 'Anyway, it was a long time ago. I'm fine now.'

'You're so lovely,' said Leila. 'I'd have killed the bastard.'

'What?' said Joe.

'I'd have blown his brains out.'

'I wasn't carrying my gun,' said David.

'Cool! You carry a gun as well?' said Leila.

'I was kidding,' said David. 'Why, do you?'

'Of course. There are some nutcases out there. I've got to be able to protect myself.'

'A gun's a bit extreme,' said David.

'It's okay for you lot, but it's different for us. We can be raped. I think it's possibly the worst thing that can happen to a woman.' Again, Ryan winced.

'What have I said now?'

By this point, David was rubbing his forehead, with his eyes closed.

'What?' said Leila. Then suddenly understanding the situation, 'Oh my God! No! David! You weren't?'

Tears began to run down David's cheeks. Joe sprang up and within seconds was holding David tightly, squashing his face against his own. Both their faces became wet.

'Ryan,' said Leila. 'I wish you'd told me.'

'It's not the kind of thing . . .' said Ryan.

David interrupted. 'Leila, it's okay. Really.'

'Still, I'm sorry for bringing it up.'

Leila was quiet for the rest of dinner. She and Ryan cleared away the dishes and made drinks for David and Joe. Leila started yawning.

'What time did you set off at?' said David.

'I was up at nine. The train was at twelve.'

'Don't let us keep you up,' said Joe.

'We're cool at the moment,' said Ryan.

'You two haven't been alone together for a while,' said Joe.

'Just one more drink,' said Ryan.

'Let me get it,' said Joe. 'How about some dessert wine.'

'I love dessert wine,' said Leila.

'Your wish is my command,' said Joe. 'Anyone else want wine?'

'I'll stick to whisky,' said Ryan.

'A man's drink,' said David.

'I just don't want to be sick,' said Ryan. 'I've drunk too much already.'

Joe went onto the kitchen and brought back the drinks.

'Are you going to stay in London?' said David.

'I'd like to,' said Leila, 'but I have to find somewhere to live.'

'You can stay here until you do,' said Joe. 'That's if David doesn't mind.'

'No,' said David. 'Of course I don't mind.'

'Wow!' said Leila.

'More than wow,' said Ryan.

'That's kind of you,' said Leila.

'I'm not here much,' said Joe. 'I should have discussed it with David, but in eight years, we've seldom disagreed.'

'Because I'm always right,' said David. 'You'd be stupid to disagree.'

'Yes honey,' said Joe. 'That must be why.' They both made an exasperated expression.

'Anyway, we could do with some fresh . . .' David paused, and licked his lips. 'I mean, new blood around the place.'

Leila laughed, and David joined in with a dramatic, Dracula-style laugh. When everybody's response to this finally died down, the conversation continued, winding up and down, meandering and at times dying. Keys, tubes, and landmarks were all discussed. Ryan lay flat out on the floor.

'Let's go to bed,' said Leila.

'I'm coming,' he said, not moving.

'Come on,' she said.

Joe could see she needed help.

'I'll show you where the bedroom is,' he said. 'Come on, slug-boy. Your lettuce awaits you.' Joe helped him stand and led him upstairs.

Standing on the landing at the top of the stairs, Joe swung open their bedroom door. On the walls were circles painted in primary colours. Where they overlapped they created new colours, combinations of the colours overlapping. The ceiling was covered in half spheres, in all of the colours on the walls. In each corner there was a light fixture. From these hung hundreds of tiny white fairy lights. They looked as though they were falling to the ground.

On seeing the room Leila said, 'Cool.'

'Sorry,' said Joe. 'I'll turn the heat up.' Leila gave him an expression showing she thought his comment was dry. 'It *is* late.'

'I'll forgive you,' said Leila. 'But tomorrow I expect wit, wit, wit, and sharp.'

'I'll see what I can do,' said Joe in mock apology.

'Now begone.'

'Okay, ma'am.' Joe started to close the door.

'Hey, wait,' said Ryan. Joe raised his eyebrows. 'Give me a kiss.'

'Sorry,' said Joe. 'I thought it too familiar.'

'Shut up and get here.'

Joe went to Ryan, whom he tried to kiss on the cheek. Ryan turned his head. Joe bent his neck to compensate, following Ryan's cheek. Ryan turned back. Their faces hovered, neither sure which way to go, until Ryan got hold of Joe's face with his hands, and kissed him squarely on the mouth.

'Why, sir!' said Joe, pretending to hide his face out of embarrassment behind a fan.

'Me! Me! Me!' squealed Leila.

This time Joe didn't bother being coy, and just kissed Leila on the lips.

'That's better,' said Ryan. 'We'll train you yet.'

Joe left, saluting at the door. As soon as it closed, Leila said, 'So fill me in.'

'About?'

'David.'

'There's not much more to tell. He was raped, and beaten up badly.'

'Poor thing!'

'Yeah. He's such a softy. At the time, he used to live with this woman called Flora.'

'What, as a couple?'

'That's right. She was a bit dodgy though. He'd been living with her for years when he met Joe, but I think he began to realise he was gay.'

'Poor cow.'

'Yes and no. She did some weird stuff.'

'What like?'

'She sent him some shit.'

'You mean drugs?'

'No, actual shit.'

'What!'

'Go figure.'

'Was she a psycho?'

'Well, yeah, kind of, I guess. Anyway, Joe found out that she'd sent the shit, and confronted her.'

'It's like a film.'

'I know. Unreal, hey! Listen, Flora managed to convince David that Joe sent the packages.'

'Wow! I'm beginning to like her.'

'She must have noticed that David liked Joe. Apparently Joe made it clear that he liked David. I guess she hoped it would ruin their friendship.'

'Did it work?'

'Yeah, for a while. They didn't see each other for ages.'

'But how . . .'

'They bumped into each other on the tube, just by chance. David was living with this other guy called Rob by this point. He was nice.'

'So, David, and Joe lived happily ever after?'

'Well, kind of. It's quite romantic. You should get David to tell you. He loves to talk about it.'

'So, what happened?'

'To cut a long story short, they started seeing each other.'

'What happened to the bitch from hell?'

'I don't know. They don't speak to her.'

'It's hardly surprising. Esta loca?'

'Love does scary stuff sometimes.'

'Please, don't ever love me like that.'

'Okay.'

'Promise?'

'I promise.'

4

David and Joe were alone in their bedroom. Unlike the rest of the house, this was much more sombre, even relaxing, and had a slightly autumnal feel to it. Mustard, salmon, turquoise, amber, and plum bands, about a quarter of a metre thick covered each wall, joining at the corners to circle the whole room. A thin line painted with black gloss helped define the bands. Joe started to change the sheets on the bed, but David grabbed his arm and said, 'Shouldn't we dirty those first?'

'Okay, governor,' said Joe, sounding like a character from Oliver Twist. David found it surprisingly sexy. They kissed. As they did, Joe felt David's hand at the side of his face. 'What . . .' David cut him off by putting something in his mouth.'

'Acid,' said David.

'No!'

'You'll believe me in about twenty minutes.'

'Is it really?'

'Yes.'

Joe thought for a moment. 'I guess, I don't have anything planned tomorrow.'

'I know,' said David. 'I checked your diary first. Now you probably understand why all the inane questions at breakfast too.'

Joe thought back, and smiled. 'Oh yeah. You sly bugger.'

'Are you okay about it?'

'God yeah! Well, here goes.'

'Let's have a joint in the bath and wait to come up.'

'Nice,' said Joe.

'Where was I?'

They kissed again, but more passionately, and longer. Pulling apart, David took off his T-shirt, revealing his torso.

'Even nicer,' said Joe.

David threw his T-shirt on the bed and headed towards the bathroom to run the taps.

'We should get Ryan to work on this room,' said David, loud enough to be heard in the other room.

'Please! I'm sick of it,' said Joe.

In the bathroom, each wall was painted with a luscious purple gloss, and in contrast the ceiling was fluorescent green. There was writing on both, in thick black marker. It gave the impression of graffiti, but on closer inspection it wasn't so chaotic. Each line was evenly spaced and done very neatly. The bath was high up on a scaffolding platform, the drainpipe on show, curling around in a corkscrew underneath. The whole floor was slanted toward a small grate, so overflow drained away. Access to the bath was from one end, by an aluminium ladder. David put the plug in, ran the taps, climbed down the ladder, and went back to the bedroom. By this time, Joe was bent over, peeling off his jeans.

'Jesus,' said David. 'Your buns look amazing.'

'They feel even better.'

David kissed Joe, and cupped his arse.

'You're right. They're so fucking hard.'

'Told you.'

'I love you,' said David.

'I love you, too.'

'Which two?'

'Flora.'

'Now, I know you're kidding.'

'Get in the bath,' said Joe. 'I'll rub your back.'

'It's a deal,' said David, taking off his jeans. He walked towards the bathroom naked. For a moment, Joe watched him. David's waist was still slim, his shoulders still broad, but his body had got more natural, since he'd stopped modelling.

'You look the best I've seen you,' said Joe. David turned around in the doorway and posed as though for a photo, but more extreme. 'Ugh! I take that back.' David relaxed and smiled. 'That's better,' said Joe. 'God, you're beautiful.'

'Must be all the cream cakes I eat,' said David, and continued into the bathroom. Joe followed. Again, Joe watched as David climbed the stairs into the bath. When David's arse was at head height, Joe got hold of his thighs and buried his face into it. Resting on the side of the bath, David bent forward, arching his back.

'Jesus!' he said. 'I love that.'

Joe pulled his face away slightly, leaving his nose in the crack of David's arse, just far enough away to be able to focus on the tiny blond hairs, yet near enough to smell the skin.

'I know you love it. Why do you think I do it?'

'Because I pay you a shilling a week,' said David.

'Oh yeah.'

'Get back to work.'

'Yes, sir,' said Joe. Then he licked right up David's crack, and said, 'Um!' Then he pushed his tongue deep into the actual hole.

'Fucking hell!' said David.

'No. Fuck in the bath.'

'Wherever! You know me.'

'I do,' said Joe. 'That's why I can't wait.'

David continued up the ladder, climbed into the bath and sank into the water. He went right under, blowing bubbles out of his nose.

Joe sat on the floor, rolling a joint. Every now and then, he looked up.

David leant on the side of the bath, with his chin resting on folded arms. 'Come on, baby,' he said, with an exaggerated moan in his voice. 'Get in.'

'I'm coming. There you go. Finished!'

Joe lit the joint, and waited while David dried his hands. Then he passed it up.

'Lovely,' said David, taking a long drag, and sliding back into the water.

'Okay. Get ready, I'm coming.'

'I'm ready.'

Joe climbed the steps two at a time. His legs were pale, hairy, and very solid. By the time he got to the top, he had a hard-on.

'Where do you want me, front or back?' said Joe, his dick bouncing in front of David's face.

'There was talk of a backrub.'

'Okay. I guess that's behind.'

He stepped in behind David and slid his legs around either side of his hips.

'That feels nice,' said David. 'But what's that lump?'

'Nothing.'

'It doesn't feel like nothing.'

'Okay it's not nothing.' He started to rub David's neck. 'How's that, baby?'

'Incredible.'

'So you like my lump?'

'You know I love your lump,' said David. 'But I was referring to the massage.'

'That'll be another shilling, governor,' said Joe, in the same cheeky accent as earlier.

'Two shillings to rub my back and lick my arse? What's the world coming to?'

Joe continued in the same voice. 'I've got me missus and five young 'uns to feed, sir.'

'So sell some of them?'

'I've sold three already, governor. I only got a farthing for the lot.'

'All right, you can have your shilling.'

'I'll lick your arse good, governor. You won't be sorry.'

David turned over in the bath. The water overflowed, fell in a single sheet, and splashed onto the floor. He nuzzled into Joe's hairy chest, then kissed down the ridges of his stomach to his abdomen. Joe pushed his pelvis towards David's face. The head of his dick rose out of the water. David opened his mouth around it, and took it as far in as he could. When he came up for air the front of his hair and eyelashes were wet.

'Do you know what you look like?'

'No,' said David. 'Tell me.'

'The most beautiful thing on the planet. That's what.'

David rested the side of his face on Joe's chest, feeling completely content. He closed his eyes and started to daydream. When he acknowledged his thoughts next, he realised the acid was taking effect. David opened his eyes. Slowly, he shifted his body, in an attempt to look at Joe. Again, water splashed out of the bath. For a moment, David's thoughts ran with this idea. He imagined the water hitting the ground. Only it was falling on top of him. He was under the bath and could hear them above, like giant sea creatures moving in the water. The squeaking of skin against the side of the bath became their cries. Tired, ancient and sad they tried to communicate. Once more, he acknowledged his thoughts. He had been distracted for some time. The bath water was getting cold.

'Baby?' he said.

'Fuck!' said Joe. 'That acid's strong.'

'You're telling me.'

'For a while, I thought I was still downstairs, only the whole room was filled with mud.'

'Err!'

'It was quite nice,' said Joe. 'Until the water started to go cold.'

David watched Joe as he spoke. He'd never realised before how much he looked like Flora. Joe broke David's train of thought.

'Let's get out, before we catch a cold.'

'Okay. You first,' said David. 'Baby. Will you do me a favour?'

'Anything.'

'Will you stay at the bottom of the ladder, in case I slip.'

'Sure. You must be pretty fucked-up.'

David made a face that meant very fucked-up. Awkwardly, he managed to turn around in the bath so he faced Joe and could see him as he climbed out. As he did, David noticed the hairs under Joe's arse joining in little peaks of water. For a second he became engrossed in them, noticing how filled with light each drop was, as it formed, hesitated, then dripped off the skin. He couldn't concentrate on anything for more than a few seconds at any one time. By concentrating, Joe made his way down the steps. As his head went below the side of the bath, David thought Joe was drowning, but then realised how ridiculous this idea was. He put his own head over the side and watched. Joe shook his head like a wet dog, causing him to lose balance, so leant against the washbasin until he finished drying off.

When he was done, Joe looked up, and said, 'Come on baby.'

'I can't be bothered moving. Do I have to?'

'No, but I'm not getting back in, so if you want to stop lying in cold water, and have sex with me, you'll have to.'

'You drive a hard bargain.'

'If I didn't, I'd still be getting a shilling a week.'

'Are you complaining?'

'No, governor.'

'Okay,' said David. 'I'm coming.'

With great care David made his way out of the bath and down the steps. As he got to the bottom, Joe took hold of him round the waist and, lifting him, carried him, still dripping, out of the bathroom.

'Put me down,' said David.

'When I'm good and ready.'

'And when might that be?'

'Now,' said Joe, as he let David down onto the bed.

'Let me dry off.'

'You'll dry soon enough on the sheets.'

Joe pulled a blanket up over his head and lowered himself onto David, covering them both. They fell into each other, their faces becoming wet with sweat, and saliva, their bodies hot and slippery. They welded together, gasping, penetrating, and smearing into the bed.

Even though the sex lasted over two hours, their acid was still in full swing. Without the sex to focus on, the acid began to play with their minds. Joe understood this could happen, and tried to relax, whereas David began to get a little scared.

'Joe. Will you give me a hug?'

'What's wrong?'

'I don't know. I feel scared.'

'Come here,' said Joe and held David. 'What's going on in my baby's head?'

'Crazy stuff.'

'That's acid for you.'

'How come you don't?'

'I have crazy thoughts, but I check myself and try not to let them consume me.'

'Easier said than done.'

'It's actually something you can learn.'

'If I keep talking, I don't get scared.'

'This may sound obvious,' said Joe, 'but that's because you're concentrating on speaking.'

'So, I should try to concentrate on something?'

'That's right, baby. Or carry on talking if you want. I'm happy to talk. If I get tired I'll just listen.'

'Don't go to sleep,' said David, slightly panicky.

'I won't, baby. In fact, I can promise I won't go to sleep before you.'

'But what if you do?'

'Well, you could wake me, but like I said, I won't. You could take something to be extra sure.'

'I don't have anything,' said David.

'I have. How about a special Joe cocktail.'

'What, a long hard screw up against the wall?'

'I was thinking more a comfortable cuddle, then a snooze.'

'What's that?'

'Some Valium and Rohypnol.'

'That sounds nice.'

'Hang on, I'll get them.'

'No,' said David. 'Don't go.'

'I'm only going to the bathroom.'

'Please don't go.'

'That's where the tablets are. Come with me.'

David thought for a moment, a confused look on his face.

'Okay.' He jumped to his feet like a kid.

'Get on my back,' said Joe. David did, and instantly felt better, distracted and loved. Joe walked into the bathroom, making racing car noises.

'I'm not a baby,' said David.

'You are. Well, I hope you are.'

'Don't tell me – I'm you're baby.'

'You got it.'

Joe got a bottle of Valium out of the cupboard and passed it over his shoulder.

'How many, doc?'

'Two should be enough. So take three.'

'Four then?'

'Good boy. A man after my own heart.'

'Got that years ago.'

David handed the bottle back to Joe, who put them back in the cupboard. Joe took the Rohypnol in his hand.

'Back to bed?' said Joe.

'What about the Rohypnol?'

'You think I'd miss an opportunity to have you turn to putty in my hands.'

'What was I thinking?'

'Stupid!'

They went back to bed. Joe must have kissed David more than fifty times before he gave him some Rohypnol, then more than another fifty before David began to breathe very heavily.

'Are you asleep?' said Joe.

David didn't answer.

Joe was still tripping, and without David to attend to, he began to have thoughts he didn't like. He felt it was a shame to waste the acid, so decided to go downstairs and watch tv until he was sleepy. Taking the duvet off the floor at the bottom the bed, he slipped on some boxer shorts and left David sleeping peacefully.

Joe put the duvet on the bench, and made a nest with cushions. He got a six pack of beers from the fridge and generally enjoyed his acid. For about an hour, he watched a horror movie. When it was over, with the choice of an Open University programme on molecular biology, or twenty-year-old sitcoms, he turned off the tv. Lying with his eyes open, he began to notice what little light there was in the room. Headlights from cars going by outside darted into the room and across the walls. Yellow and red lights turned in the corners of the room, then chased towards the kitchen door. An ambulance went by outside, and instantly, the room was chaotic with white and blue shards of light. The room appeared to twist; deforming, then reforming, as the ambulance passed, only fading as it drove on down the street. For over thirty minutes Joe watched the room, hallucinating wildly, seeing shapes form out of previously unnoticed areas of light and shadow. Every now and then, he'd close his eyes and embark on a series of involuted thoughts that would fracture and shoot off in different directions. At some point, during a visit inside his head, he fell asleep.

Joe dreamed vividly. Sexual images merged one into the other. Figures transformed, mutating from somebody in one period of his life to somebody he'd seen on tv just that night. The woman from the corner shop, flipped violently on the ground, becoming an old teacher from school. David re-occurred, often. He took many forms. Sometimes he was simply himself, but usually he was a combination of other people. Still, it was David, although only a part of him, his laugh, his concern, or his anger. Joe fused with another Joe, then became a bull charging towards a toreador. Only he wanted to kiss this man. Joe knew if he did, it would kill him. He would bleed and die in shame. A crowd watched this fight. Joe was taunted. He charged and caught an arm. Again he charged and caught a leg. This time he went for the kill, the lips he wanted to kiss. Joe felt a throbbing in his balls, and continued to run. As far as he charged, his hooves smashed into the ground. The toreador was the same distance away. Still, this throbbing. Joe wanted to cum. There was golden stitching on the toreador's waistcoat, crammed with flowers, stars and tiny motifs. The detail was intense. It had a smell, and a sound. It glistened in the Spanish sun. The light took shape, shooting above and dropping like broken glass. Then this shed; this cloth, this colour, texture and skin. This young man stood in the stadium, yet he hung like a carcass in an abattoir. This bacon, beef, barely animal now stood waiting to be speared. He was muscle and meat, turned on by the crowd, by the attack from the bull approaching. Although still dreaming, Joe's attention switched to himself. He began to wake. His dick throbbed. Something prodded his arse. David must still be horny.

'Yeah,' is all that Joe could think to say. For a moment he thought of Ryan. Slim. Smooth. Precious and smiling. Licking and sucking. 'I'm going to cum,' he said, into the darkness.

'Cum, please . . .' said a voice, intending to say more, but eager to take Joe's cum, closed around his dick.

5

David sat waiting in Gaia's room. He couldn't help wondering if this was because she was busy, or it was a device for dealing with people who were early, possibly showing that boundaries couldn't be crossed. Whatever the reason, he resigned himself to cleaning the nails of his left hand with the thumb of his right. Also, he thought a little about what he wanted to talk about that day. Nothing came immediately to mind. He looked around the room, trying to discern anything more about his therapist than he had already worked out. No. There was nothing. It was a blank environment, not the wood-panelled executive style portrayed in Hollywood, or the rundown council type funded by the British government. The room was as nondescript as it could be. The walls were off-white, and the carpet grey. The fixtures and fittings merged with both. David heard some noise outside the room. Still, Gaia didn't appear. The telephone rang. He assumed the answer machine got it, because he heard no talking.

At three o'clock precisely the door to the room opened. 'Hello,' said Gaia.

'Hello,' said David.

'I'm sorry I kept you waiting.'

'No problem. I was early anyway.'

'Really.' She looked at her watch. 'Not really.'

'Maybe a bit.'

'It wouldn't matter, if you were.' David looked at the floor.

'How are you today?'

It felt to David as though Gaia always left plenty of space for a response.

'Okay.'

'Just okay?'

'Life's never more than okay. Is it?'

'Is that how you see it?'

'Most of the time.'

'I remember you once told me how beautiful your walk over here was. I think you walked through the park.'

'That's right.'

'Is that a nice memory?'

David hesitated, seemingly reluctant to feel anything more than okay. 'I guess so.'

'You only guess it is?'

David thought for a moment, recalling the walk.

'No,' he said and smiled. 'It was nice.'

'Is there something on your mind.'

'Maybe.'

'Tell me about your week.'

'I've done nothing, really. Stayed at home a lot. Oh. I did some acid, after seeing you last Thursday. And, before you run with that thought, I don't think it had anything to do with therapy.'

'Are you sure?'

'No.'

'Last week you told me that Ryan was staying with you. How is that?

David smiled.

'You're smiling.'

'Ryan makes me smile.'

'Do you remember once telling me you were confused about your feelings for him?'

'Vaguely.'

'You're smiling again.'

'He's such a great kid.'

'You're no longer confused?'

'No.'

'It's a long time since I did acid, but I remember it being confusing.'

'That's an understatement.'

'Do you think you wanted to be confused?'

'What do you mean?'

'About Ryan.'

'No!'

'There is a certain comfort in confusion.'

'Possibly.' Then a little defensively, 'You're usually right.'

Outwardly Gaia didn't appear to react to this comment. 'Maybe you miss how you used to feel about him.'

'No.' David paused, and looked confused. 'Do you think?'

'I'm not certain.'

'Maybe,' said David lost in thought.

'What do you think?' said Gaia.

'It makes sense that I'd miss how he was. He was an incredibly sweet boy.'

'How do you feel about him now?'

'He's an incredibly sweet teenager.'

'More able to make up his own mind.'

'I wouldn't have it any other way.' David hesitated. 'Don't you think?'

Gaia smiled for the first time that day. 'Yes. I believe you love Ryan.'

'I do.'

'I believe you wouldn't do anything to harm him.'

'Never.' David looked upset.

'You wouldn't want to hurt him like you were hurt.'

David's features began to tremble. He lifted his hand to cover his face, and bowed his head. Gaia knew what this meant and reached for the tissues on the floor beside her chair. She stood up, walked over to

David and handed him the box. This was the closest Gaia ever came to comforting him. It was enough. David imagined the gesture meant she was feeling something and wanted to do something to help. Also, possibly, it showed she cared, in a way that was allowed within the boundaries of their relationship.

For a few minutes David cried and Gaia sat watching him with her fingers interlaced on her knees. Her head was at an angle and her eyes never left him. This David understood as concern, possibly even pity, definitely a learned therapy technique.

'I'd never hurt him.' He cried with more force.

'But somebody hurt you.'

David tried to say yes, but his tears wouldn't allow him. After a couple of minutes he said, 'I'm sorry.'

'There's no need to apologise. I understand. You nearly died.'

David folded into himself, bent forward and sobbed. He stayed this way for several minutes. It was a difficult position for breathing. Every few seconds, he gasped, drawing in chunks of air. Eventually, he lifted his head. The whole of his face was wet, and the area around his eyes was red.

'The attack changed your life.'

'I couldn't model any more.'

'I was referring to how it made you feel. How scared you were. You didn't like being outdoors, or around other people.'

'How could anybody do that?'

'I don't think you're asking how, but why. More specifically, why you?'

'I guess so.'

'There's no reason. Nothing that would make any sense.'

'It's such a horrible memory.'

'Of course it is. Being attacked goes against the most fundamental human instinct to protect oneself. Being sexually abused is particularly traumatic. You might feel as though you weren't just violated physically, but emotionally, also.'

It helped David, having Gaia talk about what happened to him. By doing so, she demystified the experience, took away an eerie element. David could never really know why it happened, but he could at least put it in some kind of perspective. Vile things happened. People could be cruel. This was sometimes random, and often meaningless.

Gaia continued to watch David. At least look at him.

'What are you hoping to see?' said David. Gaia looked confused. 'When you watch me.'

'People don't only communicate with words,' said Gaia.

'What am I communicating now?'

'A certain amount of hostility.'

'Does it frighten you?'

'No. Should it?'

'Of course not.'

'Let's try and keep hold of this thought,' said Gaia. 'But first I want to go back.'

Gaia pressed her lips with three fingers of her right hand. The other she left palm up on her lap. She looked as though she was thinking. 'You said that I was watching you. What do you think I see? Rather, how do you see yourself now?'

'You mean after the attack?'

'Yes.'

'I'm not as purdy as I used to be,' said David, sounding like a character from an old cowboy film.

'Your features are the same. I'm sure you're aware of that.'

'Well, yes, but I'm scarred.'

'Some people think scars are attractive. What I'm getting at is that your image of yourself may be a fantasy to some extent. Do people say you look different?'

David thought for a moment. 'I guess not.'

'I think maybe we could look further at what the fantasy is.'

Now it was David's turn to watch Gaia. He nodded to show he was listening, understanding, and even agreeing. 'We can come back to this. You mentioned something else.' Again she got into her thinking position. For a moment she looked to her side, onto the floor. 'Oh, yes. That's it.'

'Fire away.'

'It's not clear to me yet. Something about you thinking I might be afraid of you. Again, I can't help thinking this could be about Ryan.' David looked puzzled. 'Like I said, it's not clear. I'm wondering if you don't still have feelings for Ryan, but you're scared of hurting him, afraid of your own rage. These feelings could be linked to you being hurt. I'm sorry. This isn't well thought out. Does it mean anything to you?'

David shook his head, but recalled being in bed with Ryan. At that time, his nephew was only seven years old, but the feelings David had were adult and sexual. These thoughts took only a fraction of a second, but it was long enough to make blood rush into his dick. There was movement in his jeans, at his crotch. Gaia noticed. Quickly, she looked away. It wasn't quick enough. David noticed, and blushed. Gaia looked into his eyes. It was as though she knew what he was thinking. He felt uncomfortable, and looked to the window, focusing neither on the glass, nor the tree outside. 'Gaia,' he said. 'Am I,' he paused, 'a paedophile?'

6

On hearing a key in the front door, Ryan and Leila turned to see who it was.

'Blah, blah, blah,' said David as he walked in.

'Well, are you fixed?' said Ryan.

'No. Crazier.'

'I could have done that for you,' said Leila. 'You could have paid me.'

'Of all people,' said David, 'you definitely make me feel sane.'

Leila was sitting on the floor painting the nails on her toes. Ryan was finishing the surround of the door.

'Nice!' said David, referring to the paper on the walls. Ryan had used A0 size photocopies. The image was a photograph Joe had taken of the road outside their house. 'How much were the photocopies?'

'The first was five pounds, then three-fifty each one after that.'

'Bargain.'

'It still cost nearly forty quid for the whole wall,' said Leila.

'That's cheap, right?'

'No!' said Leila. She then lifted a foot and blew at her toes to dry the nail varnish.

'How long did it take?' said David.

'Including her distracting me, about four hours.'

'Do you charge the same rate for distractions?' said David.

'No. But you might want to check her rates. It must have been labour intensive.'

'The red paint looks good, too,' said David.

'Yeah. But Hammorite's a bugger to use. It's kind of sticky and if you don't put enough on, it doesn't look hammered.'

'I know all about Hammorite. It's a favourite of Joe's. Why do you think we got you to do it?'

'So you could see me without a shirt on.'

Leila looked up to see David's eyes skim quickly over Ryan's torso. 'Have you ever been in the sun?'

'I try to avoid it.'

'I've never seen such white skin.'

'It's beautiful, isn't it?' said Leila, still watching David's eyes.

'Yes, it and he are completely beautiful,' said David. Leila smiled, seemingly satisfied, then continued with her nails. Ryan blushed and blew his hair out of eyes.

'You may as well get used to the idea,' said David. 'I think you're perfect. I always have.' Ryan looked him in the eye, but David's face showed no expression, giving nothing away. 'Does it make you uncomfortable?'

'No,' said Ryan. 'But I suddenly feel very naked.' He held a straight face for a moment then burst out laughing. 'Come here you idiot. You sound like an old queer from the Fifties.' He held out his arms to hug David. 'Why should it bother me? Would it bother you if Leila fancied you?'

David pretended to think about it. 'I guess not.' He paused again. 'Why, what are you trying to tell me?'

David was closer now. Ryan got hold of him. He put his arms around him and pulled him in. David couldn't help noticing the smell that came up from Ryan's armpits. He put his face into Ryan's neck and kissed him. He suddenly felt lecherous, and uneasy. These thoughts were overpowered by a sexual urge. He felt very excited. He became aware of a sugary, pungent smell, but more than this, he felt skin, so soft. David was sure he could taste Ryan. That uniquely adolescent flavour of boy skin, boy mouth, boy cum. Did his mouth open even on Ryan's neck? Or was it his imagination, a fantasy? David could feel heat rising off skin that had never seen the sun, skin that had never been touched by a man, never been enjoyed by a mouth that asked, 'Can I fuck you?' Images crammed into David's mind, Ryan's lower back as it stretched, trying to reach the top of the door, Ryan's slim waist, flat chest and stomach, Ryan. Fuck. Instantly, David got a hard-on. With these kind of feelings he'd usually gorge, let his sexual self charge forward. Desire. Kiss. He wanted to have sex with the thing in his arms. He wanted Ryan. Must have something of him. Stop. Cool. This was wrong, inappropriate, broken. At least, out of context. David pulled away.

Ryan noticed something strange about the way David let go of him. 'What's wrong?'

'Nothing,' said David, before even thinking. He knew this was the right thing to say. He felt very different.

Ryan was concerned. This wounded David. It made him want Ryan more, but within a matter of seconds he felt hatred for Ryan, and contempt for Leila. David thought quickly and said, 'It's probably a post-therapy thing, I imagine.' He turned to see Leila dip her nail varnish brush in the Hammorite. She was applying it to her big toes.

'What do you think?' she said. 'I like red and green together.'

'Very doorway,' said David, not sure what he really meant to say, or what he meant by what he had actually said.

'When you guys were busy bonding I had to entertain myself somehow.'

'It's good camouflage,' said Ryan, and winked.

'My point exactly. You can never blend in too well.'

Again a key turned in the front door. They all looked round. Joe walked into the living room, headed towards David and kissed him. 'Baby, you're sweating?' He looked around at Ryan and Leila. 'I feel like I've interrupted something.'

'Yeah, important interior design talk,' said David.

'All interior design talk is important,' said Joe. 'Nice job, Ryan. It looks great.'

'It's your ideas.'

'Ideas are easy. Making it happen is more difficult.'

'I agree, but you also made it happen by asking me to do it.'

'I suppose so. Can't I credit you for anything?'

'For looking amazing whilst doing it.'

Joe looked at Leila, who was also watching him. 'Okay, she looks amazing whilst you're doing it.'

Leila looked down at her toes, not sure if Joe was flirting with her or teasing her.

'Well,' said Ryan. 'A credit's a credit.'

'Listen,' said Joe, 'I was thinking, David, do you fancy taking these two out on the town?'

'Where were you thinking of?' said Ryan.

Joe shrugged. 'Tragic?'

'I've heard of that place,' said Leila.

'Is it still cool?' said Ryan, acting as though he cared about such things.

'Cool's not a word I'd use for Tragic,' said David. 'Hot is more appropriate.'

'As in hawrt,' said Leila, with a non-specific American accent.

'No,' said David, 'As in, everybody's dripping with sweat.'

'Sexsey,' said Ryan.

'Well, are you all in, or not?' There was silence. Joe pulled a bunch of things out of his pocket and threw them down on the floor in front of them. 'I thought this might help persuade you.' Leila's eyes widened.

'Jesus, what's all that?'

'It's party time,' said Joe. 'Are you in?'

Ryan looked at Leila, who looked back and grinned. 'We're in,' she said.

'David?'

'We're in too,' said David.

'Crazy cow,' said Joe. 'Oh yeah! I forgot it's therapy day.'

'What's the plan?' said Ryan.

'Either sleep or not, and we'll go out about three.'

'Cool,' said Leila in an exaggerated way. 'Sorry, I mean hot.'

'What's in the stash?' said Ryan.

Joe picked up some wraps and casually gave them out. 'Here's a little something to make sure you're ready to go.'

'Coke?' said Leila, not hiding her excitement.

'You got it, sister,' said Joe, counting out, picking up and handing each of them three tablets. 'This is to make sure you're in the right mood, and make you like me.'

'Ecstasy!' said Leila.

'You're good at this,' said Joe. 'Finally, just a little something in case we start flagging.'

'Speed,' said Ryan, before Leila had a chance to speak.

'Very good,' said Joe. 'You kids have obviously done this before.'

'Joe!' said David. 'That's my nephew you're talking to.'

'All the more reason we should set a good example,' said Joe. 'Show them how to do it properly.'

'Sounds good to me,' said Leila.

'Yeah, sounds sweet,' said Ryan.

'Judy will kill me, if she finds out,' said David. 'Promise you won't tell her.'

'Okay,' said Ryan. 'Mum's the word.'

'Ha ha. Seriously, please promise.'

'I promise! What do you think I am?'

'I'm not sure yet,' said David.

'Set your watches,' said Joe. 'We'll rendezvous here at two. I like to have a drink before I get there. I hate to arrive sober.'

'Do you drink with Ecstasy?' said Leila.

'I'm afraid so.'

'Hard-core,' she said.

'Aren't I.'

'Haven't people died from that?' said Ryan.

'Exactly,' said Joe.

'You can't not drink,' said David. 'How would you get drunk?'

'You don't have to on E,' said Leila.

'But it helps,' said David. 'It gives you something to do at least. I'm hardly just going to stand there and be high. It would be tedious.'

'You could twitch, and wiggle like everybody else,' said Joe.

'Like a first-timer,' said David.

'What's a fist-timer?' said Ryan.

'Somebody who's never taken Ecstasy before. There's a routine. They have to sit down when they're coming up, because they're rushing. Then they get sick, somewhere close, like beside the chair they're sitting on. Usually, a friend is on duty, not because they care. They're beyond this. They're already up on their drugs. But, it gives them something to do. It's quite a good look, also. It makes them appear kind. Not that anybody gives a fuck about this at Tragic. After about twenty minutes, the adorable, jaw-grinding, eye-rolling, fidgety first-timer has found a confidence they never knew they had. Now they can dance, sweat, and flirt with any man they like. Suddenly, there's nothing to hold them back. So they can be funny, sexy and clever, to men they ordinarily believed out of their reach.'

'Enough!' screamed Leila, 'We choose to witness this?'

'I haven't finished,' said David.

'Yeah, I want to hear what happened to the man on first-timer duty,' said Ryan.

'Well,' said David, taking a deep breath and smiling. 'It goes something like this. Duty looks real pretty by now. He has vomit coating his trainers. His face is withdrawn and his body sinewy because he's so dehydrated. His eyes are bulging as though they no longer want to be a part of his face. He looks around the room and tries to focus, but can't. The muscles in his face move so much, it appears to churn. He's almost pure drug now. Duty's become Ecstasy-man, an undulating, sweating, paranoid freak that would make you jump in fright if you saw him in day-life.' David took another deep breath. 'Picture this. Duty's hair is sticking to his face, his jeans are soaked, and he's spent the last of his money on Ecstasy, so he becomes predator now, amidst many others in varying states of ecstasy. He doesn't want to leave, not yet. If only he was sexy again, sparkling and funny, but his high has faded.

'Anybody who can afford a cab home looks attractive. If they're cute physically, it's a bonus. When so high, it doesn't really matter. He would have liked that guy showing his big dick at the urinal earlier, but he was last seen smeared against some muscles in hot pants. Then he remembers the dealer who asked if he could take him home, with the chat-up line, "I've ev'ryfing at 'ome, even Viagra. And I love to fuck." An offer Duty can't refuse.

'They leave with a bunch of other wet-faced, jaw-grinding monsters, presumably dropping en route. Duty presumed wrong. Back in suburban-rainy-Sunday-daylight, they all pile out of the cab and into a small room that looks like it belongs to somebody's grandma, but with fluorescent lighting and techno music.'

'Bleak,' said Joe.

'We're only just getting to the good bit,' said David.

'There's some knocking on the ceiling, so Dealer turns down the music. "Old man," he said. "Just lost his wife." That was more information than Duty needed. Now he pictures the man upstairs, lonely, sad, and he's wishing he hadn't left the club. It was warm and safe there, familiar, and full of mates who go every week.'

'I'll have to take a toilet break,' said Leila. 'Or I might never touch another E again.'

'God forbid!' said Ryan.

'Let me finish,' said David.

'Sure, but I'm out of here,' said Leila, and left the room.

'Light-weight,' said Ryan. 'Go on Unc.'

'Across from Duty there's someone on a beanbag giving dirty looks, and whispering too loudly to his boyfriend. There's been a shitload of negative humour flying around since they arrived. Duty decides to make coffee, mainly to get out of the room, but also hoping it will stop him feeling so monged-out. The kitchen is cold, and can't ever have been cleaned. He fishes out cups from the fluid in the sink that actually stinks. He starts to make fifteen coffees, all with three or more sugars, but there aren't enough cups, so he makes some of them in bowls. Back in the living room, Dealer gives another tab to everybody, so it's not long before everybody's rushing again. As you all know, a rush this late on isn't like the first. It kind of staggers through your system, scratching along the way. It's less of a rush, more of an attack, with no euphoria, just the feeling that there are chemicals in your system.'

'Please stop,' said Leila as she re-entered the room.

'No. I want to know what happens to Dealer, Duty, Fidgety-first-timer, and all the Ecstasys at the chill-out.'

'Yeah, please let me finish.'

'You lot are bloody masochists,' said Leila.

David barely hears what she has said. He's keen to carry on with his story. 'There isn't even a whiff of sex for Duty. Dealer's in the middle of the floor, dancing to his favourite track. His feet are creating wads of fluff as his trainers scuff the carpet. He's already kicked over two coffees, but says it's not a problem. Dirty Look, and some more of the Ecstasys join him. Dealer hands out another tab, and already it's time to leave for More. Everybody thinks this is a great idea. Dealer knows the doorman, so the whole party is sorted.'

'What's More?' said Ryan.

'Another club, much the same, on Sunday.'

'It's very different,' said Joe, defensively.

'Okay, tell me how.'

He thought for a moment. 'Tragic's on Saturday. More's on Sunday.'

'Oh, I understand,' said Leila. 'What you actually mean is Tragic's on Saturday, whereas More's on Sunday. I get it. Will we end up at More?'

'No!' said David. 'It's crap. We're going to Tragic.'

'Keoul,' said Leila, with her American accent again.

'No, hawt!' said David.

'Right!' said Leila. 'That's what I meant.'

David's story finally ended when Leila distracted him enough, and they all went to bed.

At half-past two, David went in to Ryan's room, opened the curtains to darkness, and said, 'Rise and shine. It's a beautiful . . .' He froze. 'Oh I think my clock might be wrong.' Then he pounced onto the bed and began to roll around.

'David! You heavy thing,' said Leila.

'I don't want you two falling asleep again. Your Uncle Joe's been up since the crack of dawn, chopping and mixing.'

'You're having us on,' said Leila, wide-eyed.

'No, he isn't,' said Joe, walking into the room in pair of pyjamas. He had a mirror in one hand and a glass jug in the other.

'Firstly,' said Ryan. 'What's in the jug? Secondly, you can leave that mirror with me.'

'Long Island iced tea. And wait your turn.'

'First things first,' said Leila, and clicked her fingers sternly. 'The mirror.'

'That's my kind of gal,' said David.

'I want to hear more about Duty, Dealer, Dirty Look, and the rest of the Ecstasys,' said Ryan.

'Good memory!' said David.

'Hey those guys are family.'

'Don't worry. You'll see them all later. I'll make sure I introduce you.'

'No thanks,' said Leila.

'You'll like them, I'm sure.'

'I don't think so,' said Leila.

'I do,' said Joe. 'You'll be one of them.'

'Let's do a line first,' said Leila. 'I don't think I can bear the reality of it all otherwise.'

'Hear, hear,' said Joe. They both stooped and banged heads.

'Coke whores,' said David.

'Finish your story, granddad,' said Leila.

'I warn you David,' said Ryan. 'She gives as good as she gets.'

'I don't want to hear about your sex life,' said David.

'Can we please cut the bawdy humour for one second,' said Ryan. 'There's an innuendo every other sentence in this house.'

'It's part of our rich culture,' said Joe.

'Which, gay?' said Leila.

'No. British.'

'You mean,' said Leila, 'the fact that we're repressed as fuck.'

'Exactly,' said Joe matter-of-factly. 'So we find subtle ways of communicating those frustrations.'

'Hardly subtle,' said Ryan and Leila simultaneously, before bursting out laughing.

Joe suddenly felt old, embarrassed, and separate.

7

Three-thirty. Outside Tragic. A cab pulled up. Contorting faces stood in the rain, watching, grateful for the distraction from simply waiting. David and Joe got out either side, and Joe went to pay the cab.

Ryan put out a hand. 'Is it still raining?' he said.

'Come on, Nelly,' said David.

Leila knew people were watching, so took her time. 'Shit,' she said, whilst still sitting in the cab. 'Look at the queue.'

'Don't worry,' said David. 'Come on, I'm getting soaked. What are you waiting for?'

'Dramatic effect,' said Leila.

'It's working. I suspect people think you're in a wheelchair.'

Leila put finishing touches to her lipstick, closed her compact, and popped them in her bag. She stepped out as though to a ball. She'd made a special effort. Her hair was sticking up in twisted spikes, and she had a fine layer of gold shimmer all over her. She had on a silver metal-link dress and spectacles that you could only pull off if you were an old lady or a supermodel. She looked magical.

'I can't queue,' she said.

'I said, don't worry. Joe will sort it out.'

'Oh, my God,' said Ryan. 'Joe's Dealer, isn't he?'

They cleared the cab and headed towards the entrance. The queue on the right was for regular punters, the one on the left for those on the guest list. Joe disregarded both, and approached the man with the guest list. The bouncers pulled in tight around him.

'Josef Oltzmen!' said the man.

'Lee!' said Joe.

'Gird ta see ya. Har meny av ya got wiv ya?'

'Just three.'

'Let this lot frew,' said Lee to the bouncers. They lifted back the metal barriers. Lee gave Joe four tickets and giggled.

'Let's have a drink later,' said Lee.

Joe liked Lee. 'I'll save you a spot on my dance card,' he said.

'Thet word bey charming,' said Lee, as near as he could to an old-fashioned, very proper accent. It was hopeless. His east end accent shone through. Joe ruffled his hair. Again, Lee giggled, and shuffled his feet, looking about seven years old.

Inside the door, they heard muffled music. The air was moist and warm. Two cashiers took the tickets Lee had given them, and gave attitude. Joe didn't recognise them. Another person stood to the right of the cashiers, with a rubber stamp.

'I feel like I'm on a conveyer belt,' said Leila.

'Yeah, to hell,' said David.

Finally down just a few steps, at the first bend in the stairwell, yet another person checked the stamps.

'Joe Holtzman!' said the stamp checker.

David turned to Leila. 'You get used to this. I can tell when people don't really know him. They use his surname. That's how they think of him, the celebrity Joseph Holtzman.'

'Is he that famous?' said Ryan.

'I hate to be cynical,' said David. 'But gays love it when someone is even remotely famous and gay as well.'

'It makes sense,' said Leila. 'It's validating.'

'Yeah,' said David. 'Like what you said.'

Joe led them further down the steps. They could feel the heat rise up their bodies as they descended, until it engulfed them completely.

They stopped at the second bend in the stairwell. From here they could see the whole of one room. Everybody had their shirts off, so there wasn't much colour, only varying flesh tones. Occasionally, a plastic bottle of water could be seen shaking above someone's head as they danced. There were a couple of neon wristbands, the kind that first appeared at the very beginning of Rave. David sighed when he spotted them.

'Why do you pretend to be stupid, David?' said Leila. 'It's obviously an act.'

'It's cute,' he said. 'Isn't it?' He paused. 'Marilyn did okay on it.'

'Marilyn was working within a different world,' said Leila. 'In those days women . . .'

'Okay!' said David. 'Enough serious talk. We're meant to be mindless.'

'When should we start?' said Ryan.

David looked at his watch, 'Twenty-two, twenty-three. Now!'

'In that case, I'm off to find my mates, Duty and Dirty Look.' He looked over the crowd. Ryan pointed at somebody. 'There he is.'

'That's not Dirty Look. That's I'm-very-sexy-look-at-me.'

'It can't be,' said Leila.

'It is,' said David.

'God, he's changed,' said Leila.

'Let's get a drink in the café upstairs,' said Joe. 'It's not so gym-like.'

They turned around and headed back the way they came.

'Had enough already?' said Lee as they passed the front door.

'I'll be back for you later,' said Joe without stopping.

They entered a less chaotic room, with table and chairs.

'The café,' said Joe. 'Better?'

'I guess so,' said Leila.

They claimed a table. Ryan and Joe sat down, Leila remained standing, and David went to the bar. Leila took hold of the hem of her dress.

'Here we go,' said Ryan.

Leila lifted her dress, but instead of stopping at head height, she continued lifting it over her head. She took it off completely. Nobody took any notice. Leila rolled up the dress and stuck it in her bag.

'I wondered how long that would last,' said Joe.

Underneath the dress, Leila wore a lilac bra and a pale green slip.

'You look amazing,' said Ryan, a mix of lust and awe in his eyes.

'I'd have to agree,' said Joe.

Leila seemed to respond more to Joe's compliment than to Ryan's. She pouted her lips and sighed. Ryan didn't relate her reaction to Joe's comment, but registered something slightly off-kilter. Ryan wasn't being vigilant. Tragic, with his uncle, was the last place on earth he'd feel it were necessary.

David came back with the drinks. 'Somebody could have helped me.'

'We were kind of busy,' said Leila.

'Doing what?' said David.

'I'm not sure,' said Leila. 'Oh yeah, changing.'

A bunch of sweaty men came up to the table; shirtless, with shaved chests. They talked, and flirted for about five minutes, then moved en mass to the bar.

'They go to the gym where I work,' said David, as if it were an explanation.

'They look like uncooked sausages,' said Ryan.

'I don't understand,' said Leila. 'They all seem to be holding each other up.' Joe laughed, and David burst out laughing. 'An amazing feat, considering they were all so wet and slippery.' Leila shuddered. 'Ugh! They're grotesque.'

'They're really popular,' said David.

'You're joking. I'll never understand you boys,' said Leila.

'Boys is so patronising,' said David.

'It was meant to be,' said Leila. 'But, I was only kidding.'

'So was he,' said Joe.

'Let's take an E,' said Joe, not sure if he liked the negative tone of the conversation, and hoping to distract everyone.

'Yes,' said Ryan, a bit too quick off the mark.

'You're keen,' said David.

'Well, what are we waiting for?' said Ryan. 'It's not as though we'll stand out.'

'Yeah! Let's merge,' said Joe.

'Is that safe?' said Leila.

'It depends who you merge with,' said Joe.

'You, for example,' said Leila.

'Are you asking if he has HIV?' said David.

'I don't know,' said Leila.

'In that case,' said Joe, taking an E out of his pocket and popping it in his mouth. 'Here goes.' He made a face, as though it tasted horrible and reached for his drink. 'I wish somebody would sugar coat these fuckers.'

'Hear! Hear!' said David, doing almost the same set of actions exactly; pop, grimace, drink.

'Ryan?' said David.

'Why not?' he said, and followed suit.

'Leila?' said Joe.

'I've already done mine,' she said.

'When?' said Ryan.

'Back at the flat,' she said.

David raised his eyebrows, and shook his head in disbelief. 'So, do you love me yet?'

'Probably,' she said.

'Do you love everybody yet?' said Joe.

'I guess so,' she said.

'Do you love yourself yet?' said Ryan.

'I only had one,' said Leila.

David and Joe laughed. Ryan was used to this type of answer, so he half-expected it. The conversation carried on in much the same vein for a long while. The sausage men returned and left again. Lee came, bought the table drinks and sat on Joe's knee while he drank his. A bedraggled-looking drag queen came, and asked could she borrow Leila's lipstick. Although a little disgusted, Leila was pleasant. The drag queen loved the colour so much, she insisted Leila write down the name and brand.

When she finally left, and was out of ear-shot, David said, 'Your E must be good.'

'We'll have to get them again,' said Joe.

'Or put them in the water at home,' said Ryan.

'Why don't you lot eat shit,' said Leila.

'That's better,' said David. 'You scared me for a minute. I thought you'd OD'ed'

'I thought the poor bitch could do with some help,' said Leila.

'There's the Leila I know and love,' said David.

A mischievous look came over Leila's face. 'I'm glad I have you all together. I've been meaning to tell you this, and believe me, it's not the E talking.' Leila burst out laughing. 'But I love you guys.'

They talked some more shit for a while, mostly oblivious to their surroundings. They took another E. A different kind. It was more 'trippy' and 'mongy.' This had the effect of making them speak less and stare into space more.

'This is bollocks,' said Leila. 'Let's do some speed.'

'I can't move,' said David.

'Me neither,' said Ryan.

'I'm up for it,' said Joe, 'if I can keep hold of you on the way.'

'Just like the sausage men,' said Leila.

'I feel half-sausage at the moment,' said Joe.

'I'm more vegetable myself,' said David.

'Sounds delicious,' said Leila. 'But for some reason, I have no appetite.'

Joe stood up and said, 'I feel as though I've never done this standing thing before.'

'Come on,' said Leila. 'You'll get your E-legs in a minute.'

'Good luck,' said Ryan.

'Yeah, good fuck,' said David. Leila and Joe were already too far away to hear. Ryan looked shocked. 'Sorry. I don't know where that came from.'

'Try the abyss.'

'Possibly.'

'You're a weird mother-fucker David.' Ryan paused to think, but his train of thought went askew and wound up in mathematics. Not that he had the cognitive ability to do more than think how sound affects numbers. This went on for some time. Then he seemed to come round. 'David. Can I put my head in your lap? I could do with less sitting up.'

'Sure, puppy.'

Ryan fell to one side, as though collapsing. David caught him, and lovingly stroked his head. 'Ryan. Are you happy at our house?'

'God, yeah.'

'I'm glad. I'm going to blame this on the E, but when you were a kid, I always hoped we'd be able to hang out.'

'Shucks, grandpa,' said Ryan. 'I lurrrv you.'

'I lurrrrrrrrv you too, Bobby,' said David.

'E's a wonderful thing isn't it?'

'Sure is.'

As Leila and Joe passed the front door Lee stopped them. He gave them a bump of K, which made their journey that much harder. He also demanded a kiss, which lasted longer than Leila wanted it to. She twisted her hair, trying not to notice them. She eventually pulled at Joe's arm, which worked. They all laughed. Once more Leila and Joe headed towards the toilets. Lipstick Drag Queen stopped them to enthuse about the new colour of his lips. He now had only one heel and rambled on about how kind and beautiful Leila was. His makeup was barely on now, just stains and smudges. He put his arms around Joe and Leila, spilling his drink down Joe's T-shirt. Joe unhooked himself, pulled the T-shirt off and stuck it in his back pocket. It didn't actually go in his pocket, but fell into the black paste on the floor, unique to clubs all over the world. The drag queen made a fuss about Joe's hairy torso, and said what a lovely couple he and Leila made. Luckily, he needed to go to the toilet to check his makeup. He needed the women's because of the lighting. Joe and Leila went into the men's. Only two people were waiting, so it wasn't long before they were in a cubicle.

The toilet bowl was covered in blood. Because it was against white, and because there was acid in their E, it looked very vivid. They stared at it for a few minutes, before remembering they didn't actually need to use the toilet.

'It's quite pretty, really,' said Leila as she closed the lid.

'I was thinking that,' said Joe, and stood waiting.

Leila waited also. 'You've got the stuff,' she said eventually.

'Oh, yeah, sorry.'

Joe chopped the speed as efficiently as one would expect on so many drugs. Leila did hers first, then Joe.

'It tastes sweet,' said Leila.

'It doesn't burn, either,' said Joe. 'At least we know it's not wallpaper paste.'

'What?'

'It's a long story. I'll tell you sometime.'

'Maybe we'll get a rush from the sugar.'

'I think we're beyond being affected by such things.'

Leila got a little serious. 'I find when I'm this high, sugar does affect me. I think it's when I haven't eaten for hours . . .'

Joe leaned forward and stuck his tongue into her mouth. He let the whole weight of his body press against her. She returned the kiss, and stuck her hand down the front of his jeans.

'Sorry, drug dick,' said Joe.

This space gave Leila the time to think. Not so much think as react. Instead of continuing, she slid out of his embrace. Joe was so high he didn't think much of it.

'I'm sorry,' said Leila.

'What for?' Joe wasn't being cool. His thoughts really had moved on to something else.

'I like you Joe, and I think you're fucking gorgeous, but we've got to think about David and Ryan.'

'Oh, yeah.' Joe agreed because he was on E.

They finished the speed, and the kiss was forgotten. They fumbled with the latch, got out of the cubicle and made their way back to the others. They'd been gone about thirty-five minutes.

'That was quick,' said David. 'I thought you'd be ages.'

'We were. I think,' said Leila. 'Oh, the adventures we've had.'

'At least, you'll have some tales to tell your children,' said David.

'No one can say I haven't lived,' said Leila. 'There's a whole world out there in the club.'

Ryan opened his eyes. 'I'll have to try it sometime,' he said. 'But maybe not today.'

'You guys should get out more,' said Joe. 'There's so much going on.'

'Can't you just tell us?' said David.

'I guess so. Help me, Leila. There was Lee on the door. That was interesting. Then there was that bouncer.'

'Yeah,' said Leila, 'That was interesting. Then there was that place downstairs with the wobbly people.'

'Oh, Leila. You don't do it justice. There was that giant woman with the lipstick.'

'Yeah! Half-beast, a quarter woman, and a quarter man. Oh, the things we've seen.'

'Okay, we get the picture,' said David. 'You went to the toilet, saw the dance floor from the stairs, and you bumped into that drag queen.'

'No doubt,' said Leila, 'you two have been doing something much more stimulating.'

'We've been melting into the chairs,' said David.

'As well as each other,' said Ryan.

'And every plastic cup, and cigarette end that got in our path.'

'It's great here, isn't it?' said Leila, and finally they all laughed as much as they could be bothered.

'I love you lot,' said Ryan.

'You've done that joke already,' said Leila. 'I think. Well, one of us did.'

'You kids have fun,' said Joe with a renewed speed-induced burst of energy. 'I'm going to see who's here. Do you mind?'

'No,' said Ryan.'

'Are you going by yourself?' said Leila.

'No,' said David, getting up faster than he'd moved all night. 'I'm with you.'

'Okay?' said Joe.

'We're cool,' said Ryan.

They both disappeared into the crowd.

'Thanks!' said Leila sarcastically.

'We're okay here, aren't we? Did I tell you how fantastic you look?'

'You said amazing last time.'

'I'm not bugging you, am I?'

'No.' Leila looked around as though what she was about to say was top secret. 'Listen, I've an idea, but first you have to say whether you're in or out.'

'Out. No, I mean in.'

'In that case, follow me.'

Leila led Ryan to the toilets. There were men and women in jumbled lines outside each. The only distinction between the male and female toilets at Tragic was that one had urinals, and the other a couple more cubicles. Leila took Ryan by the hand and led him to the front of the queue in the women's. The people waiting were dazed and silent.

'What do you think you're doing?' said a women wet with sweat.

'Don't worry,' said Leila. 'We work here. We've got to get back to the door.'

'You weren't there when I came in,' said the girl.

'We've got to start now,' said Leila. 'Listen, do I have to get security?'

Like a slug in salt, the girl recoiled, her mind a mass of fear; of being thrown out, of being high with nowhere to go.

Her eyes darted, eager to avoid contact. Eventually, she said, 'Sorry, I didn't know you worked here.'

'No worry,' said Leila. 'You weren't to know.'

'The music's great tonight,' said the girl. 'The best ever.'

Leila nodded and smiled in an overly patronising way. She looked at her watch, as though conscious of being late. Feigning impatience, she sighed and knocked on a door. Just then, a door opened, and a man came out wafting the air in front of his face. Leila assumed this meant he'd had a shit and it smelt. When he cleared the doorway, Ryan and Leila slid in. Leila was right. It did smell, but as a bonus the man had left shit splattered all over the side of the pan. Leila closed the lid and flushed the chain with her foot. She opened the door again and asked somebody for some matches. The man who'd caused the smell was still there, apologised and gave her a box of matches, telling her she could keep them. Once a match was lit, and the smell dealt with, Ryan sat on the floor with his back against the door and Leila sat on the lid of the toilet. She opened her bag, and rummaged.

'There,' said Leila.

'What. . .?' Ryan stopped as he realised what she was holding.

'Don't look so shocked. It's just a bit of coke.'

'Just a bit of coke in a syringe.'

'Sssh! Give me your belt.'

Ryan undid it, slid it out of his jeans, and marvelled at the ease with which his girlfriend put it around her arm.

'You've done this before.'

'You know I have. Don't act so shocked.'

'I hope one of them isn't for me.'

'I hope it is,' said Leila.

'What, here in the toilet?'

'Why not?'

'I didn't imagine the first time I shot up would be in a toilet.'

'Where else?' said Leila. 'It's perfect. Don't you see?'

Ryan thought for a moment. 'Actually, I do.' He smiled mischievously. 'But, you'll have to do it for me.'

'Naturally. I couldn't at first. You get used to it.'

'Not too used to it, I hope.'

'Now I associate the needle with the feeling afterwards.'

'Should I bother asking?'

'You'll see.'

'Actually, I better do you first,' said Leila, taking the belt off her own arm. 'I won't be in a fit state afterwards.'

'Okay.' Again, he paused. 'I really didn't picture it like this. I can't imagine what I did picture.'

'Dancing girls? Ponies? Acrobats?'

'Okay!'

'Which arm?'

'I don't know.'

'This one's got the best vein.'

'You sound like a vampire.'

'You'll be grateful. Just you wait and see.'

Matter-of-factly, she took hold of Ryan's arm and put the belt around it, tightened it, tapped on his vein and injected. For a second she watched him, as his eyes began to widen, and his back stiffened. She took the belt off his arm and immediately got on with her own. Again, she tightened the belt. The area where she was about to put the needle looked particularly dirty, so she licked it to clean it and took another quick glance at Ryan. He was staring ahead of him. He swallowed hard and said, 'I love you.'

'You mean you love the feeling,' she said. 'Intense, hey?'

There was no answer. Leila assumed he was enjoying it, so went to put the needle in her own arm, then stopped. She looked up again.

'Ryan?'

By now his face looked like it was going to pop. He was sitting against the door. He started to bang his head backward.

'Baby, don't,' she said, worried they'd be thrown out of the club. He banged harder.

'Baby!' Vomit spewed out of Ryan's mouth, splashing all over Leila's lap and legs. It was mainly alcohol, so just ran off her. In a state of shock, Leila watched Ryan as he closed his eyes and slid towards the wall.

'Ryan!' There was no answer.

Leila leant forward, undid the belt around her arm, and quickly did it up again around his waist. She didn't bother putting it through the belt loops. Next she put the two needles in the sanitary towel bin, pulled open the door, and squeezed out.

'My boyfriend's passed out. Will somebody help?'

Outside the queue had changed little, except the sausage men were splashing themselves with cold water.

'Let me deal with it,' said one of them, sounding surprisingly sober.

He and Leila squeezed back into the cubicle.

Ryan already had his eyes open. 'What's going on?' he said.

'You passed out,' said Leila.

'Let me take a look at you,' said the man. He checked Ryan's pulse. 'What were you guys doing in here?'

'Just a bit of coke,' said Leila.

There was a knock at the door. It was David. He squeezed in.

'It's nothing to worry about,' said the sausage man. 'They've just been overdoing it a bit.'

'Thanks, George,' said David.

'No problem,' said George. 'Can you stand?'

'Sure,' said Ryan. David and George helped him to his feet, but instantly Ryan slouched and fell into George, who caught him and laughed. Ryan looked very pale. Leila pulled the toilet roll out of its holder and dried the vomit on her legs.

'Let's get him some fresh air,' said George. 'David, you maybe should think about getting him home.'

'That's probably not a bad idea,' said David.

'But we've just got here,' said Ryan, barely using real words. Awkwardly, they all bundled out of the toilet.

Joe arrived. 'What happened?'

Again, George spoke, assuming the voice of authority. 'They've just been overdoing it a bit.'

'Let's go home,' said David. 'Thanks again, George. I'm glad you were here.'

'I didn't do anything,' said George. 'He's fine.'

'Wait till Judy hears about this,' said Joe, raising his eyebrows, and shaking his head.

'Jesus!' said David.

'It's my fault,' said Ryan.

'That's not how she'll see it,' said David.

They made their way to the front door. They might have been embarrassed they were in such a dishevelled state, but they were too high to care. There were lots of cab drivers touting for business. As they walked out onto the pavement, Joe spotted a black cab on its way toward them. He whistled. The cab stopped, and they all got in. Ryan lay with his head on David's lap, moaning dramatically.

'Had a rough night?' said the driver.

This ignited something in David; disgust, hatred, or anger. He turned to look at the driver. For no apparent reason, David disliked him. Joe saw David's response, put a hand on his knee and gave him a questioning look.

'You okay, baby?'

'I think so,' said David. 'I suddenly felt really scared.'

'It's probably just the drugs.'

'I know. But . . .' David's voice went quiet enough for only Joe to hear. 'Don't you think he's creepy,' he said gesturing towards the driver with his head.

'No!' said Joe. 'He's just some poor man trying to make a living.'

'There's something about him. He gives me the creeps.'

'Baby! My sweet-sweet-scared-kitten-thing. It's the drugs, trust me. He's probably as normal a man as you'll ever meet.'

'What are you two talking about?' said Leila. 'Apparently, it's rude to whisper.'

The driver looked into his rear-view mirror. 'Yeah! There's no whispering allowed in this cab. How do you think I take my mind off the job.'

'Don't take your mind off the job too much,' said Leila. 'It would be nice to get home safely.'

'There ain't no one safer on the roads.'

David looked in the rear-view mirror, listening to the driver, watching his forehead suspended within the small rectangle. For a brief moment, eyes replaced forehead, then darted out of sight. David thought him familiar. His thoughts were jumbled. Realising he was fighting a losing battle with the drugs, he resigned himself to believing that he'd simply had the same driver some other time. Leila farted, Ryan said something funny, and David, settling down into Joe's lap, forgot about his suspicions.

It wasn't long before the cab smelt of vomit, and the driver complained. To distract him, Ryan chatted. It was quite nonsensical, but the driver responded well, even seemed to like Ryan. Because of this, and opening the windows full, they got home without being thrown out. The cab dropped them right outside their house. As they got out David took a closer look at the driver. David didn't recognise him, so finally let go of what he now believed to be drug-induced paranoia.

Ryan was left to pay, then ran after them. 'You must have driven him mad,' said Leila, as he approached. 'The poor thing has to rest.'

'What do you mean?' said Ryan.

'He hasn't gone yet.'

'He's probably clocking off.'

'Cashing up,' said Joe, agreeing.

'What? With no lights on,' said David.

8

By the time they got into the house, Leila was dying to have a bath. Ryan ran upstairs to prepare it. He put lots of bubble bath and lavender oil in it to make it smell nice. He joked that it would have a calming effect. In reply to this, Leila suggested they do peppermint instead of cocaine in future. Everybody agreed.

David warmed some hot milk, and although nobody felt like drinking it, on his advice that it would be good to put something in their stomachs before sleeping, they did. Ryan brought Leila hers in the bath. Then he climbed in behind her. Soon David went looking for them and sat on the floor talking to them. Eventually, Joe arrived too, and stretched out across the floor. This kind of disrespect for the normal way of doing things, treating rooms in ways you wouldn't ordinarily, was common to being on drugs. It was slightly liberating, but was generally forgotten once sober.

Both David and Joe were invited into the bath, and they accepted. The only way they would fit in was sideways. All four of them sat with their legs over the side. They knew it must have looked ridiculous, but they all found it surprisingly comfortable and comforting. At one point Leila took it upon herself to get out, and pour water over each of them with a jug she got from downstairs. The heating had been put on full when they came in. Hence, Leila didn't bother putting a towel around herself, but ran down to the kitchen naked. She didn't even dry herself, so was covered in patches of suds. They all found this very funny and couldn't stop laughing. Something they found even funnier was when Ryan stood up and decided that he would climb over everybody else, pretending he was on an army assault course. Luckily, there was a scaffolding railing for him to hold onto, otherwise it could have been dangerous. He slipped a couple of times, and was caught by the others. The water splashed over the sides, but the taps were left running continually, so the bath stayed full. Ryan was obviously feeling much better after his ordeal at the club, so Leila suggested they finish off the drugs. This consisted of two Es and two wraps of damp coke. They split the Es into halves, regardless of how much each of them had already done. The coke was too damp to snort easily so David had the idea to put it in a drink. He rooted around in the cupboards downstairs, again not bothering to get dressed, and made a cocktail. When quizzed, he couldn't remember what he'd put in it. They all made faces when they tasted it, but eventually voted it the best cocktail 'in all the land.' Joe got bored of the bath first, complaining that it must look really clichéd, like a photo by Herb Ritz. They all cringed and reluctantly got out one by one, putting on towelling robes David supplied. Ryan was left in last, playing with the bubbles. He loved the idea that he could splash as much as he wanted and the water just poured over the sides and went down the drain. He slid backwards and forward, and almost emptied the bath without pulling the plug.

Joe was already downstairs, putting on music. Instead of choosing chill-out music he went upbeat, and turned the music up full. It was a detached house so there were no neighbours to think about. He sang along at the top of his voice. Soon Leila and David joined him. Occasionally, Ryan could even be heard howling upstairs. It seemed to have little to do with the track, but worked somehow.

By the time Ryan got downstairs a nest of quilts and pillows had been made on the living room floor. The blackout blinds, bought especially for such occasions, were down. The music was slower, sweeter, and candles had been lit. Leila was lying on her front, her knees bent and her feet crossed, wiggling in the air behind her. Joe rested on his elbows, his head in his hands. David knelt over Joe's back, massaging his neck.

'Cosy,' said Ryan.

'Fucked,' said Joe.

'Completely cunted,' said Leila.

'All the above,' said David.

'What a charming bunch,' said Ryan. He fell onto them clumsily.

'You must get that seen to,' said David.

'I've been meaning to,' said Ryan. 'But it's such fun.'

'Such a pain in the neck,' said Joe.

'That's what's fun about it,' said Ryan. At this Joe pulled at Ryan's towel and it fell off. Ryan picked it up quickly and wrapped it around him again. 'Isn't that illegal; necrophilia, or nepotism, or something?'

'Do you mean incest?' said David.

'That's the one,' said Ryan.

'Technically, I'm not related,' said Joe.

'So we can do whatever we like?' said Ryan.

'Whatever,' said Joe.

'Thanks a lot. I'm flattered. All you get me doing is decorating.'

'I'm afraid there is a reason for that,' said Joe.

'Do I want to hear this?' said Ryan.

'I don't know what you were hoping,' said David. 'But the reality is we just couldn't get anyone else at such short notice.'

'Thanks for not being mean, David,' said Ryan, and he crawled forward on all fours and gave him a lingering kiss on the lips. Instantly, David got a hard-on.

Ryan spotted the bulge and tried to grab it. 'Uncle David's got a hard-on,' he said.

David squirmed, but not before his robe had been pulled open. 'You little bugger.'

'Nice dick!' said Leila.

'Yeah, a real beauty,' said Ryan.

'How would you know what a beauty was?' said David.

'Us straight boys still know a good dick when we see one.'

'You surprise me,' said Joe.

'You gays,' Ryan said, pointing his nose in the air. 'Are not the only ones with an aesthetic appreciation.'

'Get you,' said David.

'Yeah, shut up,' said Leila. 'You wouldn't know a beautiful dick if it hit you in the face.'

'Now there's an idea,' said David.

'I think enough rubbish has been spoken this evening,' said Joe. 'It's time for...' From under the corner of the quilt they lay on, Joe pulled out a box. 'Rohypnol.'

'Yippee!' said Leila. 'I love them Rohies'

'Who doesn't?' said Joe.

'Don't,' said Ryan.

'Why?'

'I haven't told you about Rob and David?'

'No.'

'David will fuck you when you're asleep,' said Ryan.

'I *was* going to fuck you,' said David.

'I was gonna fuck Leila,' said Joe.

'There's no way then,' said Ryan. He looked at Joe. 'I wanted you to fuck me, Leila wanted David.'

'You'd be asleep,' said Joe. 'How would you know who did what?'

'It's the thought that counts,' said Ryan.

'I must admit, I've never heard that expression sound quite so warped before.'

'I like to know who's been up my bum,' said Ryan.

'You're so old-fashioned,' said David.

As they spoke, Joe popped tablets out of the blister packets and put them into their mouths.

'One!' said Leila.

'Sorry!' said Joe. 'I didn't know you were such an old hand.' He put another in everybody's mouth. 'Fairs' fair.' He smiled a ridiculous evil smile and rubbed his hands together. 'Ha, ha, ha! There, there, my pretties.'

'We better get in sleeping positions, before the Rohypnol hits,' said David.

'Baggsy the middle,' said Leila.

'I hate to use the word, but baggsy the other middle,' said Joe.

'No couples together,' said Leila. 'I don't want to be woken up with the sound of kissing and cuddling.'

This left little option. Leila lay with David and Joe either side, which left Joe in between Ryan and Leila. For the next twenty minutes, the conversation meandered, until eventually it slurred, and stopped mid-someone's sentence. Daylight had already arrived, but it didn't get through the blinds. Darkness returned. Ryan manoeuvred his head onto Joe's chest, and Joe responded by putting an arm over his neck. Leila was cuddled up behind them both, with her face squashed against Joe's back. David spooned around Leila, holding her tight. At some point, David woke to go to the toilet. He became aware he was holding somebody, and that it was a woman. The first cloudy thoughts that came to his mind were of Flora. This made him only mildly anxious, because he was still saturated with Rohypnol. Thoughts jumbled about, then smeared into place, and vaguely he understood. They wove their limbs in and around each other like worms as they slept. Many positions later, David woke. Without moving, and looking straight up at the ceiling, he said,

'Moaning!'

Joe made a growling noise.

Ryan replied with a noise that could have been the same language, then managed, 'Monday, or Tuesday?'

'What a wonderful sleep,' said Leila. 'But, my bum feels sore. Curious!'

'Mine does,' said Ryan. 'How odd. We must have picked something up at Tragic.'

'Yeah,' said Leila, 'David and Joe.'

'Joe, honey,' said David. 'You might want to cover up.'

Joe was lying with no covers on and his robe wide open.

'Ryan!' said Joe. 'What were you up to?'

Ryan opened his eyes for the first time and became aware of exactly where he was lying.

'In your dreams, mate,' he answered, lifting up his head and flopping back on the pillow.

'In my dream you had a lovely time. We all did,' said David. 'Including Judy.'

'Ugh!' said Ryan. 'I hate Ecstasy.'

'Why?' said David.

'You can't pretend you forgot what happened the night before,' said Ryan.

'The worst thing is not minding,' said David.

'I think that's because there's still some drugs in your system,' said Joe.

'Hooray for drugs still being in the system!' said Leila.

'Food, anybody?' said David. To which there were retching sounds from everybody. 'The latest research shows, it's really good for you.'

'Good-shmood,' said Joe.

'My thoughts exactly,' said Leila.

This anti-energy, barely functioning attitude lasted all day. The most nutrition any of them could stomach came via the nuts and milk in a Snickers bar. At some point, David felt he could stomach something more serious, so forced down some Sugar Puffs. Joe surprised everybody by getting dressed, leaving the house, and making it to the video store. They spent the rest of the evening watching episodes of Star Trek: The Next Generation, whilst melting into the floor more and more. By eleven o' clock, it was the most anybody could do to pull themselves up the stairs, using the banister, brush their teeth, and get into bed

9

After doing drugs, the loving, open sense of wellbeing is overwhelmed by insecurity, irritability, and a closing off. Thoughts become difficult to direct, impossible to shape.

It's only Monday. There's Tuesday, and, worse still, Wednesday to get through, before Thursday, which is more reasonable, and, eventually, Friday, which is usually only the beginning of a return to normality.

David lay in bed, not wanting to get up, waiting for less day to get through, tomorrow to be nearer, more of the week to have passed. He tried snoozing, but his tiredness seemed to have run out. The reassurance of sleep and dreaming was overtaken by being awake, and the dis-ease that came with it. He tried counting. Fear interrupted. He thought of blackness, but jumbled uncomfortable negativity kept shining through.

Leila tried a different method, although it wasn't so conscious. She got up early and cleaned. Neurotically, she dusted things. The usual cleaner did a good job, so it wasn't necessary. Still, Leila wiped the edges of things, vacuumed under things, and behind things. She emptied cupboards, rubbed the contents with a cloth and put them neatly back again, often in exactly the same place, but with everything facing the same way, the right way.

Ryan attempted to simply chill, relaxing in a hot bath, smoking a strong joint. The grass didn't calm him, only made him paranoid. After half an hour he gave up.

Joe decided to work on his exhibition. His post-drug-contorted way of seeing things was an ideal time to root around in such ideas as desperation, suffering, and hopelessness, and, by default, safety, passion and kindness.

Reluctantly, David got up. He didn't want to bother with being challenged, so had Valium for breakfast. Shortly after his second cup of coffee, he felt more able to deal with living. In case he'd missed anything important in the world, he put the tv on. In the living room, he found Leila bent over a pad, writing a letter to a friend.

'Are you sure that's a good idea?' said David.

'She's used to it,' said Leila, then paused a second. 'Are you sure that's a good idea,' she said, pointing to the tv with her pen.

'What, the news?'

'You mean gossip, and usually unpleasant. Apart from the cutesy-feelgood story they throw in at the end when they realise their viewers might commit suicide, so roll on the puppy story they keep in reserve and everything's okay. The world's not so bad.'

'I suppose that's one way of looking at it,' said David. 'Does the phrase good mood mean anything to you?'

'Good food? Of course! I'm not stupid,' said Leila. After a slight pause, she added, 'Just cranky, and only too happy to share it.'

'I don't think the word happy should be anywhere near that sentence.'

Ryan came into the room, wearing a bathrobe. 'Hello,' he said loudly, feigning good spirits.

'That outfit's so two days ago,' said Leila.

'One, actually,' said Ryan. 'It was Sunday. I'm not that old-fashioned.'

'Get you, Mr Pernickety,' said Leila.

'Shall I go out, and come back in again?' said Ryan.

'Or just stay out,' said Leila.

'Hey, kids!' said David. 'This is a house of lurve.'

'Now look who's behind the times?' said Ryan. 'That was Saturday, and I think I'm right in saying it was probably due to the E.'

David turned off the tv and sighed. Joe walked into the room. Everybody turned and looked annoyed. 'Jesus!' he said. 'What a sight. You lot remind me of that film The Time Machine. What were those things called?'

'Morlocks,' said Leila.

'My God, that's right,' said Joe. 'I love those things.'

'I should hope so,' said David.

Joe went over and squeezed David's cheeks. 'My bute-iful Morlock.'

'Why are you in such a good mood?' said David.

'I made some headway with my exhibition.'

'What's this exhibition?' said Leila.

'It's just a little show I'm putting together. I was having a bit of trouble with some of the ideas, but it's all coming thick and fast now.'

'Not too thick, I hope,' said David. 'You make it sound like a gardenparty.' He paused. 'It's not, is it?'

'What do you think?' said Joe.

'Knowing you,' said Leila. 'I'd say not.'

'Thank you, in more ways than one. Your CD is the cherry on the cake.'

'CD?' said Leila.

'The barking,' said Joe.

'Oh yeah! My party CD,' said Leila.

'And the tv jingles?' said David.

'That's my cultural CD.'

'You should hear the sad CD,' said Ryan.

'What's on that?' said David.

'Babies,' said Ryan.

'Babies crying,' said Leila, explaining more thoroughly.

'Why do you listen to babies crying?' said David.

'It makes me cry,' said Leila. Joe smiled.

'Why would you want to cry?' said David.

'I think it clears something,' said Leila. 'I don't know what.'

'I know what you mean,' said Joe. He put his head to one side and squinted slightly. His focus left Leila and rested a couple of feet in front of her.

'What are you thinking?' said Leila.

'I don't know, really,' said Joe. 'Something about you as a baby.'

Leila smiled in a coy way. Ryan saw this and looked at Joe.

'Sorry, can we just rewind a little. Why babies?' said David.

'Its something to do with them being so helpless, and a little to do with wondering what's making them cry. Poor little bubbies.'

'But it's only a recording,' said David.

'They're still upset about something,' said Leila.

'I guess so,' said David.

For a short space of time there was silence. David thought Leila was kooky. Leila thought David was obvious and a little flimsy. Ryan thought Leila was powerful. Joe thought they were all affected by the weekend. Leila pulled a smile at David. He did the same back. Ryan nodded at Leila. She winked back. David had a flashback to the first time he saw Ryan. Joe noticed David's facial expression. It puzzled Joe. The sun shone brightly through the window, and caught the tiny hairs on David's forehead. He seemed to glow. This was exaggerated by the fact that David was sun-tanned and wearing a turquoise T-shirt. More than this, the wall behind him was matt-black, and appeared to absorb light, whereas David reflected it, making him radiate.

Leila saw Joe staring at David. 'My God,' she said. 'I never realised how detailed that wall was, Joe.'

'That's David's handiwork.'

David turned around to look at the wall. 'It's hardly handiwork,' he said.

'How did you do it?' said Ryan.

'It's just black paint with marker pen over the top,' said David. 'It looks okay in this light, doesn't it.'

'He's used different coloured markers,' said Joe enthusiastically. 'Each one gives a slightly different hue.'

'Cool effect,' said Ryan.

'Yeah, beautiful,' said Leila.

'I was just thinking how beautiful David looked in front of it.'

'You guys are so corny sometimes,' said Ryan.

'You ain't seen nothing yet,' said Joe. He got hold of David and squeezed him.

'Joe gave me free reign. He said to draw anything I wanted. I can't draw for shit, so I kept it simple. Anyone can draw a teardrop.'

'But doing them different sizes creates perspective,' said Joe.

'I noticed that,' said David. 'But I have to confess, it was an accident.'

'Still, it is beautiful,' said Leila.

'What are you doing today, Ryan?' said David, trying to change the focus of the conversation.

'Don't know. See a film. Buy a book.'

'Good luck,' said Joe. 'That's like trying to find a person you like.'

'I agree,' said Leila. 'But we've all managed it.' She looked at Joe, then acted at brushing something off her skirt.

'What about you?' said Ryan to David.

'I was thinking of the gym.' Everybody looked at him startled.

'You're not being serious!' said Ryan.

'It was just an idea,' said David, a little embarrassed.

'We should all go,' said Leila. 'A family day out.'

'At the gym?' said Joe.

'It might be just what we need,' said Leila.

'Yeah,' said David. 'We could just do bicycle. Anything to get the endorphins going.'

'Who going?' said Ryan. 'Dorphins?'

'That's what dolphins have,' said Leila.

'They're dorsal fins,' said Joe.

'Endorphins are what make you feel nice,' said David. He looked at each of them with a "How about it?" expression.

'I'm up for it,' said Ryan. 'I guess.'

'If we're only guessing, then, you can count me in,' said Leila.

'I'm not going to sit here on a comedown by myself,' said Joe. 'I'll have nobody to take it out on.'

'Super,' said David.

'Did you say stupor?' said Leila.

'Who knows?' said David. 'But first, coffee. Coffee?'

'Here!' said Joe.

'Here!' said Leila.

'Here?' said Ryan.

'So, that's three hearing aids,' said David.

'How about a coffee while you're there,' said Ryan.

'What was that?' said Leila.

'I said, and some toffee for the bear,' said Ryan with exaggerated lip movements.

David headed to the kitchen, and half-heard Leila say that too much toffee wasn't good for the bear. He sighed and couldn't help rolling his eyes, despite nobody being in front of him to see this.

'It's actually the body's response to pain,' said Joe. 'Endorphins, that is.' He paused, his mind clearly racing. 'Fuck!' At this he ran out of the room, leapt upstairs, and across the landing.

Leila and Ryan were left in silence until David returned. 'Thank God for coffee,' he said.

This was followed by exaggerated smiles, followed by silence. They all fell into another round of looks and responses, reactions and misunderstanding. After a couple of minutes Joe came back into the living room panting and smiling.

'Fill us in,' said Leila.

'Just an idea,' said Joe.

'Energetic idea,' said David.

'I think it's worth it,' said Joe.

'Tell!' said Leila.

'You'll see,' said Joe.

David looked at Leila, puckered his lips, and smiled. She had no idea what he meant by this.

'We might be able to give you some useful feedback,' said Leila.

'I wouldn't bother,' said David. 'He won't budge.'

'You can give me feedback at the exhibition,' said Joe.

'In that case I hope it's soon,' said Leila.

'A couple of weeks,' said Joe.

'Fantastic!' said Leila.

Ryan noticed something in her expression, and in a singsong voice, he said, 'Leila's got a crush on Joe.'

Leila looked shocked. David looked confused. Joe blushed.

Ryan noticed Joe blushing. 'My God. I've hit something.'

'If you say enough stupid things,' said Leila, 'one day you might say something clever by mistake.' She screwed her face up. 'But not this time.'

'You could have fooled me,' said Ryan.

'Well, that wouldn't be too difficult,' said Leila.

'Now I know it's true. You wouldn't be so horrible if it wasn't.'

Leila looked at Joe, giving too much away.

Now David realised it was true also. 'If you don't shut up, Ryan, we'll go to the gym without you.'

Leila looked at David feeling grateful for his interception. David looked at Leila and smiled with concern. She saw a kindness in his eyes she'd never seen in him before.

David threw a bit of rolled-up tissue at Ryan. 'You're confused,' he said. 'It's me who has a crush on you.' This embarrassed Ryan enough to shut him up.

After several more cups of coffee and lots of encouragement from David, they all got out of the house. They got on the tube and off it again in Covent Garden. The gym was only a five-minute walk from there. When they arrived, David was greeted with smiles, judging, hellos, and varying degrees of hate. A man sitting having a coffee at the bar looked Joe up and down.

'What!' Joe said to the man, who looked into his coffee, swilled it around, finished it and left.

'Was that necessary?' said David.

'I can't stand it when men do that. What the fuck does it mean?'

'It probably means he fancies you.'

'So why can't he speak?'

'Because he's been oppressed all his life, because he's intimidated, he's not confident. Shall I go on?'

'Okay!'

'We could have gone to a straight gym,' said Ryan. 'It might have been less . . .' He paused, searching for the word.

'Paranoid?' said Leila.

'Cruisey?' said Joe.

'Friendly?' said David, looking at Joe.

Ryan rubbed his chin. 'I was thinking, complex.'

A group of men came walking towards them, laughing and screeching.

'David!' said the one at the front. He nudged cheeks with David and made a kissing noise. Then he continued a sentence into the air that he must have been in the middle of when he saw David.

When they left Leila said, 'Has he got hygiene issues?'

'Far from it,' said Joe. 'I've seen him on all fours at Fist.

'What's Fist?' said Ryan.

'A leather/fetish/bondage club,' said Joe.

'Maybe he'd lost his keys,' said Ryan.

'Lost his mind more like,' said Joe. 'His prissiness at least.'

'Please, baby!' said David. 'I've got to work here.'

'Oh, that's why we've come,' said Ryan. 'I wondered why.'

'Duh!' said Leila.

'So, we don't have to pay?' said Ryan.

'Exactly!' said Joe.

David went off to sort this out. Some men at a table a few feet away looked at Leila and started laughing.

'Watch out,' said Joe. 'We're being bitched about.'

'How do you know?' said Ryan.

'Well, which do you think it is,' said Joe. 'Either they're saying something flattering about us, or they're bitching. Take a guess.'

'They might be talking about the weather,' said Ryan.

'So why aren't they moving their lips?' said Joe.

'Because they're secret agents,' said Ryan.

'Cute,' said Leila. 'Or because they recognise us from the toilet in Tragic when you were almost carried out.'

'Can I just remind you that it was your fault,' said Ryan.

'My fault that you can't handle your drugs?' said Leila.

The men burst out laughing. Leila turned to look at them. One of them said something. The other pursed his lips, then said something back. The first looked shocked. To which the second pursed his lips and nodded slowly, his chin disappearing into folds of skin on his neck. Then they both took their coffee cups to the counter, made smile faces in Leila's direction, turned, and left. Leila wanted to make a smile face back, but felt so much hatred, she hadn't the command of muscles needed to achieve this.

David returned, grinning. 'Sorted!'

'Not more drugs,' said Ryan.

'Just caffeine,' said David.

'Was that a joke?' said Leila.

'Barely,' said David. 'It's the Monday after.'

'Fair enough,' said Joe.

'It will have to be,' said David. 'It's the best I can do.' He quickly looked at each of them in turn and pulled an expression of slight pain. 'Shall we get started?'

Joe winced.

'What?' said David.

'Can I wait here?' said Joe. David scowled. 'Please dad?'

'Really?' said David.

'I'm tired,' said Joe in a whiny voice.

'Okay already,' said David in his version of a New York Jewish accent.

'I didn't know it was that easy,' said Ryan.

'It isn't,' said David. 'Don't even think about it, young man.'

'But he . . .' Ryan started to say.

'But he'll make up for it. That's right, Ryan.' David was determined that nobody else would get out of gym duty. He thought for a moment. 'By cooking dinner.'

'Okay dad,' said Joe.

Leila laughed at their playacting. 'Come on, then. That's if we're still doing it.'

'I'll just sit and read,' said Joe.

'All right,' said David. 'See you when we're full of morphine.'

'I wish,' said Leila.

Leila was directed into the women's changing room and David and Ryan headed into the men's. Ryan undressed unselfconsciously. David couldn't do the same. He was aware that the men in the changing room all looked at each other. It seemed that because he worked there, everybody looked even more. An Asian-looking man came back from having a shower and stood too close to David. He let his towel drop to the floor and stepped on it, keeping his feet dry. David had to back away from him, especially when he started spraying deodorant under his arms.

In his new space, another man appeared and wanted to get into the locker behind him. David felt suddenly claustrophobic, so picked all his clothes up and dumped them in the largest unoccupied space he could find. Ryan thought it was overly dramatic, so laughed. David pulled off his jeans and sat down to change his socks. There were several jackets hanging on hooks. David noticed the Asian man peeping through. The man looked away when David caught his eye. Two men came back from the showers, without drying themselves. They talked loudly about work, and women, and left a trail of wet footprints. David found their behaviour verging on passive-aggressive, possibly even homophobic. Most members couldn't help wondering why straight men would go to a gay gym. If asked, David would shrug and say, your guess is as good as mine. To which there were about three main responses. Raised eyebrows, the comment that they must be closets, or a saucy smile. David had grown to despise all three.

Leila was stretching by the time David and Ryan had finished changing. This impressed David. Firstly, that she'd got ready so quickly. Secondly, that she looked like she knew what she was doing.

'Get you,' said David.

'I haven't been to a gym since I trained for the last Olympics,' said Leila.

'You are kidding,' said David. Then, uncertain, he said, 'Aren't you?'

Leila only smiled. This made David smile.

'I never know with you,' he said.

'You probably never will,' said Ryan. 'She always keeps me guessing.'

'What should we start on?' said David.

'We're doing more than one thing?' said Ryan.

'No,' said David, pretending he was trying to cover up a lie. 'What I meant to say was, what shall we do?'

'How about bicycle?' said Ryan.

'Or the step machine,' said David. 'Get that bum of yours in shape.'

'What shape?' said Ryan.

'I like it the shape it is,' said Leila.

'It will get the morphine circulating,' said David.

'Sounds good to me,' said Leila. 'But can't we just use a needle?'

'No more needles,' said Ryan.

'Needles?' said David.

'It's just a running joke,' said Ryan, realising he'd said too much in front of David.

They made their way to the step machines. From there they could see Joe sitting in the café.

'Joe!' shouted Ryan. Joe looked up. Leila stuck out her tongue and waved. Joe waved back. He watched them for a moment as they decided who was going to use which machine. He thought them comical, but a treat to look at.

'Excuse me,' said a deep voice.

Joe looked around. A man stood beside him. Because Joe was sitting, he came up to the middle of the man's stomach. For a fraction of a second, Joe thought about leaning toward the man, unbuttoning his fly, and sucking his dick. 'Do you mind if I sit here?'

Joe's response was little more than to look the man up and down quickly, then gesture with his hand to the chair in question. 'Thanks. I'm fucked. I don't know how I'm going to get through this workout.'

Again, Joe had sexual thoughts about the man. The word "fucked" had set off a stream of images. 'The name's Don,' said the man.

'Joe.'

'Have you finished?'

'No. I came with that lot,' said Joe, pointing. 'But I was too tired.'

'Big weekend?'

'Yeah,' said Joe, folding the page of his book and closing it.

'Sorry, am I interrupting?'

'Don't worry. It's no big deal.'

'I could shut up.'

'No, really.'

'Do you want anything?' said Don, standing up.

'I'm all right, thanks.'

Don walked toward the counter. Joe watched him. He thought Don was the sexiest man he'd ever seen. His T-shirt was snug, his jeans baggy. His clothes bulged in all the right places. Joe wanted to see him naked. He imagined this. Don turned to catch Joe looking at his arse and smiled. Joe blushed. Then he blushed more because he'd blushed in the first place. Suddenly, he felt teenaged, awkward.

Don came back to the table. 'Why are you blushing?'

'I'm just hot,' said Joe, and blushed again.

'I'll say.'

For the fourth time Joe felt himself blushing. By this point he felt ridiculous.

'Are you okay?'

'I thought so.'

'Until?'

'Until you came in. Do you always have this effect on men?'

'I don't know.'

'You do know this is a gay gym.'

'I know. I work just round the corner.'

'Where?' said Joe, unsure if this was the only reason Don came to this gym.

'The fire station.'

Every word Don said made Joe more attracted to him.

'You're a fireman?'

'Yeah, what about you?'

'Good question,' said Joe. 'I guess I'm . . .' He paused. 'An artist?'

'Shit! I've never met an artist before.'

Joe had a feeling in his stomach that was usually reserved for David. It made him uncomfortable. He looked over at David, who was sweating by now. He felt things he acknowledged as good. Relieved, he looked back at Don. Fuck! He was sexy. His forearms were huge, thick with swirling hair. His hands might have been cartoon, his fingers were so thick. He had a tattoo on the back of one of them of five straight lines, worn, obviously old.

'Nice tattoo,' said Joe. As soon as he'd said it, he felt very gay. "Nice tattoo." His awkwardness was crippling. Don didn't even bother answering, but gulped his coffee. Joe imagined that all the men that came to the gym must coo over Don. A fireman!

'Do you not get sick of all the attention you get at this gym?'

'No.'

Joe ran with a fantasy of Don not being straight. Then he felt pathetic for even having this thought. He imagined himself sitting talking to Don, and saw himself as corny and desperate, fawning. But the way Don's T-shirt hugged his stomach was fucking beautiful. Joe found it difficult to have the simplest conversation with Don without loading it with sex. Don spoke, and his voice was sexy. He said nothing and his silence was sexy. The way he held his cup, his lips, his throat and his jaw. Joe watched. Aware of this, Don looked back as he drank. Then he put his cup down and laughed.

'Sorry,' said Joe. 'Was I staring?'

'I don't know. Were you?'

Joe was silenced. He didn't know what to make of Don.

'Probably.'

Don laughed again, but longer.

Leila appeared at the table. 'What's so funny?'

'I don't know,' said Joe.

'Who's this?' said Leila.

'Don,' said Joe. 'This is Leila.' Then to clarify, 'A friend of mine.'

'Hello, Leila. Is that Persian?'

'It is, actually,' said Leila, charmed that he knew. She took hold of his hand and kissed it.

'Ladies never kiss my hand any more,' said Don.

'This one does,' said Leila.

'Shall I leave you two to it?' said Joe.

'Jealous?' said Leila.

'Maybe,' said Joe.

'I just came to see if you were okay,' said Leila. 'Clearly, you're doing fine.'

'Not really,' said Joe.

'No?' said Don.

'Am I?' said Joe.

'I'll let you figure this out,' said Leila. 'Those guys are staying on the step machines. I want to work out properly. Are you okay for a while?'

'He's okay,' said Don.

'I'll leave you in good hands,' said Leila, and did a dramatic kick into the air in front of them.

'What's that? A teenage mutant ninja turtle?' said Joe, thinking he was being up to date.

'No. Turtles are out,' said Leila. 'It's kung-fu this week.' She did another kick to near Don's head, but in slow-motion. 'Seee hyoo late ta,' she said. Then she jumped, and span mid-air, before running off.

'She's fun,' said Don.

'Yeah,' said Joe. 'Leila and her boyfriend are staying with me.'

'Cosy!'

'It's not like that. We're kind of related. Her boyfriend is my boyfriend's nephew.' Joe felt odd saying the word "boyfriend."

'I understand,' said Don. 'I think.'

Pointing again, Joe said, 'The blond one's David, my boyfriend, and the other one's Ryan.'

'Leila's boyfriend,' said Don. 'Your boyfriend's nephew.'

'You got it.'

'Happy family,' said Don.

'It is, actually.'

'Listen, I'd better get started.' He stood up. 'But . . .'

'Spit it out,' said Joe.

'I'd love to see your work.'

'I've got an exhibition soon.'

'Where is it?'

'Spitalfields.' Joe paused. 'Do you fancy seeing it?'

'Yeah!'

'I'll be setting it up in a couple of weeks. You could see it before it opens.'

'A preview?'

'Kind of. I could show you around it one evening.'

'Shit!'

'I better warn you. It's not paintings.'

'What is it then?'

'You could call them sculptures.'

'Shit!'

'Well, not exactly. They're animals.'

'Ah.'

'There's nothing cute about it.'

'What is it then?'

'I don't know.'

'What do you mean?'

'Wait and see. It will be easier to show you.'

'Woo, mysterious!' said Don. 'When do you want to do it?'

'You've probably a busier schedule than I have.'

'Maybe you could call me nearer the time.'

'Great!'

Don pulled out a felt tip from his denim jacket pocket and scribbled on a napkin, using the palm of his other hand to rest on. 'Here's my number. You can give me the address and stuff when you call.'

'Great,' Joe said again, a bit surprised at how forward Don was. 'I'll call.' Don turned and saluted. Joe watched as he walked away. Don's jeans were a baggy cut, but his thighs still seemed to be squashed into them. Joe's eyes stayed on Don until he turned the corner, enjoying the view. Joe stared into space for a second, then his sight drifted towards the step machines. David was drying his face and neck with a towel, and talking to Ryan. All with his eyes on Joe.

10

Joe called Don, several times. They got on well on the phone. As the time drew near to seeing Joe's work, Don got excited. Joe did too, but for different reasons. Although David and Joe had a relatively open relationship, other people didn't usually keep their interest for long. David was concerned that Don would. Joe seemed keen on him.

On the evening Joe left to meet Don, David pottered around the house, feeling awkward, as though he didn't quite fit the space. One moment he'd be too hot, the next too cold. He couldn't find anything to do that kept his attention for more than a few minutes. He decided to heat some milk, hoping it would help him relax. He zoned out, then remembered what he was doing. He caught the milk just as it was about to boil over. He poured a cup, and added some artificial sweetener. The doorbell rang. David opened it, cup in hand.

'Judy!'

'Thanks for getting him to call.'

'I can't make him call.'

'He got the messages, I presume. I hope.'

'Of course he did. Do you think I kidnapped him? And yes, it's nice to see you, too.'

'Oh yeah,' said Judy, clearly distracted. 'Is he in?'

'No, but you can still come in.'

'Thanks,' she said as she walked in.

'I know you must be upset, but don't take it out on me.'

'I wasn't. I mean, I'm not.'

'You mean you're always this rude?'

'No,' said Judy and gave David a hug. 'I'm sorry. I just got bored of waiting for him to call.'

'Lots of kids leave home at sixteen.'

'He wasn't meant to. I mean, I didn't want him to. He has to finish his education.'

'He didn't say anything about that.'

'He wouldn't, would he? He's meant to be going to the local college next term.'

'If I remember rightly, that's soon.'

'Very.'

'Do you want anything to drink?'

'Tea would be great.'

'Do you have a preference?'

Judy frowned. 'Ordinary, please.'

'English Breakfast?'

'English Breakfast! No. Teabag tea.'

'It is teabag tea.'

'*You've* been living in the big city too long.'

'Do you mean PG, or Typhoo. Something like that?'

'Yes!'

'Sorry, we don't have any.'

'Well, whatever tastes the most normal.'

'I guess that's Lapsang Souchong then.' Judy made a smile shape with her lips. 'Just kidding!'

Judy shrugged. 'Your London jokes are wasted on me.'

'Right,' said David. Facing away, he rolled his eyes, and headed into the kitchen.

Alone Judy couldn't help but inspect the room. Something caught her attention, just above the doorway. She stared, trying to understand. As David came back into the room, she said, 'It's not right.'

'What?' said David.

'Putting chocolate on that cross.'

'It's just a joke.'

'If God's not for you, fine. There's no need to mock.'

'It's not about mocking God, but about questioning the things we worship.'

'I don't worship chocolate.'

'It's not just about chocolate. It's about all large companies, consumerism, capitalism generally, the worship of money and success, that kind of thing.'

'I don't worship those things.'

'But some people do.'

'It makes sense to,' said Judy.

'Do you think?'

'Money is power, and in a way it has depth.'

'You're losing me,' said David.

'It can move mountains, make the blind see and the lame walk, etc, etc.'

'Now I see what you're getting at. It makes Joe's joke seem petty.'

'All things are petty in the presence of God.'

'That sounded both biblical and trashy all at the same time.'

Judy ignored David's remark. 'What I mean is, for some, God is their quietest, most severe and pure self. So comparatively, most things will seem petty.' David was silent. 'Don't you think?'

'I don't know.'

'Maybe your ideas are more about yourself than God.'

'Maybe.'

'But that's the beauty of God,' said Judy with an exaggerated evangelist zeal. 'It is whatever we want. Whatever we dare imagine.'

'Maybe.'

David got quite introspective.

'Where've you gone?'

'Inside.'

'Nearer your God?'

'Maybe. I hadn't looked at it that way before.'

Judy smiled. It was obvious she'd got through to David.

'Stop me if you like, but I presume you don't believe that there's this guy in the sky.'

'No!'

'Phew. I thought . . .'

Judy interrupted. 'You could have asked me.'

'God's not the kind of thing that comes up in small talk.'

'This small talk you speak of. Whose idea was it?'

'I don't know.' David was uncomfortable.

'It's not my fault,' said David.

'What?'

'That Ryan came here.'

'If you weren't here, he wouldn't have come.'

'I mean, it's not my fault he left home.'

'What makes you think I thought it was?'

'You seem intent on making me look a fool, or something.'

Judy's expression switched, as though a different program had been downloaded. 'I'm sorry. I didn't mean to make you uncomfortable.'

'That's even more disturbing. If it wasn't your intention it makes me wonder what's going on in your head.' He paused. 'Judy. Do you even like me?'

'I like you. I'm just not sure about your lifestyle.'

'What do you know of my lifestyle?'

'David, I'm not stupid.'

'I didn't think you were.'

'I know what you get up to.'

'How?'

'It's written all over your soul.'

This remark made David think she was completely insane. At the same time, he felt as though she could see into him. He blushed and tried to distract attention away from this by washing the dishes, making a lot of noise.

'David, you haven't changed. Always the blusher.'

Ryan walked in. David turned.

'Oh, Ryan. I didn't hear you come in.'

Seeing Judy, Ryan pulled a shocked face. 'I'm not surprised. All that banging.' He casually threw down his bag and kissed Judy on the cheek, then did the same to David.

'I was washing the dishes. I know it's weird.'

'I think he was trying to drown me out,' said Judy.

Ryan nodded and made a comical resigned expression.

'Look at your hair,' said Judy.

'Why, what's it doing?' said Ryan.

'I couldn't tell you,' said Judy.

David scuffed Ryan on the head and said. 'If you're going to have hair that misbehaves, it may as well be beautiful.'

Ryan looked at the floor. He wasn't acting. 'So, what brings you south of the wall?'

'I 'ad to get some goose fat,' said Judy. 'Before Saint Swithen's day.'

'Nice accent,' said David. 'What century was that?'

'Sixteenth.'

'Something tells me you've got eighteenth and seventeenth, too.'

Judy nodded and smiled so much that all of her top teeth showed. She let out a stifled, 'Ha, ha.'

'Mum's quite the comedian,' said Ryan as he poured himself a huge glass of skimmed milk.

'Healthy!' said Judy.

'He doesn't have much choice,' said David. 'Oh yeah, what's this about college?'

'It's where people get learning,' said Ryan.

'I know what it is. What I didn't know was that you were meant to be going.'

'Neither did I.'

'You know that's what your father and I wanted.'

'Are you sure?'

'Yes! And I'll forget about the smoke, or whatever you call it.'

'What about the next time?'

'There'll be a next time?'

'There's always a next time.'

'Does there have to be in this case?'

'Mum!'

Judy knew what this meant. She winced and reluctantly said, 'Okay.'

Ryan smiled. This made David smile. This and seeing that they were really communicating.

Judy let out another, 'Ha, ha!'

'I know I'm going to sound a hundred years old, but you're really lucky that you can talk to your mum like that.'

'This is lucky?'

'I'd hate to see unlucky.'

'I'll show you unlucky,' said Judy, trying to sound like a mum.

'So what will you be studying?' said David.

'Hey! We're jumping ahead a bit.'

'Sorry,' said David. 'What might you be studying?'

'English and drama. There's quite a good drama course.'

'It's one of the best in the country,' said Judy.

'It's one of the only ones,' said Ryan.

'Best. Only,' said Judy. 'Don't split hairs.'

'So, you're going to be an actor?' said David.

'Already am.'

'That he is.'

'Quite an actor, is our Ryan,' said Judy. 'He can lie like it's the norm.'

'Isn't it?' said David.

'Please don't encourage him.'

David dried the things he'd washed and started rooting through the fridge. It was spray-painted black and stuffed with food.

'You keen on shopping?' said Judy.

'It's something to do.'

'Are you short of things to do?'

'Sometimes. I could live to sixty, what with new medications these days. I have to fill my time somehow.'

'You could go to church,' said Judy.

'Believe me, I've thought of it,' said David.

'Never miss a chance, hey, Mum?'

'I don't mind,' said David. 'She's got a point, too.'

'There's only so much socialising, reading, drug taking and sleeping one can do. I could do with something other in my life.'

'So learn a new language,' said Ryan.

'It doesn't hit the spot,' said David.

'Have you tried?' said Ryan.

'Si.'

'You speak Spanish?' said Judy.

'Un poco.'

'Cool,' said Ryan.

'Before you get excited. I can only ask for beer, where the sauna is, stuff like that.'

'The necessities, then,' said Ryan.

'I got by just fine,' said David.

'Well, you're blond,' said Ryan. 'They must have loved you.'

'Over and over again,' said David.

'Spare us the details,' said Judy.

'Tell me later,' said Ryan, and winked.

'It's nice to see you're having a good influence on him,' said Judy.

'I like to think we help him broaden his horizons,' said David.

'As long as that's all you're broadening.'

'Judy!' said David, truly shocked that the idea came from her mind.

Ryan laughed. 'I told you mum was a comedian.'

'It's not that funny,' said David.

'I'm laughing at mum saying it, not the idea of you doing it.'

'Oh,' said David, then realised he was beginning to blush. Ryan also looked uncomfortable.

After several seconds of awkward silence, David began to move things around on the table. Judy broke the awkwardness, saying,

'What a pickle.'

First Ryan, then David, then Judy laughed.

11

Dusk. Smithfield meat market. As his cab pulled up, Don glanced at his watch. On the other side of the road another cab pulled up. Although silhouetted, he could make out that it was Joe. Don paid, put his fingers in his mouth, and whistled. Joe heard this as he got out of his cab, and raised his hand in recognition.

'I like a man who's punctual,' said Joe.

'Me too,' said Don.

'Any trouble finding it?'

'No. I got a black cab.'

'How are you?'

'Good!' said Joe. 'I had a good day.'

'What does good entail?'

'You know, no death in the family. Didn't come across any starving children. I didn't catch any incurable diseases.'

'You *did* have a good day. How did you manage to avoid all that?'

'I stayed in bed.'

'All day?'

'Sure did.'

'You lazy bugger.'

'Thank you. What did you do?'

'I saved a mother and her baby, trapped in a burning house.'

'You're not kidding, are you?'

Don smiled, then looked at his watch. 'So, the gallery's closed now. There'll be no one there?'

'Only the security. Why, what have you got planned? And it's not a gallery, ordinarily.'

'What is it?'

'It's a disused shop. A butcher's.'

Joe rang the bell. An old man answered the door.

'Hello Shawn.'

'Hallo, mate.'

'Everything okay?'

'Yeah. It's nice to have company. It gets spooky here at night.'

Are you thinking of staying long?' said Shawn.

'As long as it takes,' said Joe. 'An hour. Maybe a bit longer.'

'Well, I'll be here if you need me. I can't hear them if the telly's up loud.'

'Okay,' said Joe. 'See you in a while.' A cry came from down the corridor. Joe winced. Don looked confused. 'I'm afraid that's where we're heading.'

'Nice!' said Don.

The corridor was lit by single bulbs, so one was never too far away from darkness, corners that couldn't be seen. Joe pushed open two big wooden doors. As he did, the whole spectrum of noise could be heard, crackling, moaning, and whining. The noises sent a shiver up Joe's spine.

'Jesus!' said Don. 'I feel like I've just walked into hell.'

'Great response,' said Joe. 'It's not too late to change your mind.' Don faltered. 'Really, it's not. You probably see enough hideous stuff at work.'

'That's kind of my feeling about it.'

'Let's skip it.'

'I think I get the idea.' Joe took hold of Don's hand and led him out of the exhibition space. 'Sorry.'

'No. I'm sorry. Well, that's how I'm meant to feel.'

'What do you mean?"

'I hope I have some kind of conscience about creating this.'

'I'm sure you do.'

'Thanks, but I can't help wondering if I'm just really fucked-up.'

'That sounds like a good start. I would have thought it essential for an artist.'

'Well-counselled.'

'We get training in it.'

Joe burst out laughing. His voice echoed through the corridor. With the doors closed to the exhibition, the sounds of it were muffled, but still audible.

'Let's get out of here,' said Joe.

'I'm right behind you.'

They went back through the same corridor, feeling more on edge.

'Shawn,' said Joe. 'We've changed our minds.'

'No offence, mate, but I'm not surprised.'

'None taken.'

'So, when's the official opening?'

'In two days. I started putting it together about a week ago. I wanted it to be ready before the press saw it.'

'Is it?' said Don.'

'Let's say, it's how I imagined it.'

'That's good,' said Don. 'I think.'

Joe raised his shoulders, frowned and then smiled at the same time. 'I guess so.'

'Good night to you both then,' said Shawn, and pulled open the door to the street.

'Thanks, Shawn. I'll see you Tuesday, unless there's a hiccup.'

'Tuesday it is, then,' said Shawn, and closed the door behind them. On the street, they had to walk a few streets to get a cab. It was a beautiful evening, the air warm.

'God, look at the moon,' said Don. They stopped.

'That's the kind of moon people fall in love under,' said Joe.

'Or turn to werewolves.'

Joe turned to face Don, who said something else about werewolves, and love being connected. Joe could only watch him. It was bright, so Joe could clearly see Don's lashes, and his mouth. Joe stared at his lips. It was as though they were saying something else, something about being kissed. It might have been the way they moved, puckering needlessly, or the look in Don's eye, his pupils large, or the angle at which his body leaned forward. Surely it wasn't necessary for Don to make the breath from his speech be felt against Joe's nose. Joe became saturated, smelling, tasting, and breathing Don in deep. Before he knew it, he had pressed his lips against Don's. They were warm, dry, and gave in to Joe's. After a few seconds, Joe pulled back.

'God! I was dying to do that.'

'I think you're a beautiful man . . .' said Don, then paused.

'It sounds like there's a but.'

Don made an expression like it was painful to say what came next.

'But?' said Joe.

'I'm straight.'

'Jesus. I didn't think there were any of you left.'

'Sorry.'

'Hey, there's nothing to be sorry about. We didn't do anything. I was just checking I guess.'

'That's fair enough, and I must admit, a real ego boost. You must be able to get anybody you want.'

Joe pulled Don's arm to continue walking. 'Obviously not,' he said. The night still felt beautiful.

12

Flora sat in her studio, restless. All week she'd been working on a design, an art-therapy theatre space for the elderly. It was within the shell of an old factory that had been used for many things since being built, including ammunitions packing and a tea warehouse. It was a big project, but was finally finished. Not wanting to begin anything new, she answered e-mails, faxed a couple of things, and wiped her desk with some antibacterial spray. It occurred to her she was killing time, but she wasn't ready to leave just yet. She imagined she was possibly waiting for rush hour traffic to clear. No. Maybe she didn't look forward to going home to an empty house. She decided to clear her computer of extraneous stuff and defragged it, hoping to speed up her hard disk. She opened and closed folders one after the other, sometimes deleting, other times rearranging them. A folder titled "Miscellaneous" caught her attention. It had been a long time since she'd seen it, let alone opened it. If computer files could gather dust, this would have a thick layer. As expected, there was all sorts of stuff in it, letters, personal and work-related, a schedule for a job a year previous, a recipe for Christmas cake, even a couple of poems. Within it she found a file titled "You." She opened the file, her eyes glancing quickly over it. It was prose, a letter, but clearly not for anyone else to read. It was as though Flora had written to herself. Fascinated, she read on, became more involved, then recalled the feelings that went into it, remembering the pain. When finished, she immediately started at the beginning again. She snickered a few times, then began to laugh. Suddenly self-conscious, she looked around to see if anybody had overheard. She was alone, the room empty. When she'd finished it for a second time, something began to grow within. At the same time, it fuelled and burned her. She had to let it out, so began to write.

"Love. It filled me as much as emotion can, and it emptied me. I never want it again. Maybe it wasn't love, and I still have that to look forward to. If it was, then love stinks. Abandoning me as quickly as it engulfed me. Making me rotten as slowly as it made me grow. Romantic love is small, fleeting and arbitrary.

The love a mother has for a child. That is true love. It needs her. It can't live without her. It is a part of her and belongs to her. I believe there is no greater love. The child doesn't even have to reciprocate. Still, the mother knows. This love doesn't have to be fed by flattery, explanation, or sex.

Joe and David have a silly love. It will last as long as their desire. It is superficial. Deep within him, David still loves me. Things like that can't be stopped by a change of the mind.

Our love is eternal. Rather, as long as we both live. Joe is insignificant, an inconvenience. More than this, he's an annoyance. David's my baby."

Flora closed the file and shut down her computer. She sighed deeply and stared ahead of her. Slowly but definitely her lips pulled in tighter and her eyes squinted. There was a clanking noise. A door opened behind her.

'Sorry miss,' said the cleaner. 'I thought everybody was gone.'

'Don't worry, I'm off now.'

'What should I do with these drawings?' said the cleaner, referring to a huge roll of photocopies.

'Actually, we're done with them. We didn't get the job. You can bin them.'

'Didn't you have your heart set on designing that place?'

'Uh huh.'

'Oh! I'm sorry, honey.'

'It doesn't matter. There'll always be babies, so hopefully there'll always be a need for nurseries.'

The cleaner picked up the roll and set off down to the bins. Flora, taking her cue, decided to leave. She collected a few things off her desk and headed home.

On the street, there was still a post-work urgency, everybody eager to get home. The traffic was thick; inches apart in places. Once home, she felt weary, bored. The telephone rang.

'Baby! How's your arse?'

'Round, hard, a little hair in the crack.'

'I mean. How does it feel?'

'Beautiful. You should check it out sometime.'

'I don't think I could be accused of neglecting it.'

'I suppose you're right.'

'Are you hooked yet?'

'Course!'

'I knew you'd like it.'

'I understand why gays do it now.'

'Don't even think about it. I lost one boy to gays already. I'm not about to lose another.'

'Only fooling. I like breasts squashing against my back whilst I'm getting fucked.'

'That's my boy. You just keep thinking that.' The man's voice fell silent. 'Is my baby okay?'

'Yeah,' he said, a bit of whine in his voice.

'What's wrong?'

'Nothing. I'm just a bit down.'

'I know what you need.'

'Go on.'

'I know a few shops in Knightsbridge that stay open late for their good customers. How's about I give them a call and we go burn some of that stuff.'

'I think it's called money.'

'Yeah, yeah, yeah!'

'You earn too much.'

'There's no such thing. Apparently one can't eat too much chocolate, lose too much weight, or earn too much money.'

'Says who?'

'Hello! magazine.'

'Known for their highly accurate facts and subtle reportage.'

'That's the one,' said Flora. 'Listen, I'll just make some calls, jump in the shower, and pick you up in thirty.'

'Thirty it is.'

'Bye!' Just as Flora took the receiver away from her ear, she heard the man speak. 'What? Sorry, I didn't hear you.'

'I said. You won't make me pay you back for this in some hideous, twisted, fucked–up, sexual way?'

'Of course!'

'Good. See you in thirty.'

Flora went to the toilet, brushed her teeth, reapplied her lipstick, changed her tampon, and left. Rush-hour traffic had thinned, so she made good time. Driving down a central street, Flora pulled over and honked. Within seconds the car door opened and a man jumped in. They sat for a moment looking at each other. Then smiles broke out on their faces. Flora pulled a joint from behind her ear, slapped the man on his thigh and shouted in an over-excited way,

'Ready parrrdner?'

'Yahoo!' said the man, and they tore off up the street.

As promised, the shops she'd called were open. The couple spent over an hour in the first shop alone, totally engrossed by what they were doing, not noticing when occasional passers-by stopped to window shop and ended up watching them. Leila was one of these. A pair of shoes had caught her eye; pretty, with primrose straps, and what looked like mother of pearl stones all the way round the soles. Assuming they'd be too expensive, she decided not to bother even trying them on. The man inside got his arms caught up in the sleeves of the jacket and was trying to wiggle into it. Instead of sliding smoothly, the jacket seemed to cling to him. As Leila turned back towards the street, the waving of the man's arms caught her attention. As the jacket finally slipped into place, the man turned to face the mirror. He stepped forward and turned to see how the jacket fitted at the back. For the first time, she got a good look at him, and the woman behind. Leila recognised Flora from photos, and having had her pointed out a couple of times. What surprised Leila was seeing her with Joe's friend, Don. She immediately felt awkward, unsure whether she should say hello. If she tapped on the glass, she would feel trashy, and she didn't particularly want to meet Flora. Her thoughts were at odds with themselves. Within her head, dialogue started, and got too loud. She caught herself making facial expressions that expressed the jumble of thoughts and feelings within. It was dark at the front of the shop, near the window, so it gave a good reflection. Leila realised that the people next to her could probably see her face. She backed away, embarrassed. With a pathetic voice and barely a gesture, she said 'Taxi.' The cab didn't have its light on. It sped by, the driver shaking his head and pointing above him to the unlit sign. The man who'd been standing next to Leila coughed, cleared his throat, and checked his tie. The woman next to him chewed her cheek, straightened her skirt, then rubbed the window with a finger. She made an appalled, almost cartoon face, and said, 'Uh! It's filthy.' The couple allowed themselves to be distracted by this. They continued to appear to be looking in the window, until she was far enough away so they could relax.

13

The exhibition opened at six. David and Joe turned up at seven. When they arrived, they had to make their way through reporters and protestors. Joe was getting used to this on opening nights. His exhibitions were getting more attention each time. The Times newspaper wrote that 'It shouldn't be possible for Holtzman to go further with this exhibition than his previous, but it would be expected.' The Sun wrote a less coherent tirade, with the heading, 'Lock him up.'

Don was invited and, to Joe's surprise, came. Joe was doing his duty, talking to the people, at least the ones he could be bothered with. At one point when talking to David, he was tapped on the shoulder. He turned.

'Oh, my God! Flora,' said Joe.

'What are you doing here?' said David.

'That almost sounds like I'm not welcome.'

'Of course you're welcome,' said Joe.

'Nice stuff,' she said with an over-dramatic gesture of her hand.

'Nice?' said David.

'Yes, nice. How are you, David?'

'Fine.'

'And?'

'That's it, I'm fine.'

'That's nice,' she said sarcastically.

'Okay you two, be nice. Sorry, I forgot. Flora, this is Don.'

'Hello, Don.'

'Hi.'

'Haven't we met before?'

'I don't think so,' said Don.

'You look kind of familiar.'

'It's probably the man on the porridge commercial. Everyone says that.'

'Oh, my God! That's right. "Eat them good and hot."'

'Everyone says that as well.'

'Sorry.'

'That, too.'

'I better shut up.'

'Yep, that too.'

Flora winced, then made a zipping action across her mouth. All the while, Leila watched their play-acting, slightly confused. She had been told about Flora, so wasn't too surprised.

'A friend of mine said she was coming,' said Flora. ' And so here I am.'

'How nice,' said David.

'Thank you, dear,' said Flora.

'You two,' said Joe. 'I won't tell you again. This is my night, okay?'

'Sorry,' said David.

'Oh, yeah, sorry,' said Flora.

'I need to go to the toilet,' said Leila. 'Flora, do you want to come?'

'Sure.'

Flora thought this was an ideal chance to get to know who Leila was. More importantly, what she was doing with David and Joe.

'Would somebody hold my drink?'

'I will,' said Don, instinctively.

In an over-familiar way, Flora linked Leila's arm as they headed towards the toilet. David noticed this.

'She's too much,' he said quietly to Joe.

They watched the women go through the fire exit doors, heading towards the bathroom. The women made their way along convoluted corridors, and finally entered a room that smelt like school showers.

'Do you want a line of coke?' said Flora.

'Yeah, great,' said Leila.

They both slid into a cubicle. It was a tight fit. Flora didn't mind. She found Leila magnetic, almost seductive. Emptying out a wrap onto the cistern, she chopped two huge lines, aware that she was showing off.

'Jesus!' said Leila. 'They're big.'

'They're breakfast-size.'

'You don't mind, do you?'

'No!'

'Do you mind finishing it?'

'No, that's what it's for. Anyway, don't worry, I've got more.'

Flora handed her a thin gold tube. 'You first.'

'Fancy!'

'Tiffany's, darling,' said Flora.

Leila forced a laugh.

'You've been hanging out with too many gays.'

'There's no such thing.'

'Do you do a lot of this?' said Leila, referring to the coke.

'Not particularly. I just thought this would be easier with a little help,' said Flora.

'What do you mean?' Now it was Leila's turn to deceive.

'Seeing those two again.'

'You know them well?'

'You could say that. I used to go out with David.'

'You're messing with me. He used to be straight?'

'Well, it has a bit of a curve.'

'I can't believe you used to see him.'

'Promise,' said Flora, rising from doing her line.

'What was he like in bed?'

'I knew you'd be thinking that. Good actually. You'd never know he didn't like it. I still can't really believe it.'

'I guess people change.'

'No. I mean he was really good, if you get my drift?'

'I hear you girlfriend, but I can't imagine it with David. Actually, if Ryan's anything to go by...'

'Ryan! That's not nephew Ryan is it?'

'The very same.'

'I used to tease David about him.'

'How?'

'I used to say that David fancied him. He was only a kid then.'

'Did he?'

'I don't know. I don't think so. Who knows? Well, like I said. I don't even believe he's really gay. But Joe is a dish.'

'You fancy Joe?'

'When you get to thirty, your taste becomes much more varied.'

'You mean, you get desperate.'

'Bitch! Let's get out of here, I'm getting claustrophobic.'

'Yeah, if we stay in here much longer, we'll need another line.'

'Now there's an idea.'

'I was messing.'

'Oh! I mean, of course.'

They left the cubicle.

'You're bad!' said Leila.

'And that's good, right?'

'Sometimes.'

'Only sometimes?'

'I think so.'

They stood in front of the mirror.

'I love that lipstick,' said Flora, talking into the mirror. 'Where did you get it?'

Suddenly, Leila looked serious. Leila got hold of Flora's neck and pushed her up against the wall. Her face was only inches from Flora's, but still Leila talked into the mirror. 'Okay! Let's cut the crap.'

'What are you doing?' said Flora.

'Start talking bitch.'

'You're crazy.'

'That's rich. What the fuck are you playing at?'

'Nothing.'

'I know about you and Don,' said Leila, partly guessing.

'Oh!'

'What's Don up to?'

'Nothing. He's just a tool.'

'To do what?'

'For me to fuck with their heads. It's just a game.'

'Let me make myself very clear. It's going to stop. Okay?'

'You're hurting me.'

Leila's grip was so tight that Flora could hardly speak. She made a rasping sound. Leila snarled. 'I can't hear you.'

'Okay. I said okay.'

'I'm serious, Flora. I'll blow your fucking head off.'

Leila loosened her grip on Flora's neck and went back to the mirror. She wet her finger and groomed an eyebrow. Then she went into her bag, pulled out an eyebrow pencil, and left her bag open.

'Flora, will you pass my mascara? It's in my bag.'

Flora went into the bag, and spotted Leila's gun. She stepped back in shock.

'That's right,' said Leila, watching Flora in the mirror of her compact. She snapped it shut and said, 'Let's get out of here. They'll be wondering what happened to us.'

They left the toilet and went back to the others.

'Girl talk?' said David.

'Yeah,' said Leila, 'girl talk.'

Flora laughed nervously. Ryan noticed. David did too. It was so out of character. Joe excused himself.

'Do you need any help?' said Don.

'No. All I have to do is open some doors to another room.'

'Why the mystery?' said Flora.

'You'll see.'

A couple of minutes later, there were photographers' flashes, and gasps.

'What's he gone and done now?' said David.

'He's kept it secret from you?' said Don.

'Just for the fun of it.'

'Let's go see,' said Leila.

'Yeah, let's,' said David.

They joined the crowd. On seeing the exhibit, Flora tried to think of something witty to say, but couldn't. Everybody was speechless.

14

The phone rang. Flora rushed, and caught it, falling clumsily on her bed.

'What?' she said, with a mouthful of fruit salad. Juice squirted from her lips and dribbled down her chin. She swallowed as much as she could, and spat the rest into her hand. Steadying the phone between her ear and shoulder, she reached for a tissue.

'Flora?'

'Who'd you expect?'

'I don't know. I might have dialled the wrong number.'

'But you've got speed dial.'

'Oh, yeah. Anyway, how are you?'

'And since when have you been ex-directory?' said Flora. 'It says withheld on my display.'

'Uh! Since today?'

'Why?'

'I don't know.'

'You funny bugger,' said Flora putting a flame to the tissue in her hand. It set alight easily and rapidly. She let it drop into an ashtray. Immediately, she lit another, and watched it burn, mesmerised. Silently it glowed, changing from bright orange and incandescent, to matt black and crinkled. The tissue burnt itself out with the same dynamic as a city going to sleep, full of life. 'So, listen. I was thinking about those two.'

'You mean Joe and David.'

'Who else?'

'Why do you let them get to you?'

'The first time I didn't really have a choice. This time it's just sport.'

'I don't like hearing you talk like that.'

'What's changed? It didn't used to. Do you like them?'

'No!'

Flora thought for a moment. 'Anyway, I'm over them. They bore me. You can drop them. That's if you're not too attached already. Joe's a seductive bugger. And you know what I think of David.'

'I don't, actually. Well, I'm confused. You said you loved him. That's not what it looks like.'

'Love often turns to hate.'

'No love I know. Obsession maybe.'

'You're getting all soft on me,' said Flora. Then, with a tune in her voice, she sang, 'Don loves Joe!'

'Get bent, Flora.'

'Sounds like you already are.'

'Right!'

'Don loves Joe!' she sang again.

'That is so irritating.'

'Only 'cos it's true!'

'If you don't take that stupid tune out of your voice I'm going to hang up.'

'Like I care.'

'Okay, bye.'

'Don! Stop.'

'Give me half a reason.'

'I was only teasing you. Have I hit a nerve?'

'Absolutely anything said with that voice would hit a nerve.'

'How about, "Eat my pussy!"' she said with the same inflection and the same melody.

'It doesn't sound sexy.'

'Are you sure?'

'Maybe. Try some more.'

'Suck mama's nipples!'

'I'm warming to it.'

'Bet you are.'

'You're a twisted cunt, Flora.'

'That sounds painful.'

'Probably is.'

Flora giggled and rubbed her toes into the goatskin rug at her feet. Suddenly, there was a loud crash at her window. Flora gasped.

'What!' said Don. 'Are you okay?' There was no answer. 'Flora! What's wrong?'

After a pause, she said, 'I don't know.'

'What happened?'

'Something hit the window.'

'What do you mean something. You're quite high up.'

'I know, that's why it surprised me.'

'What was it?'

'A bird?'

'This would only happen to you, Flora.'

'It's probably very common.'

'What kind of bird was it,' said Don.

'I don't know. A pigeon?'

'What did it look like.'

'Black and white, maybe?'

'Sounds like a magpie, not a pigeon.'

'What's with the sudden ornithology interest?'

'It's bad luck.'

'What!'

'One magpie's bad luck.'

'Give me a break.'

'One's for sorry. Two's for joy.'

'Maybe it was two then.'

'Come on, the likelihood of two magpies simultaneously smashing into your window are slim.'

'And your waist is very slim. When does this get interesting?'

'Some people would think a magpie crashing into your window was quite interesting.'

'Yeah, my granddad, and his fascinating drinking buddy, Jeb.'

'Flora, you're so cynical.'

'Thanks!'

'I said you're cylindrical.'

'I know, thanks! Women are supposed to be.'

'Yours is leaner and more muscular than most.'

'Joe's is even more. Does that means he wins?'

'God, Flora. I was just trying to give you a compliment.'

'Yeah, yeah, yeah, Don and Joe. I bet you've been hanging out together all the time.'

'I'm hanging up. Four! Three! Two! I'm hanging.'

'I'm pregnant!' said Flora with enough urgency to make Don stop in his tracks. He couldn't move, or reply, simply looked into the corner of the room, his focus more in his head than on anything in the room. 'I'm stagnant, or a sad cunt. Depending on how you want to look at it.'

'Jesus Christ!' Don paused. 'Is it mine?'

'For the moment, it's nobody's.'

Don was silent. He tried to digest what he'd heard and wondered about possibilities. Then, timidly, he said, 'Might you keep it?'

'Might.'

'If?'

'If I feel like it.'

'What does it depend on?'

'I don't know yet. I'll get back to you.' Again Don found a little refuge in silence. 'Listen, honey,' said Flora. 'I've got to get something ready for FedEx? Can I call you later?'

'I'll be out.'

'I'll page you then.'

'Okay. Talk to you later.'

They both put their receivers down. Don was shocked. He left the bedroom, and walked onto the landing. The floor was covered with a blackwatch tartan carpet. The walls and ceiling were painted in the same design. It was striking, and oppressive, but cosy, and usually caught the attention of anybody who walked through it. Not Don. He drifted through the hall and plodded down the stairs, turned into and through the living room, then entered the kitchen.

'Hey! What's wrong?' said Joe.

'Bad news?' said David.

'I'm not sure,' said Don.

15

Gaia's office was still, empty, without character. It gave nothing, yet it was the perfect environment for her to give support, encouragement, and at times, love. David felt this. They'd even discussed it. David told her that he'd begun to love her. She smiled sweetly and said that she loved him too.

'Are we allowed to say things like this in therapy?' said David.

'We can say whatever we like,' said Gaia.

This was exactly the reason David had begun to love her. Gaia never resorted to clichés for ease, but did and said what she felt was most compassionate, sensible, human. Once, David asked her, if they came across each other in the street, were they allowed to say hello? She looked puzzled. 'It would be weird if we didn't. Don't you think?'

David's response was, 'Definitely!'

Gaia was warm, kind and genuine. The things David hoped for with friends, exactly what he got from Joe. He knew it was rare, so cherished Gaia. He'd been seeing her for several years now, since shortly after he was raped. She'd helped him through it and then took it further. David felt she taught him something nearly every time he saw her. Some kind of love was bound to grow between them. Neither he nor she was worried about the shape their relationship took. It felt completely natural for both of them.

David looked up. He had been daydreaming. Gaia stood at the

door. In her hand she held a folded piece of paper.

'These are my holiday dates. I wrote them down for you, so you wouldn't forget.'

'Thanks. Isn't it simply that you're away for three weeks?'

'Well, tell me what you think of this. I thought I'd see you the day before I leave and the day after I got back, although those aren't the days I'd usually see you.'

'That's very thoughtful of you. Am I your only patient?'

'No.' Gaia chuckled, and put her head down. She moved her fringe from out of her eyes, and lifted her head again, still smiling. 'I just thought you might like that.'

'You mean need it,' said David.

'Do you need it?'

'I guess so.' David watched Gaia. He noted what she was wearing, although it meant little to him. Aware that she was under scrutiny, Gaia caught David's eye and smiled. 'You seem happy today,' he said.

'I am.'

'Is there a particular reason for it?'

'It's Wednesday?'

'That's so corny.'

'Corny's okay.'

'I guess so.'

'It only sounds corny because you've heard people say it so many times before. Why do you think that is?'

'Because it's true, or something, maybe.'

'Well, I'd say lots of people probably feel it.'

'It's still corny.'

'I know, but that's like saying I love you is corny, but when you feel it, as you'll have experienced, nothing else will do but those three words. It's corny as hell, but if you feel it, what should you do, hold it inside, or . . .'

David butted in. 'Say it, no matter how corny it is?'

'I think so,' said Gaia.

'You're a lovely woman.'

'Thank you.'

The window in the therapy room was open. There was noise in the street, children screeching and shouting. Some unpleasant memories came back to David, of playgrounds, of not fitting in.

'What's on your mind?' said Gaia.

'How did you know there was anything?'

'Your face changed.'

'I must try to control it better,' said David.

'Why would you want to do that?'

'I don't see why you should have to suffer because my mind is on something.'

'I presume you are referring to me as another person, because as your therapist it's my job to deal with what's on your mind.'

'I meant as another person. Others shouldn't have to see what I'm thinking, or feeling.'

'But what if they want to? People spend time with you because they choose to. I'd imagine they'd like to share your thoughts and feelings.'

'I hadn't thought about it like that.' There was a pause. David looked at Gaia and she back at him. 'Still, people don't need to hear every neurotic comment to and from myself.'

'I'm afraid I can't agree with you. It sounds quite fun.'

'It's only because you're a therapist that you find it interesting.'

'No. I'm a therapist because I'm interested in people, not the other way round.'

'Ah! You've got a silk tongue, so you have,' said David with an Irish accent he'd learned from his father's side of the family. Again Gaia laughed.

'You're funny.'

'That'll be my long feet and my curly teeth.'

Gaia covered her face with both hands and suppressed her laughter.

'Why do you cover your face when you laugh?'

'Do you really want to know?'

'Yes.'

'Firstly, I used to be self-conscious about my teeth as a little girl. Secondly, I was eating some raw spinach before you arrived and was afraid it might have stuck to my teeth. Thirdly, I'd rather the image you had of me in your head wasn't me laughing. It's too easy to misconstrue.'

'I'm not that paranoid.'

'Still, laughter doesn't always mean happiness.'

'I don't understand.'

'I'm thinking of those clowns at funfairs.'

'You're showing your age. Weren't they a Fifties thing? And, anyway, I don't think of you like that. They're horrible.'

'You see my point, though? Laughter can be very cruel. Nobody likes to be laughed at.'

'Why is that?'

'I'm not sure, but I'd guess it's because it's so potent. When somebody laughs, it takes a lot of effort. Imagine the feeling when that's turned against you. It's quite scary.'

'Right!'

'It makes me think of when dogs bark,' said Gaia.

'They really *are* scary.'

'It might be for similar reasons. Possibly, something very natural.'

Gaia put her head to one side. Her face relaxed into a pleasant expression, one that David imagined was comfortable for Gaia. He believed because it was natural for her.

'You never told me what was on your mind, before, when you heard the children playing outside.'

'I was taken back to my schoolyard.'

'This can be a source of so much unhappiness.'

'And happiness,' said David, pleased that he was being positive.

'Of course. Are you saying that it was for you?'

'No.'

'That's what I imagined.'

'From my face?' said David. Gaia nodded and smiled in a way she often did. To David it meant she understood. Also that she was concerned, even cared. David started to cry. Through his tears he managed to say, 'Can't I get through a single session without this shit?' His acknowledgement made him cry more ferociously. He was determined to not let his emotions rule him, so he forced out more words. 'What's this about?'

'What were you thinking of?' said Gaia. As she'd done many times before, she handed David a box of tissues.

'Someone poking me.'

Gaia was silent. Clearly, David was very upset, and being picked on at school probably wasn't the reason. Gaia became more serious. This made David cry harder. Through a mass of emotion, he thought he knew what was on her mind.

'You think this is connected to the rape, don't you?'

'Possibly.' She put three fingers over her lips and looked pensive. David wondered if it meant anything besides that she was thinking. Fragments of thoughts dwelt on this idea, whilst at the same time he continued to cry over more immediate responses.

'Why?' said David, and immediately felt like he'd said something trite.

'There's no reason. Nothing connected with you, anyway.'

'There must have been something I could have done.' Again, he questioned how it sounded. A character off a tv movie came to mind. Nobody, or no movie in particular, just a victim. 'I feel like a victim.'

'You were a victim.'

'When will the memories go away?'

'I doubt they will, but you'll become more able to deal with them.'

David stopped crying. 'Will I?'

Gaia nodded in a sure way, and pulled a faint tranquil smile.

Again, voices could be heard on the street below. A bee flew through the window, buzzing noisily. It looped the room and left. Outside. Inside. Therapy. Real world. Voices. Gaia. David looked down, taking comfort in being distracted by the speckled pile of the carpet. For seconds, he and Gaia didn't say anything. There was silence, but for distant city sounds. Then David burst out laughing. Gaia's expression didn't change.

'I was just thinking how much I cry here. I wonder how much water I've left in this room, over the years.'

Without missing a beat, Gaia said, 'Enough to keep a flower alive.'

At first, David didn't get the double meaning of this, so looked towards the open window, thinking it was simply beautiful imagery. Then it clicked, and he turned back to face Gaia, who was already smiling in acknowledgement.

16

Leila's parents hadn't seen, or heard from her for a while. They loved her, and liked nothing more than spoiling her, but they'd asked her to go home so that her finances could be reviewed. It was really just an excuse, and they knew she'd go, if her allowance were in jeopardy. They were right.

On Friday night she left. Ryan took her to Euston, the train station from which most northbound trains departed, to Manchester, Liverpool, Preston, many places they'd both rather forget. Leila's destination was Wilmslow, an affluent strip on the outskirts of Manchester.

Ryan looked up at the timetable. 'The train's in ten minutes,' he said. 'Let's grab a coffee.'

'Okay amigo,' said Leila.

'Ouch! That accent was rotten,' said Ryan.

'Sorry. How about Si, Señor?'

'Worse.'

'Oui, mon ami?'

'Lovely. Your French is pretty. I'd wish you'd use it during sex.'

'I do,' said Leila. 'In my head.'

'What good's it doing there?'

'It does *me* good.'

'You could share it.'

'I'd feel stupid.'

'I think that's meant to be part of the deal. Like dressing up, or playing roles. It's liberating.'

'Have you been seeing David's shrink?'

'No,' said Ryan. 'Her name's Gaia, by the way. Nice name hey?'

'I suppose so. Weird surname though,' said Leila. Then, into the air, 'Computer! A tearful goodbye, hot!'

'You might just get it, captain.' They walked to their platform and looked up at the board. The train seemed to be stopping at so many other stations. Leila made a resigned expression. This made Ryan smile. Then he looked overly earnest. 'You will write me?'

'If I have time for recollections of the heart,' said Leila. 'Sometime, perhaps, between engagements, if I find myself at a loss, I might put pen to paper and send news of my affection; its health and vitality.'

'Right! Call when you get there,' said Ryan. 'When you walk through the front door, then it's just sitting, drinking tea, and anything else you think to do,' he paused. 'Without me!'

'So,' said Leila. 'That's every twenty minutes. Sounds good to me. If I get nervous, can I cut into that?'

'You mean like fifteen minutes, or something quirky like that?'

'Precisely. If after reading the periodicals, setting my affairs in order, or taking in the waters, and if it's sooner, can I presume to call?'

'Certainly,' said Ryan. 'But be vigilant, my dear, these things can get quite out of hand.'

Leila threw herself around Ryan's neck. 'I love . . .' she paused. 'Your sense of humour.'

'She loves you.' This was the nearest either of them had ever been to using the word love within their relationship. They both felt it. Leila looked Ryan in the eye. He did the same to her. The bustle, the people trying to get by, the noises of trains, the announcements, for this moment, nothing external was able to break through. They stood and held on to each other, kissing, their faces covered by Ryan's hair and Leila's long black wig. They pulled apart, then helplessly went back for more. Suddenly Leila pulled away sharply.

'My train!'

'Oh, my God!'

Leila ran down the platform, stopping at the bottom where the ticket collector was. She let her bags drop, turned, collected herself and shouted as loud as she was able,

'I like you.'

Ryan tapped his head with his finger, did about three moves of a country-and-western line dance, then mouthed the words, 'Mad cow!' He noticed a change in Leila's face, so added, 'I like you, too.'

Leila turned, picked up her bags and ran. She disappeared behind the ticket booth, then got on the train. Ryan went back to Hampstead, where he found David different from usual, uneasy.

'What's up?' said Ryan.

'Nothing, I think. A tv crew will be at Joe's exhibition tomorrow. It's the BBC. He's quite nervous.'

Ryan made an exaggerated expression that meant he was impressed, then said, 'Does it always affect you like this?'

'I have been known to go out, get really wasted.'

'Stress management. Sounds good to me.' David's eyes looked as though he were thinking about the idea. 'Don't think about it too much. If we all did that, we'd never take drugs.'

'I guess you're right.' He paused. 'I think.'

'Less of that thinking nonsense. I'm going to have a bath, and then I'll be ready.' David pictured Ryan naked. Ryan noticed that David was daydreaming. 'Is anybody home?'

'I'm home.'

'Good. Let's start out by having dinner, then we'll go for a drink, then a club, then get really fucking cunted!'

David burst out laughing; more from excitement than anything Ryan had said. 'I wish I'd had my hair cut.'

'You vain sod,' said Ryan.

'It's my duty to look beautiful. It's expected of me.'

'You're with me tonight, remember that. None of that gay malarkey.'

'What's that?'

'You know, eyes everywhere.'

'I don't do that. Do I?'

'Every gay man I've met does,' said Ryan. 'It's in your genes.'

David couldn't help snickering at the jeans pun, but thought better of voicing it.

'I know what you're thinking,' said Ryan. 'Your age group like their innuendoes, don't they.'

'That's because when we were kids, you couldn't be frank.'

'Frank,' said Ryan, then, in an exaggerated way, 'Ha, ha!' This annoyed David. 'So, is it a deal? No cruising?'

'I'll try my best, but if I don't know I'm doing it, how can I stop it?'

'Just focus on me.'

'It sounds like good old-fashioned jealousy.'

'Maybe. Or I just like a lot of attention.'

'Don't we all?'

'Yeah, but I'm used to it,' said Ryan, then feigned arrogance.

'You're either a good actor, or that's real.'

Ryan didn't answer, but went to the doorway, stopped and turned. He put his chin up, and flicked some hair off his neck. With only a hint of a smile, he left the room, and bounded off up the stairs.

David decided to have a nap before going out, anticipating a long night. He was too excited to sleep so took a Rohypnol. When he woke, Joe was beside him, holding him tight.

'Hey, puppy,' said David. 'Are you sure it's okay if I go out?'

'Completely. It'll be good for me to have some time alone. Plan for tomorrow.'

'That's what I suspected.'

'Are you still going to come?'

'Of course,' said David. 'I wouldn't let you down.' Joe held him even tighter. 'I love you when you're insecure.'

'Am I being too clingy?'

'No. You can be as clingy, mushy, and as clumsy as you want.'

'Where did that clumsy come from?'

'I thought I'd just throw that one in. Keep you on your toes.'

'Clumsy, and on my toes. Sounds like something from Dumbo.'

David had the sheets pulled up around his neck. They were white, so made him look very tanned.

'It may be some trick of the light,' said Joe, 'But you look stunning,'

'Ah! Just when I was feeling ugly.'

'How could you ever feel ugly?'

David contorted his face and body. 'Like this.'

'Damn! You're beautiful.'

'What are you after?'

'Your bumhole.' Joe put his hand on David's arse.

'Okay,' said David, responding as quickly as he could. 'It took a lot of persuading, but you convinced me.'

'It's just to alleviate the stress, you understand.'

'Of course!'

They rolled around and fucked for a while, until there was a knock at the door.

'I'm worried about the noise in there,' said Ryan. 'Are you two okay?' Joe and David had only just cum, and were still kissing. They laughed, covered up and told Ryan to come in.

'You guys had me really worried.'

'Were we making that much noise?'

'Let's put it this way. I had a CD on and I could still hear you.'

'Sorry,' said David. 'Was it like hearing your parents have sex?'

'What's sex got to do with this?'

'Nothing. I just wondered if Joe and I doing our exercises sounded anything like your parents having sex.'

'Oh. I see. Yes, it was very similar. Curious, hey?'

Joe tickled Ryan who squirmed about. In retaliation, Ryan did the same to Joe and David. Soon this turned into a boisterous wrestle, ending up with them all in a heap, laughing hysterically. They took it in turn to assemble their limbs and get off the bed.

'It's getting late,' said Ryan. 'That's why I came to get you. It wasn't just to ruin your fun.'

'I was bored of exercising anyway,' said David. Joe looked at David with a hurt expression. 'Puppy, I didn't mean . . .'

'I know!' said Joe. 'I'm not that soft.'

'Okay. Chop-chop,' said Ryan. Again, David sniggered. Ryan feigned a bored sigh. Joe shook his head, as if to say, 'What am I going to do with you both?' then went downstairs to make some notes.

Once out, Ryan and David got a little over-excited, and didn't bother with dinner. After a couple of hours of drinking they were quite drunk. They went to Heaven for a few hours, just to kill time and buy drugs. David bumped into a few people he knew, but nobody he wanted to spend time with. When Heaven closed, they went to Tragic. It had been the plan all along, although neither had mentioned it. It didn't really have to be said. The next few hours were unpunctuated, a stream of haphazard shapes, personalities, and attitudes, one blending with the next. Noise and colour merged with cigarette smoke and neurosis. The evening mainly consisted of drinking, snorting, popping, squeezing past bodies slippery with sweat, monotonous beats, dancing, more chopping and popping, the odd suggestion of a melody within one seemingly continual track, confused, racing thoughts, and more repetitive beats. Then resting, sitting, zoning out, intimate conversations with strangers, erratic obsessions, irregular shifts in mood, then the sudden emptiness of the toilet cubicle: The chaos of its stillness, not changing colour, or flashing, or banging, or heaving, or catching somebody's eye, or noticing somebody's tricep as they lean and order a drink. Without all this distraction, it's easy to turn inside, turn over thoughts, useless ideas that lead nowhere but the next stream of consciousness. Occasionally, a practicality arises, like focusing on pissing, trying to open the cubicle door or navigate the stairs. Then there's safety, sitting, talking nonsense, and, by chance, arbitrarily making sense, but more than normal. At least that's how it seemed to David and Ryan. Things were somehow deeper, loaded with meaning.

'I can't believe you slept earlier,' said Ryan, his mouth moving more than was necessary to say the words.

'Why?'

'I was too excited. I get that way if I know I'm going out.'

'I did have a little help.'

'No? Was it about so big?' Ryan held his forefinger and thumb about three millimetres apart. 'I'm seeing purple?'

'How did you guess?' said David. 'But, fact check, they're green now.'

'Why?'

'They contain dye.'

'Why?'

'So you could see it if someone had spiked your drink.'

'What's the fun in that?' said Ryan.

'Go figure!'

'I can't hear the word Rohypnol anymore without picturing you and what's-his-face.'

'Rob,' said David. 'How do you picture it, if you don't know what he looked like?'

'In my head he's just an amorphous figure. He changes even within the same scene.'

'Sounds like it's stained your memory.'

'It has.'

'I'm sorry, puppy.'

'It's not a problem.' Ryan paused, looked around him, took a gulp of his vodka and coke and said, 'I like it.'

'Let me get this straight. In your head, I'm with this monster thing, right?'

'No. It's not like that. He is particular people, but changes, like on a pop video.'

'Morphing,' said David. Not getting a response from Ryan, he said, 'The technique's called morphing.'

'Oh! Well, sometimes he's Joe, other times he's the last person I saw you talk to.'

'It sounds very hectic.'

'It doesn't feel like that.'

'How does it feel?'

'It usually gives me a hard-on.'

'You freak.'

'Sometimes, the other person . . .' Ryan stopped for a second.

'Don't tell me, Leila?'

'No. Good guess. Nearly! Sometimes, it's me.'

'I take that back. You're not a freak. That's very sensible, Master Ryan.'

'It doesn't feel that sensible.'

'You don't know until you've tried it.'

'I guess so,' said Ryan. David thought Ryan looked adorable, so pulled him forward to give him a hug. Ryan leant forward, but mistaking the gesture, opened his mouth, and kissed David. When finished, they pulled apart.

'God! Your tongue is soft, puppy.'

'Your nephew snogs you, and all you can say is, your tongue is soft?'

'That's not all I thought.'

'What did you think?'

'Considering it was, maybe only thirty seconds, quite a lot. I thought if I wasn't so high, I'd be fucking shocked! Then I rambled through the years, one image of you tripping over the next. I remembered how beautiful you were the first time I saw you. You were seven. I had my usual, but brief, dilemma about you being so young. Then I quickly moved onto the hundreds of times I have jerked off about you. I had a lot to get through, nine years of jerking off, and the different images I've had of you in my head during that time. Then I wondered, should I be questioning the fact that we're related. I justified this by thinking that's more an issue if we were going to have children. Which I assume we're not. Finally, I abandoned myself completely to the moment and kind of poured myself into you. And it was this which led to the comment about your tongue.'

'So, should we, or shouldn't we?' said Ryan.

'I'm way ahead of you. I'm on, who does who?'

'You sleep. I have fun.'

Responding in an unhurried, not too keen, very measured way, David said, 'Okay.' Then, after finishing his drink, 'I've had enough here.'

'You took the words right out of my mouth,' said Ryan.

'Shall we split?'

'That's a bit forward. We're not even together yet.'

They stood, balanced, and made their way upstairs. Once outside, they chose one of the shouting, haggling cab drivers to take them home. Whoever they chose was guaranteed to rip them off, so they went with one because David liked the colour of his T-shirt. In the cab they kissed again. They both felt they had been waiting years for this moment. At home, they kept quiet, so as not to wake Joe. Collecting beer from the fridge, they went up to Ryan's room. Although part of David wanted to stay awake, he took three Rohypnol. Ryan rolled a joint as they drank. They smoked, talked, and kissed, stripping each other down to their underwear. David started to slur his words. At some point when reaching for his beer he stopped. From swallowing the tablets, it took about twenty minutes before David was out cold.

Ryan finished the joint he was working on, then lay down beside David. He put his arm over David, and could feel the heat from his body. It felt lovely. He rubbed his lips against David's chest then rested his head down on it. For over five minutes Ryan lay still, gazing ahead of him. Then he eased off David's boxer shorts, and turned him over. Ryan threw the pillows on the floor, for fear of David suffocating whilst he slept. He took off his own underpants, pushed David's legs apart, knelt between them, and lay on his tummy with his face close to David's arse. Ryan pushed his hips down, clenching his bum, and squashing his now hard dick against the sheets beneath. As he raised his hips, his arse opened, showing the inside of his crack. When he thrust forward his cheeks formed two hard, hairless, bumps. Ryan breathed in deep, hoping to absorb some of David. For a moment Ryan's face hovered over David's arse, before nuzzling into it. Again, he breathed in deep. David smelt musky, gorgeous. More wonderful than Ryan had ever imagined. More so than any of the boys he'd ever had sex with. David was an adult, a man, his sexy uncle, and for now, whatever Ryan wanted him to be. For a moment he knelt upright again, and looked down at the sight below. It was good to look at, plain and simple. Ryan wanted to remember it. For seconds he thought about consequences, then threw them aside in favour of absolute sensual indulgence. Almost falling, he pushed his face into David's arse. He stuck out his tongue, licked around the hole, prodded it by making his tongue stiff and pointed, then slid it right inside. It was incredible. Warm like a mouth, but more erotic. Like Leila's cunt, but less moist, with a completely different taste and smell.

For half an hour, Ryan kept his face never more than three inches away from David's arse. Slowly he began to come down from his drugs. With each passing minute he questioned himself further. What did this mean? Would he be expected to do it again? What would their relationship be? What would Leila think? Would they tell her? Would he be given a choice?

Within minutes, Ryan pulled back, emotionally and physically. He didn't want to be inside David anymore. Fear took a hold, overcoming his desire. He turned and sat on the edge of the bed.

Suddenly, David seemed foolish, naked, with his legs apart; so vulnerable, careless and stupid. Head in his hands, Ryan sat, steadily feeling less high, and increasingly wretched. Tormented, he pulled the sheet over David's feet, the backs of his knees, thighs and shoulders, everything that only a short time before he'd wanted to coat with himself. Already, he'd begun mourning something that wasn't allowed to happen. This quieter, internal self was hushed. He took one last look at David's face, kissed the side of his head, smelled his lovely smell one more time, then said goodnight in his ear, and went to the doorway. He thought back to a Christmas nine years before. Infatuated, he'd cuddled and squirmed into David giving him a hard-on. Ryan felt like he wanted to smile, but something inside him wouldn't allow it. He switched out the lights, closed the door, and went downstairs to sleep on the sofa.

17

Joe wore a black fitted suit, and had his hair slicked back. He was clean-shaven, and looked well-groomed.

'So, to round up,' said the reporter. 'Would it be too simplistic to say you believe art is more important than life?'

'Yes,' he said. Then realising how this could be misunderstood. 'I mean it *would* be too simplistic.'

The camera pulled in to a close-up of the woman interviewing Joe. She gave a quizzical, reporter kind of look, as though Joe had just said a curious punch line; she didn't quite get it, and she'd leave it for the viewers to work out. Joe thought she'd already made it clear what she thought their response should be.

Knowing he was out of shot, Joe reached for his drink. He saw David, who stuck his thumb up as he walked towards Joe.

'Well done, puppy,' said David. 'That was great.'

'How long have you been here?'

'About twenty minutes.'

'I didn't see you.'

'The light was in your eyes.'

'Oh, yeah, I forgot, you're used to being in front of a camera.'

'Not any more.'

Joe stepped closer to David and spoke quietly into his ear. 'Do you think they got it?'

'They'd have to be stupid not to.'

'Just between you and me, I think they are.' Joe walked away and returned with another drink. 'How was last night?'

'Interesting. I think.'

'Did you have Rohypnol?' David nodded. 'That's why I don't like taking them. If I'm going to go to such lengths to have fun, I at least want to remember.'

'Good point. I just hate coming down.'

Again, Joe spoke into David's ear. 'Don't quote me on this,' he said. 'But I'll be glad to scrap this fucking exhibition.'

'Right!' said David not really concentrating. 'Did you see Don?'

'No, but did you see Flora?'

'You're kidding?'

'I'm not. I saw her helping herself to the refreshments. Did Leila tell you?' David paused.

'About seeing Don and her together?' said Joe.

'Weird, hey?'

'I don't get it,' said Joe. 'I trust Don.'

'Do you think that's wise?'

'I don't know now. I just find it hard to believe he'd go along with any nonsense. What do you think?'

'I don't know.'

'Do you like him?' said Joe.

'He sort of intimidates me.'

For a moment Joe looked surprised. Then he said, 'I can see why.' He thought for a moment. 'Of course, nothing Flora does surprises me.'

'She went beyond that a long time ago. Do you think she's up to something?'

'Probably.'

'Do you care?'

'Maybe.'

'I'm not sure.'

He looked about him. 'Where is Mad Cow?'

'I saw her heading towards the stairwell. Which reminds me, I have to piss.'

'You know where it is,' said Joe.

'Yeah.'

'Good luck, if you see M.C.'

'Thanks,' he said, kissed Joe on the nose and turned to go.

'Baby,' said Joe.

David stopped, feigned annoyance. 'What?'

'I love you.'

'I know,' said David and strode off in a comical way. The toilet was in the basement down two flights of stairs, so David prepared himself mentally for the long haul. As he was about to leave the room Ryan stepped in front of him.

'Ryan,' he said.

'David. You off to the toilet?' David nodded. Ryan put out his arms. They hugged clumsily. 'I feel a bit awkward, but . . .' He paused. 'Did we have fun?' Ryan nodded with a cheeky smile. 'You weren't there when I got up, so I began to worry. Thought maybe I'd scared you away.'

'That'll be paranoia. Probably the drugs.'

'That's what I was hoping.'

'Don't worry. Nothing has changed. And yes, I still love you.' David managed a half-baked smile. Ryan sensed his uneasiness, took hold of him and squeezed him. 'You silly-manilly.'

'Phew.' David opened the door to the stairwell. 'Thanks Ryan, for being you.'

'You corny bugger. Get out of here. I'm going to get a drink. Come over when you get back. I'll be with Joe.'

'Okay. Won't be long.' Once out of the main exhibition space, David noticed how much quieter it was, and away from the lights much cooler also. The hallway was packed with screens, paints, brushes and cartons of white spirits. Flora was nowhere to be seen. David plodded down the concrete steps slowly, and loudly, like a child, listening to the echo. He began to sing notes, nothing in particular, just enjoying the acoustics. His voice was clear. The sound was thunderous, yet pure and sharp. He was pleased with the noise.

Ryan went to the refreshments table and got a drink. He bumped into Flora, who chatted, but seemed nervous.

Joe was getting ready for his final take when Don tapped his shoulder. 'Joe,' he said, less confidently than Joe was used to.

'Hey, dude!'

'Since when did you get all Californian?'

'Just now. Does it suit me?'

'Kind of,' said Don, and put his hand on Joe's shoulder. 'Listen, there's something I want to talk to you about.'

'They've just got to do the closing shot.'

'It's quite important,' he said with his head down.

'Can it wait?' said Joe, whilst trying to establish eye contact. 'It won't be long.'

'Yeah,' said Don. 'It can wait.'

With her face powdered, the interviewer was ready. She planned to criticise the exhibition, hoping to get the support of the viewers, then close with some pithy remark. Then she'd give her concerned but warm smile and say goodnight. She looked around at the mirror to rehearse her expression. She had to bend to see herself. Standing upright again, she fluffed her fringe gently with her fingers. As she turned back towards the set her heel caught. She tripped, and fell against a light. It tipped, hovered, and crashed onto the floor. There was a lot of commotion, and noise, as people rushed about.

Over this racket a single cry was heard. 'Fire! Fire! Fire!' In the stairwell, out of sight, it had begun only minutes before. Within a short time, flames coated the hallway, floor, walls and ceiling. The double doors set alight quickly, the wood being old and dry. Streams of smoke started gushing through the crack in between the doors. Don took charge immediately and started to evacuate the building.

Once outside, all anybody could do was stand and stare. Flora left.

Don stayed, and helped the other firemen when he could, but he knew they had a routine to follow and team roles to play, so mostly he stood beside Joe, out of the way. He thought to ask if David had gone home already. Joe looked suddenly bewildered, almost blank. Then he set off, running, towards the entrance to the building. Don caught him, pinning him down.

'Let me go,' said Joe, hardly words. 'David's inside.'

'Where?' said Don, as Joe continued to kick and scream.

'The basement.'

Don called to one of the other firemen, who in turn spoke into his radio.

✪

After last night, David's stomach felt weird, so he sat on the toilet for some time, nothing really happening. He finished, pulled up his jeans, replaced the lid, and sat back down. He pulled out a joint he'd prepared at the house, and smoked it. He felt content, good, excited. He thought of Joe and smiled. By the time David had finished his joint and got back to the stairs, the doors were covered in flames. He ran back past the toilet, hoping to find another exit. The only other door was up three flights, and was locked. He ran back to the burning doors, crying and shouting for help. He saw some tarpaulin lying under an old chest of drawers. He dragged it out and covered himself. Desperate and terrified, he ran to the door and pushed it open. He got through relatively unscathed, stopped and threw off the tarpaulin, only to discover he was in another corridor coated with flames, with nothing to protect him. He breathed in flames as the fire engulfed him, and fell to his knees screaming, 'Joe!'

18

The weather was only just fine enough for the service to be held outside. At one point the sun even moved from behind the clouds. Beams of light cut through the leaves of an oak tree leaving patterns on everybody who attended the funeral. Nobody noticed. Ordinarily, this kind of sunlight had the ability to lighten moods, but this time it didn't.

Ryan and Leila comforted Joe throughout David's funeral. Ryan loved David, he always had. Within a very short time, Leila had begun to also. Don managed not to cry, although his face twitched constantly. He'd spent only a little time with David, hardly knew him, but was aware of the impact his death had on Joe and Flora. They wrote eulogies, but Joe wasn't fit to read his. Judy offered to read it for him.

'This is Joe's eulogy,' said Judy, and began reading.

'What was David to me? It would make more sense to ask, what wasn't he? I'd like to praise him, but you all knew him. This leaves me wanting to tell you how he made me feel; loved, adored, and so at ease. When everything made so little sense, he was my sense. When I couldn't comprehend others, their actions or the things they said, he was my link. He fixed what was broken in me, making order of what I saw as chaos, simply by letting me tell him that I loved him. Through him, for the first time in my life, everything made sense. Although I was bitter, cynical, and jaded, he made me comprehend love.'

✪

As Judy finished reading, Joe closed his eyes. In his head, he had an image of David sitting at the end of their bed, facing away, so Joe could see his back, and his beautiful waist. He smiled. Judy looked over for some kind of acknowledgement, but Joe was inside, with David. The service continued.

A little later, it was Flora's turn to read what she had written. She hadn't been sure that she'd be able. Filled with doubt, she repeated encouragement, as though a mantra. She left her seat, and by the time she reached the microphone, she was able to begin. Although she sniffled all the way through, she carried on reading, determined. She read,

'Things won't be the same without you. You selfish thing. What about us? I'm sure I'll forgive you in time, but remember, I'll think of you every day, my precious, my puppy.'

She looked over at Joe, who now had his eyes open. Then she said, finally, 'Our puppy.'

At this point she began to sob noisily. Don went up and collected her. She was all little girl now, pathetic, unable to walk without being led, her eyes full of tears. Joe's heart went out to Flora. She was empty. Over the years since she and David had split, she'd taken comfort knowing he was around, if only in the same city, and with somebody else. At this moment, Joe wanted to hold Flora, make sure she was okay. They had, after all, loved the same person.

Ryan had been put in charge of calling everybody in David's address book. He had to run everybody past Joe, to make sure they weren't the dry cleaners, something unimportant. Gaia was on the list of people who were informed. She asked if she could read something at the service.

'I'm here to say goodbye to a dear man. I will miss his kindness, and his softness. He left a print. Goodbye, David.'

Before everybody left the church, through his tears, Joe told Flora to call him if she needed to talk. She called that night, and Joe was glad. The next day she called again, in the morning, when trying to face her day, and in the evening when trying to face the night. On both occasions Joe was more than happy to talk about David. He was conscious not to trample on Flora's feelings. At the same time, Flora was careful not to undermine Joe's. Flora and he began to feel comfortable with each other. They had something in common, which made their relationship up to this point seem petty. At first, they spoke on the phone. Then they started to meet; occasionally, then more often. Flora had softened, and Joe had opened. Both were more able to accept each other. Their friendship began to grow.

Flora had a scan, to make sure her baby was healthy, and was told she was carrying a boy. She was excited when she got the news, but generally she seemed to get milder, and calmer as the months went by. Joe began to think she'd make an incredible mother. Flora decided to call the baby David. Everyone thought this right somehow. As the pregnancy drew to a close, Joe helped out, more and more. Whether he realised this might be the nearest he'd come to having a baby, or there were deeper paternal instincts at work, either way, he was there when she needed him. He kept her company when bored, indulged her diet, massaged her feet, even drove her to the hospital when the time came. Flora asked if he'd be the godfather, and Joe was very flattered. He said yes. The baby was stillborn.

They stood on either side of the tiny coffin as it was lowered into the earth, and slowly, in ones and twos, the crowd trickled away. Joe walked with Flora to her car, his arm linked in hers.

Don caught them up. 'I've just been talking to the priest,' he said. 'I'll be ordained on Thursday. If either of you would like to come. . .'

'Think again,' said Flora.

'Apparently, I can still have sex.'

'Oh!' said Flora. 'In that case.'

'Is it tasteless to go in drag to an ordination?' said Joe, feigning concern.

'Surely, that depends on the dress.' All three laughed, happy for the distraction, no matter how silly. 'So. No work this afternoon. I'm completely yours for the rest of the day.'

'Are you talking to me?' said Joe enthusiastically.

'No,' said Don. 'Well, possibly. But I meant my widdle flower.'

'What was that accent meant to be?' said Flora.

'Cowboy?' said Don. 'With a bit of toddler speak?'

It took a moment after he'd finished saying this before he noticed that Flora and Joe had started another, unspoken conversation. Feeling left out, and a bit stupid, he said, 'Let me in.'

'Well,' said Joe. 'I was saying a couple of things, I miss David. And, Flora you're a lucky bitch finding a guy like Don.'

Flora turned to Don. 'It's surprising what one can say.' She paused, and smiled. 'Without words!' She kissed him to make sure he knew she wasn't serious. Next she said to Joe, as though in mid-conversation, 'And I was saying, you're very special. I'm glad that David found you, and loved you.'

Joe reached out for Flora with both hands. They held each other.

'Look what you've gone and done,' said Flora, pulling away. Joe could see she was crying.

'Don't Flora, you'll make me . . .' Joe couldn't finish his sentence, because he held his mouth firmly shut. He was trying to stop himself crying. He looked down, then into the sky, then up to Flora. At this, seeing each other so upset, and looking ridiculous, they both burst out laughing.

'Enough of this thought stuff,' said Don.

Whilst sniffling, Joe said, 'I guess we could use that speech thing, like the humans do.'

'In that case,' said Flora. 'I'll state that I've had enough funerals for one year.'

'Too many,' said Joe.

'I guess any is too many,' said Don.

'So it's a deal,' said Flora. 'No more.'

Joe smiled, despite the topic of conversation. 'It's a deal.'

19

The stage was only a few feet off the ground. The audience, sitting in rows of dining hall chairs, consisted of mums and dads, a reporter from a local paper, and a talent scout there to watch one person in particular.

A blue spotlight came up on a young man. This was his soliloquy, part of his end-of-term assessment. He felt relaxed and comfortable, verging on showing off. His stage presence was self-assured, his acting subtle and controlled. The lights dimmed to black. He spoke into the dark. Putting only the slightest melody into his voice, he started to sing the last sentence, then returned to speaking for the final few words.

Then, silence in front of him.

It broke with some hesitant clapping, which turned into noisy and vigorous applause. Someone in the audience shouted, 'Well done, kid.'

The lights came up, and Ryan stood, smiling. He put his hands together in front of him, about waist high, tipped his head forward, turned and walked off stage left. A high-pitched 'Woo!' followed him. This time Ryan recognised the voice. It was Leila's. The crowd kept clapping.

Backstage, Ryan couldn't contain his excitement. His friends squealed and patted him. Dylan, the only person at college Ryan considered a friend, rushed forward, and jumped up. He wrapped his legs around Ryan, and gave him loud, theatrical kisses on either cheek. Ryan liked Dylan's softness, it reminded him a little of David. Dylan liked Ryan mainly because he seemed more open-minded than most their age. They had little in common, but still hung out everyday, and increasingly out of college.

Dylan was not heavy, so Ryan spun him round. As they turned, Dylan leant back with his arms outstretched, screeching 'darling', and generally being outrageous. Dylan's brother appeared backstage. He looked like a larger version of Dylan, without the cute element. Instantly uncomfortable, Dylan jumped down off Ryan, and acted completely different. On seeing this, Ryan felt sorry for Dylan, but also felt he understood him a little more.

One of Ryan's tutors distracted him, and introduced him to a woman, the man's wife. Ryan was immediately struck by boredom, but managed to gather enough of his personality to entertain once more. He hated having to do this, but he did appreciate Mr Kenwood's advice, so attempted to suppress his boredom as it began to surface. Just as he resigned himself to this task at hand, Leila appeared over Mrs Kenwood's shoulder, standing at the backstage doorway. She winked, then nodded. Ryan responded making Mr Kenwood understand that there was another person he'd like to talk to.

'I'm sorry. My girlfriend's here,' said Ryan.

'Oh don't worry, I'll see you tomorrow.'

Then, as though to validate his leaving Mr Kenwood, he said, 'She had to take time off work to come.'

'Get over there. You shouldn't keep her waiting,' added Mrs Kenwood, giving what she thought the more female take on the situation.

Ryan laughed convincingly, said goodbye, and rushed over to Leila.

'You nailed it,' she said.

'I hoped so.'

'Did you hear that applause?'

'Yeah.'

'The audience was right with you. Especially that stuff about your mum.'

'Did that really work?'

'God, yeah!'

'I've got a couple of beers in my bag. Let's go find a quiet place somewhere.'

Leila knew the college quite well by now. She'd spent many a lunch break with Ryan. 'How about the refectory?'

'Good idea.'

They made their way there, only having to stop a couple of times to receive congratulations. One of these was from the agent who'd been in the audience. Ryan was surprised, but acted cool. He was given a card, with a number to ring.

Only one door was open to the refectory. It had been left for the cleaners. Inside it was empty – apart from the chairs turned upside down on tabletops. Usually full of glances, and angst, it felt strange now. Although the lights were off, it wasn't dark. The moon was full, and gave a lot of light.

'Spooky!' said Ryan.

'I was thinking romantic.'

'It's quite exciting isn't it?'

'What, the agent?' said Leila.

'Well yeah, but I meant in here.'

'Are you getting fresh?'

'Maybe.'

'Give me a kiss.'

She didn't hesitate. They kissed.

Leila pulled away, 'I . . .' she said, then stopped.

'Spit it out.'

Leila took a deep breath, and sighed, 'I love you.'

'Baby!' Leila looked down for a few seconds, then up into Ryan's eyes.

'I love you too,' said Ryan. 'Regardless.'

Leila smiled, and looked down again. This time, Ryan lifted her chin. He paused for a moment, then kissed her.

Leila felt as though she were melting. 'I've been dying to say that.'

'Me too.'

Leila's voice was breathy, 'Baby!'

'I say it in my head every time we kiss.'

'Every time?'

'Well . . .' he said, then thought hard to make sure he was telling the truth. 'Definitely when we get fleshy.'

'That sounds cannibalistic.'

'Sexy, huh?'

'I've been thinking it for ages,' said Leila. 'The love thing, I mean.'

'Why didn't you say?'

'I don't know. Scared?'

'Of what?'

'Rejection, I guess.'

'I thought it was obvious how I felt.'

'Not to me.'

'But I follow you round like a dog. You move to London, I do. You come back to Manchester, I do. Do you think I wanted to do this stupid BA?'

'Didn't you?'

'I only did it because I didn't know what else to do while you were at college.'

'You said you liked it.'

'Only so far. Could you really imagine me as a magistrate? If I'm not careful, that's what I'm heading for.'

'I think it's sexy. Your honour.'

'Oh. I guess that's okay then. That's the important thing.'

'Isn't it?'

Leila thought for a second, 'Actually, it's quite important.'

Ryan pulled Leila towards him again. They kissed. This time more passionately. Ryan rubbed his hands up her body, inside her blouse. It made her shiver. He slid his hand under her bra, took hold of her breast, and started to massage it, flicking her nipple with his forefinger. Leila responded with a deep, seemingly endless sigh. When she next gathered her thoughts, she undid his fly, and pushed her hand inside his jeans. His dick was hot compared to the cool air. Ryan pushed his tongue into her mouth. This drove Leila on. She pulled out his dick, and bent towards it. Muffled sounds could be heard from the main hall. There were glass doors, and curtains separating them.

Leila took Ryan's dick in her mouth, making him groan.

'Jesus!' he said. Leila got on her knees and took his dick as far down her throat as she could. 'You better be careful. At this rate I could cum in seconds.'

Leila got up. 'Not that I wouldn't love a mouthful of your cum, but let's take this home. I want to get naked.'

Ryan gave a cheeky expression, which meant, why not here.

'If this gets you going, wait till we can do it in a courtroom.'

'I'm way ahead of you. Why do you think I encourage you.'

'Because you think I'll make a good magistrate, and you're interested in my future.'

'That's it,' said Ryan. 'Yeah. That future thing you mentioned.'

They kissed again.

20

Flora squashed awkwardly through the doorway of a West End bar. She had a huge portfolio under one arm and a bunch of flowers in her free hand. The bar was full, but the crowd was low-key, neither aggressive nor pushy. There was some ambient music playing, low enough to talk over.

'Sorry, I'm a bit late,' said Flora, to Joe, whilst miming at the waiter, asking his permission to put her portfolio on the mantelpiece over the fireplace.

'A bit,' said Joe.

Flora looked at her watch and made a shocked face. 'God!'

'Is that who kept you?'

'Aha! Her and every other driver in London, it seems.'

'Why didn't you leave that in the car?' said Joe, gesturing to the portfolio.

'I know this sounds stupid, but I was scared of it getting stolen.'

'But you're not bothered about the car?'

'I'm bored with the colour.'

'I wondered when you would be.'

'Is it that bad?'

'Aha!' said Joe, in exactly the same way Flora had.

'Really?'

'Yeah!'

'Now I know you're teasing me. If you really thought so, you wouldn't tell me.'

'Got me. Maybe I knew you'd think that, and I'm actually telling the truth.'

Flora screamed a bit too loud. People looked around at her. She seized the opportunity, beckoned a waiter, and ordered a kir royale.

'Make that a double,' said Flora.

The waiter looked confused. 'We don't do champagne in doubles.'

'It was a joke.'

'That was extremely funny,' he said. 'Let me get your drink while I laugh.'

Flora looked at Joe, pointing to the waiter with her eyes, and said, 'Dry!'

'Crispy,' said Joe.

'Crispy. I'll have to remember that.'

'I got it from David. He had a whole list; crunchy, brittle, arid, and many more.' Flora smiled sadly, frowned, and sighed. Joe fell into a reverie.

For months after David's death, Joe blamed himself. He felt partly responsible. Therapy, and a course of anti-depressants helped him change his perspective. Eventually, he began to think less about the man he loved being burnt alive, and more about getting through each day and night, just filling time without him.

Joe had woken, ate, rested and slept with his lover every day for over four years. After his death, he had to get used to David not being at arm's length, whenever he needed a kiss, a hug, or an expression that showed he understood, or was bothered about what happened in Joe's life.

'Hey! Come back!' said Flora.

'Sorry.

'Let me guess. David?'

'Yeah, but . . .'

'Always his butt.'

'No. Well, yes, but I was actually thinking about the first time I stayed at your house.' The waiter put Flora's drink in front of her.

'That will be . . .'

Joe cut him off. 'Put it on my tab.'

'Okay,' said the waiter. Then, to Flora, 'You know, I'm still having trouble keeping a straight face.'

'Looks goddamn straight to me,' said Flora. The waiter left the table without responding.

'He looked gay to me,' said Joe.

'Oh yeah, I forgot you can all tell, can't you?' Joe nodded. 'In that case, I'm surprised I didn't fancy him.'

'Didn't you?'

'Maybe a little.'

'Your nostrils flared. Your skin changed colour. And your body temperature rose by at least four degrees.'

'Right!'

'I think you did fancy him.'

'He did have lovely forearms.'

'Probably from carrying all those trays.'

'Well, I'm glad I contributed to the look. Anyway! What about the first time you stayed at my house?'

'Oh yeah!' said Joe. 'The artwork in my bedroom. I asked David about it, but never got round to asking you. It was a crazy time.'

'Thanks to me.'

'I don't mean to put down your role, but you were only an extra.'

'Thanks, I think. Were you being bitchy, or sweet?'

'Yes,' said Joe, and raised his glass to Flora's.

'Cheers to rears.'

'Yeah! Cheers to fears.'

'And so?' said Flora.

'What?'

'The artwork?'

'Sorry! Do you still do any?'

'You make it sound like drugs.'

'Isn't it?'

'I guess so.' Flora thought about what Joe said for a moment. 'If it's so addictive, why aren't you doing any?'

'Don't feel like it.'

'Guess that's why, in answer to your question, I haven't done any since David left me.' Flora zoned out. Then in a flash returned. 'Around that time anyway.'

'It was a significant time.'

'Aha!' Flora turned away. 'Waiter! Same.' She turned back to Joe. 'Drink?'

'Beer, please,' said Joe.

'And a beer, please.'

'Do you care which kind?' said the waiter. Joe held up the bottle he'd been drinking from, and the waiter left.

'You sure have a way with waiters,' said Joe.

'What? Know how to bug them?'

'Something like that.' Joe looked at the waiter as he walked away. 'I think he quite likes you.'

'But you said he was gay.'

'Didn't stop David, did it?'

'I caught him on the cusp.'

'So that's your trick.'

'I wouldn't advise it.'

'I blamed myself, of course.'

'Of course. I've always found it difficult to grasp the idea that the world doesn't revolve round me.'

Joe burst out laughing.

'That's not to say you can't have a hell of a lot revolving around you. I mean, me.'

'Hell being the operative word. But back to the artwork. We may die of old age before we finish this conversation, but I'm not going to give up.'

'I can't wait,' said Flora. The waiter put their drinks in front of them. 'That was quick.'

'I'm quick all right,' said the waiter. He closed his eyes, sighed, turned, and left.

'Is it me, or is he completely vile?'

'He probably thinks we're vile.'

'Joe, there's a time and place for generosity of spirit and . . .'

'Don't tell me. Now isn't it?'

'Never in front of me. It emphasises my meanness.'

'Sorry,' said Joe.

'The artwork! I have to confess, you've almost got me interested now.'

'Right!' said Joe. 'So, how did you hang it?' He looked at Flora earnestly. 'I've always wondered.'

'Don't even bother.'

'No, really. I was wondering if you had any more.'

'Why do you ask?'

'I'll tell you in a minute. First, can I just run some questions by you?'

'Sure,' said Flora looking slightly puzzled.

'About painting.'

'I feel I better warn you, my knowledge is limited.'

'Maybe that's a good thing. Don't think too hard, just tell me what you feel, intuitively.'

'Fire away.'

'Okay,' said Joe. 'What do you think of Symbolism?'

'If the viewer doesn't know what the symbols refer to, it won't communicate much.'

'Impressionism?'

'Oh, come on, it's just stupid, isn't it? I guess they were ahead of their time, anticipating chocolate box design by a hundred years or so.'

Joe laughed. 'Landscapes?'

'Unchallenging. Too safe.'

'Abstraction?'

'Childish, but pretending to be adult.'

'Cubism?'

'This I find confusing. Someone has an idea, then a generation of duds reproduce different versions of the same thing.'

'Ouch!' Joe thought for a moment. 'Op-art?'

'Scratches the surface. It shows shape and colour have an effect, which is useful.'

'Very good. What about figurative art?'

'Ah! It definitely has potential.'

'So, there is some art you think worth bothering with.'

'Yeah!'

'Carry on.'

'Expressionism. It's simple, evocative, understandable, and again ,effective.' Joe nodded. 'Then there's portraiture. You can't go wrong with portraits. They're indicative of the age, yet give insight into the person portrayed and the artist. Rather, the person in that time.' Joe feigned seriousness. 'Pop art was fun. It made sense of art and industry. Mondrian had a good eye for placement of colour.'

'Wait a minute. Your tornado montage used symbolism, didn't it?'

'Very easily understood symbols. You could call them icons. They are pretty universal. A mean-looking dog, an erection, a tornado, destruction, the fragility and vulnerability of a baby bird.'

'David isn't a universal symbol.'

'Actually he is, within the Western world. Youth and beauty are understood, even if somebody isn't sexually attractive to you. Generally you still know if they're beautiful, or not.'

'Get you lady. You know your stuff.'

'Only my stuff. Don't know Jack-shit about anybody else's.'

'It's a good start.' Flora forced a laugh, unsure. 'I'm serious. What better place to start than knowing what is right and good and true for you?'

'You came over all Emerson then.'

'My God! You're not referring to his essay on self-reliance are you?' Flora nodded, shook her head, then nodded again. 'You are, aren't you?' This time Flora made her head roll around, neither nodding, nor shaking. 'Please say yes.'

Flora opened her mouth into a thin slit, just a couple of millimetres apart, and squeaked in a voice that sounded like it might belong to an elf, 'Yes!'

'Brilliant!'

'Who me, or this Emerson lady?'

'Maybe both.'

'Why, you're too kind. But why all these questions?'

'I was thinking, maybe . . . Just maybe, we could work on something together.'

'What, like an aberration?'

'I hope not. I was thinking of collaboration.'

'You're still teasing me, right?'

'No. We could have an exhibition.'

'What! An exhibition with you! But Joe, you're so famous. People will think it strange?'

'That's good.'

'Oh, my God! You *are* being serious.'

'It would be hard work. There'd be stupid journalists to deal with. I'd boss you around. I'd be a fascist about every shape and colour you chose. I'd use you, starve you, be opinionated and arrogant.'

'Sounds wonderful, but . . .'

'What!' said Joe in mock annoyance.

'I won't have you being fascist about colour. It's my baby.'

Joe winced. 'Mine, too.'

'And all you want is my soul? Where do I sign?'

'Seriously, though, if it doesn't work out, there's no harm done. It's just an idea.'

'Not for long.' Flora raised her glass to Joe's bottle.

'Needless to say, we can both back out whenever we feel like it.'

'You mean, like a relationship,' said Flora. Before Joe had time to digest this comment, she continued, 'So, how about coming back to my place?' Flora paused. 'And looking at the rest of my stuff. If you don't back out when you've seen the rest, then it's a deal.'

'You drive a hard bargain.'

'Is it a German car?'

'No, it's slang for arsehole,' said Joe. 'Waiter! Can I have the check? Sorry, are we ready?'

'Ready as I can be.'

'I'm sure your ready is enough for anybody.'

The bill was paid, attitude given, numbers swapped, sex imagined, and numbers thrown away. This was followed by rush-hour traffic. Cars inches apart. Aggression. Frustration. Exhaust fumes. Drivers cruised out of boredom. Next came parking, keys out, jacket off, kettle on, and only then, gradually, a sense of calm returned, along with Flora's private life; her more real, unoffice life.

'You know the deal. Treat this like your own place.'

'I know...' said Joe. Then, in a pretend Flora-voice, ' ...But, no decorating!'

'Have I made that joke so many times?'

'That's what's meant to be funny about it, isn't it?'

Flora felt embarrassed and lied. 'Of course!'

Joe made himself a cup of tea, and Flora rolled a joint. They kicked back, taking deep relaxing breaths.

'Phew!' said Flora. 'Better?'

'Much.'

'I'm going to have to look around a bit for that artwork. I don't think I've thrown it out.'

'I never throw artwork away,' said Joe. 'It shows where my head was at the time.'

'Maybe I didn't want to remember where my head was.'

'Sounds kind of a shame. Whatever you've been through makes

you what you are today. And I for one wouldn't change anything about you.'

'If memories are worth remembering, they'll probably stay.'

'I like to encourage some. Things about David, say.'

'Of course, but I don't have a problem remembering David.'

'Flora, I'm kinda coming raght accustomed to ya all.'

'Hey Joe, don't get all sweet on me. It doesn't suit you.'

'Sweet does suit me.'

'Since when?'

'Since I realised it works,' said Joe. 'I'd say it was when I was about thirteen.' He paused, and looked toward the window. He wasn't acting. 'I just don't have much call for it these days.'

'You soft bastard,' said Flora. Then, realising she'd been callous, she reached for Joe. They stayed in that position for a few minutes. 'Baby, you know I'm always here for you. Really, Joe, day or night, any hour of any morning.'

'Enough already! You sound like an ad for a hot beverage.'

'God! I'm never allowed a nice moment with you, Joe.'

'Sorry. I'm over nice moments.'

'I know, baby, but please don't be scared of letting me show you I care.' Joe rolled his eyes. 'I mean it, Joe. You can only avoid the feeling thang so long.'

'I know, but this is how long I'm doing it.'

'I'm sorry. I didn't mean to push you.'

'I know.' He cupped her chin with his hand. 'So, how about finding that artwork?'

'Okay, boss.'

Flora disappeared into her bedroom. Cupboards could be heard opening and closing, boxes being shifted and dragged, until Flora returned dragging a large box. Joe jumped to his feet to help her, and together they carried it to the table.

'What's the smell?' said Joe, angling his head, trying to catch the scent.

'I'd say probably a putrid mix by now. They used to all have individual smells, essential oils, boot polish, perfumes, household bleach, all sorts of stuff.'

'It's part of the art?'

'Whimsical, hey!'

'Cute.'

'Cute, like a toddler taking its first steps?'

'Maybe.'

'Somehow, I don't mind being patronised by you.'

'Good! It's part of the work package.' Joe emptied the box. He looked through the work, deliberately and carefully, considering each one. Occasionally, he'd utter, "I get it," "witty," "clever," or "ugh." Sometimes he barely formed words, but simply responded with an emotion. At one point, he pursed his lips; another time, he laughed heartily. This was followed by a frown, which continued through several pieces. Lastly, he rubbed his hands together, then clasped them. When he arrived at the bottom of the pile, he said,

'Just a couple more quick questions.'

'Fire away.'

'What is sex to you?'

'Joe. Don't get fresh.'

'I'm not.'

'Never mind.' She thought for a second. 'At best it's an expression of feelings of love. At worst, it's isolating, like how I imagine dying feels.'

'Flora, you're such a poet.' Joe took a second, then asked, 'God?'

'At best it's love. At worst it's fear.'

Joe smiled. 'I can't wait to start working with you. How busy are you this week?'

'Like, totally.'

'Next weekend?'

'Like, not.'

'Great. Let's start next week, just brainstorming. I'll bring some pads and some felt tips, and you bring your pretty brain and your not-so-pretty attitude.'

'Okay! Got it,' said Flora. 'You'll bring some lads and your svelte hips. And I'll bring the shitty rain and the platitudes.'

'So, my abandoned-for-quite-some-time-now-studio at sixteen hundred hours.'

'You sound so Batman all of a sudden.'

'Okay. My loft at tea time.'

'Now you sound all Wind in the Willows.'

'I know what,' said Joe. 'I'll call you.'

21

Chrysalids twitched in the dim light. This made some sink, others come to the surface. They made a crackling sound as they moved. The lighting became brighter, making them livelier. The more the light heated them, the more frantic they became, and the more noise they made.

'The zoom,' said Joe. 'Lovely.' Violins began to make sharp, stabbing sounds. The camera pulled out to show thousands of the grubs.

'Makes my skin crawl,' said the Scent rep.

'Makes mine tingle,' said Joe.

'The spray's beautiful. How did you make it glow like that?'

'Sorry! A trade secret,' said Joe. 'No. It's just well-angled side lighting.'

'Stunning! Really, Joe.'

'You wait, the best bit's coming any second.' The perfume mist seemed to dance in the air, finally landing on the chrysalids, coating them.

'The mist?' said the rep.

'Animated.'

'Subtle. I couldn't tell.' In fast motion, suddenly the grubs began to hatch. Many different species of butterfly started to appear. The violins began to make sense. Melody emerged out of the previous cacophony. The screen became saturated with gently fluttering coloured wings, each leaving trails of faint colour as they moved.

'Magnificent!' said the rep.

'Wait for it,' said Joe.

The voice-over was clearly an elderly woman's: 'Scent. Helps bring out the beauty in you.'

'Clever,' said the rep.

'Clean, don't you think? No nonsense.'

'Yes. Not too much, but just enough.'

'I'd never give you not enough.'

'That wasn't our fear.'

'My reputation precedes me.'

'That could be unfortunate sometimes. We nearly didn't go with you on this project, thinking you might produce something too controversial.' The rep said the word controversial as though he didn't like it being in his head, or mouth. Joe realised that he was supposed to feel ashamed, but couldn't. 'Something tells me you're not as hard as everyone thinks you are.' Joe looked down at his feet. 'I knew it. The lamb within the wolf.' Now Joe started to go slightly pink. 'They won't believe this back at the office. I made Joseph Holtzman blush.'

'You make me sound like a monster.'

'Aren't you?'

'Not that I'm aware of.'

'What about your last exhibition?'

'Not again. Will I have to carry that around my neck forever?'

'Probably. People don't forget things like that easily.'

'I should be flattered, I suppose.'

'I think it's definitely a talent to be able to cause such response, but...'

'Blah, blah, blah.'

'Sorry, does that annoy you?'

'Actually it bores me.'

'Sensitive subject?'

'Get out of here. You've got your ad, hope everyone likes it and all, but you don't pay me enough to listen to your shit as well.' Joe led the man to the front door. 'If there are any questions, e-mail me.'

The man was left outside Joe's front door confused, trying to work out how things got so out of hand. He wouldn't be able to say anything at work. It was his job to be able to liaise with people.

'He been bossing you around, has he?' The rep looked to his side and saw an old woman. She looked as though she'd dressed in as many different colours as was possible, including odd socks, and even odd shoes, one yellow and one blue. 'I'm his next-door neighbour. The name's Claire.' She reached out a hand. On it she wore a white lace fingerless glove, more Eighties music video than old lady gear.

The rep didn't think to hide his surprise. 'Cool outfit! Hello Claire. I'm Joe.'

'You must be confused. He's Joe.'

'I know, but I'm Joe, too.'

'Not Joe one?'

'Well, he's older than me, so was born first. That would make him Joe one.' Claire was no longer listening. She continued to smile, trying to decide between chicken, or beef flavoured cat food.

'Claire?'

'Yes, dear.'

'I thought you were daydreaming.'

'I was. That Joe one or two stuff didn't interest me much.'

Joe was beginning to think that there might be something in the water in Hampstead. He laughed to himself.

'Let me in on the joke,' said Claire.

'It was nothing.'

'You mean it was about me, or Neighbour Joe?'

'No!'

'Caught you out, didn't I?'

'No! Anyway, it was nice meeting you Claire.'

'Are you in advertising?'

'Yes,' he said enthusiastically.

'It wasn't meant to be a compliment.'

Joe shook his head in disbelief. He'd had enough of nutty people for one day. He walked away.

'Bye, Mister Ad-man!' shouted Claire.

Joe didn't turn around or reply. Claire stuck her finger up at him. Then, in case she was caught, she pulled down her hand and giggled.

A knocking came from the front window in Joe's house. Claire turned around, a little startled. Joe had been watching the whole encounter. Although he'd never met Claire he recognised her as his next-door neighbour. He stuck up his thumb. Claire acted as though she were bashful. Then she went to his front window and kissed it. From inside, Claire's mouth looked odd, like a sea anemone. Her lipstick smudged the glass. For a fraction of a second, Joe was fazed, thinking it perverse flirting with someone Claire's age, then he burst out laughing. His saliva sprayed onto the glass. Outside, Claire backed away from the window, but when she saw Joe's saliva beginning to dribble she couldn't help laughing, and rushed forward for another, sloppier kiss.

22

Flora was bored, and Don was worn out. He'd been up all night at work: two false alarms; then just before he got off work, his watch was called out to a huge fire in the city. There was only a security guard in the building, and because he was asleep, it quickly got out of hand.

Flora knew Don hadn't slept, but goaded him persistently.

'I'm fine. I just want to be left alone.'

'I'll let you alone when I'm ready.'

'Please! Do you have to be so bossy?'

'Sorry I'm not some little missy.'

'There is something in between.'

'Joe?'

'Christ! Let up on that gay thing.'

'Does it wound your masculinity?'

'No. It's just stupid. You can only tell the same joke so many times. I assume it is a joke.'

'The idea of you two as a couple makes me laugh.'

'You'd probably get off on it.'

'Right!'

'It seems to be in your head a lot.'

'Let's just say it's a sore point.'

'No, why don't we say, it's not a point at all.' Don paused, rubbing his temples. 'Listen, I've a headache. Can't we just be nice?'

'God almighty! You sound like my grandmother.'

'I don't care what I sound like. I just want some peace.'

'Oh. Is diddles all tired?' said Flora, as if talking to a child.

'Diddles?'

'He *is* tired.'

'It's hardly surprising.'

'What a hero.'

'Can't you just give me a break?'

'Why would I do that?'

He looked at her seriously. 'Cos you like me?'

'Now you sound like a kid.'

'Flora. Please!' He put his hands over his face and lay back on her sofa. He tried to change the conversation, lighten it. 'How was last night?'

'He was great.'

'Spare me.'

'Don't you want to hear?'

'Firstly. I know you're joking. Secondly, I hate thinking of you with anyone else.' Flora seemed to be smiling triumphantly. 'You are joking, right?' Again, her response was the smirk. 'Bitch! Whether you did or didn't, bitch!' Flora made a face as though communicating with a baby.

'Boo hoo!'

'You didn't?'

'Do you think you own me?'

'No, but I do have an emotional investment. Don't I?'

'I don't know what goes on in your widdle head.' Flora went and knelt down beside Don. Again, as though talking to a child, 'Priddy widdle head.'

If Don hadn't been so tired, he'd have been more annoyed at her, but he was grateful for the attention. She stroked his head. With more breath than actual words he said, 'That feels nice.'

'His dick was juicier than yours.'

Don couldn't help picturing this, and felt overwhelmed with jealousy.

'What are you trying to do?'

'Just playing.'

'Can't I get through to you? I'm too tired to play.'

'I'm bored.'

'So go and do something, see a film, read a book, anything, but just stop getting at me.'

'Maybe I'll give Juicy-dick-Rick a call.'

'If you're intending to drive me away, it's working.'

Although not completely aware, she was trying to push him out of her life. She was bored, not just with the day, but of their routine, and their interaction, even the sound of his voice. Things about him had begun to irritate her. Once it had started, it snowballed. She didn't like him smelling of smoke; it made her think of David. She didn't like him being so tired all the time; she found it boring. She didn't like his work hours; she could never remember them, so found it impossible to make plans. Flora found Don comforting after David's death, like a flannelette sheet, an old cardigan, or a cup of warm milk. As she began to get stronger emotionally, she had less use for him. He became an embarrassment, a reminder of how needy she'd been. It made her cringe to think she'd depended on him. Flora never wanted to depend on anyone again. These weren't thoughts with a clear beginning and end. They were feelings, causing responses. Attacking Don seemed to be a solution. If questioned, she probably would have denied being cruel, but he definitely felt it, and it muddled his feelings, and his thoughts. There were times when he couldn't even face seeing her. Sometimes, creeping back to his own home after an exhausting night was all he could bear. This wasn't the case today. He was exhausted, but didn't want to be alone. He felt insecure, and needy. The last thing he wanted was to be provoked, and made to have images in his head he didn't want there.

Flora continued to amuse herself with Don, comforting him; then, just as he was softening and letting down his guard, she'd be mean to him. When she was lovely, he couldn't refuse her, but when she wasn't he wanted to be nowhere near her. Finally, after he'd taken as much as he could stand, he said,

'I'm going.'

This annoyed Flora. He couldn't just walk out. She'd planned her day around him. It didn't make her feel sorry, but indignant, and harder than ever. 'I'll call you,' she said, and paused for effect. 'Sometime.'

'Or not,' said Don. He'd had enough of her behaviour.

'Is that a choice?' said Flora.

'I don't care.'

'In that case, not.'

'Suits me fine.'

'Nothing suits you.'

'Childish bitch.'

'Fuck you.'

'Sorry, I take that back. Just bitch.' Don picked up his jacket. 'If you stick to this, you can send my stuff round in a cab. I'll do the same.'

'If I can be bothered. I probably bought it all for you anyway.'

'I know what. You wear it. Or stick it.'

'Charming!'

'Care!'

'You sound like a teenage girl.'

'You're too much. Has anybody ever told you that?'

'People don't seem to mind.'

'What do you mean? You've only ever had one boyfriend.'

'Don't bring David into this.'

'He must have been a fucking angel to put up with you. Oh, no! That's right, he left you.'

'You fucker!' She came at Don.

He held her by her wrists. 'You're pathetic.'

She kneed him in the balls. He fell to the floor, moaning.

'Not so pathetic,' said Flora, and grinned.

Don got hold of her ankle and pulled it from under her. She fell onto her back, Don crawled on top of her, pinning her down.

'You've gone too far this time,' he said.

'As a stupid queen once said, care!'

'You are completely off your nut.'

Don got up off Flora, but she stayed sitting on the floor.

'I'm going. And you're going to have to do some pretty apologising if you want to see me again.'

'Sorry . . .' She paused. 'I ever met you.'

'Bye!' said Don. 'I can't believe I nearly had a kid with you.'

As he put his hand on the doorknob to open it, Flora shouted, 'It wasn't even yours.'

Don stopped in his tracks, slowly turned to face her. 'What did you say?'

'It fucking wasn't yours. It was Joe's.'

On hearing this, Don opened the door and left. He walked out knowing he would never see Flora again. As the door closed, she looked around, grabbed the ashtray off the table, and threw it against the door. It smashed into tiny pieces. For a moment, she had a hard expression on her face, pure anger and hatred. Slowly this softened. Flora hadn't clear enough thoughts to understand why, but she began to cry.

23

Rain poured down. Joe struggled with his front door keys, not focusing on the task, his thoughts elsewhere. Somebody tapped him from behind. It startled him. When he turned around, he was even more surprised. The old woman from next door was standing, smiling, soaked to the skin. She seemed completely unaware that it was pouring down, or didn't care.

'Come under here,' said Joe, referring to the meagre shelter the doorway offered.

'Why?' said the old woman.

'It's raining,' said Joe.

'So! Are you just trying to be fresh?' she said with a glint in her eye.

'You're getting soaked.'

'Rain, I can handle.' Joe was taken aback. 'It's umbrellas I hate.' Joe pictured a rainy day in the West End, dodging through the cattle-like tourists. He found himself agreeing with her. 'It's warm, anyway. Quite lovely, in fact!'

Again, Joe thought about what she'd said. It was warm. He changed his mind, and could no longer see why he wanted so desperately to get under cover, apart from habit. The old woman smiled as though she knew what Joe was thinking.

'It's about perspective,' she said. Joe looked slightly puzzled, not because of what she was saying, but because she'd said it. 'The name's

Claire.'

'Hey! I'm Joe. Joseph Holtzman.'

'I know who you are,' said Claire and chuckled. 'You're Neighbour Joe.' Claire shook her head as though to shake the water off, but she was only pretending. She knew that if she shook her head properly it would make her dizzy, and she'd have to sit down. 'Where's the other one?'

'Sorry!'

'The nice young man who helped me get in my house.'

Joe fell quiet. Again, Claire seemed to know what he was thinking. 'Oh dear me. No!' Joe couldn't speak.

She took the keys out of Joe's hand and opened his front door. In silence, she took his hand and led him inside.

'You sit there, sweetheart,' she said, first plumping the seat cushion. 'I'll make you a cup of tea.' She headed towards the kitchen. The house was the same shape as hers, so it wasn't difficult to work out. She stood tentatively at the doorway, took in the decoration of the kitchen, then went on smoothly, as though she'd lived there all her life. Joe sat in silence, feeling comfortable having this stranger in his house. As she came back into the room, a cup in either hand, she said, 'You've done a lovely job with the decorating.' Joe had never heard anybody use the word lovely in relation to his interior design sense before, but he accepted the compliment. Claire sat next to Joe and put a hand on his knee. 'I know how it feels. My Mickey passed away three years ago. I'm almost sure he still messes up the place.' Joe smiled faintly. He knew what she meant about people leaving residue. 'Of course, I know it's not him, but sometimes, I like to think it is.'

Joe took a sip of tea. The cup smelled the same as Claire. He was lost in thought for seconds, staring into his tea. Then he said,

'So, you met David?'

'I took a shine to him. Bet he was a ladies' man.'

'He was my boyfriend,' said Joe, a little hesitant.

'I know that! Can't you let an old lady dream?' Again, Joe was speechless. 'Do you think I'm daft? He told me your name, what you did for work, all sorts of stuff. Some things an old lady shouldn't hear. Well I guess I shouldn't have asked.' Joe smiled. 'He couldn't say anything about you without this sparkle in his eye.' This comment cut through to Joe's emotions, deeply. He was stunned, both happy, and sad at the same time. 'I know that sparkle,' Claire continued, oblivious. 'It may be hard to believe, but I've had that kind of infatuation directed at me before now.' She stopped, stared into space, and sighed. Joe was staring into space also, lost in thoughts of David. 'I miss that. Anyway, when was it that he helped me? Four months ago, I think. Yes, four months ago. I was making a cake for my grandson. It was his birthday four months ago.'

David had been dead almost a year now.

Joe struggled to remain present, and deal with Claire. 'So, you met David?' he repeated.

'Yes. A lovely chap. Much nicer than that Quentin.'

Joe raised his eyebrows. 'You're not referring to Quentin Crisp by any chance?'

'Yes Crispy, that's what we called him... When he wasn't listening, mind.' She looked pensive, then puzzled. 'His hair was so dry.' Joe was amused, and couldn't work out if she was for real or completely batty, or both. 'Ah, God bless him! Poor chap! Mind you, it was different then...' She paused. Joe prepared himself to hear something patronising, probably with the word homosexual in it. 'You just couldn't get the good hair dyes you can today.'

Joe burst out laughing.

'Did you hang out with him?'

'Who?'

Joe hated saying it, but his curiosity got the better of him. 'Crispy.'

'No, no! The brightest thing about Crispy was his rouge. Shocking! The colours he used. And he painted it on so thick. Ugh!'

'You mean you didn't hang out with Crispy because he was dull?'

'It sounds ever so cruel put like that, but yes.' Claire chuckled.

'You're a devil,' said Joe.

'That's what they say.'

'Who's they?'

'The girls at the club.'

'The club?'

'The knitting club.'

'There's a club for knitting?'

'It's just an excuse to sit and chat, really,' said Claire. 'I've known some of them since . . .'

'The war?' said Joe.

'The parties at Hugh's. I was an original Playboy bunny, one of his favourites.' Joe was unable to hide his shock. 'Just playing! Got you there.'

Joe laughed again. He couldn't believe she was so with it. Joe's face must have been giving away his thoughts.

'Not bad for such an old one, hey?'

24

Whatever she tried, Flora couldn't get the attention of the man at the bar. The air was wet and hot, Tragic climate. Joe had taken her, but had gone off to dance about an hour ago. To Flora it felt like he'd just left. It felt like she'd been at the bar over half an hour. It had, in fact, been ten minutes.

A man squeezed in beside her. He was served within minutes.

'Hey! I've been here ages.'

'You should check out the dance floor,' said the man. 'It's much more fun.'

'Ha! Ha! I would if I could.'

'What! Your E no good?'

'That's not the problem. I've been trying to get served.'

'Why didn't you say?' He gestured to the barman, and said, 'Can you get this lady a drink?'

'Sure, mate,' said the barman.

Flora was surprised how quickly he responded. Distracted by this, she had to remember what she wanted.

'Uh! Large Red Bull and vodka.' Facing the man beside her she said, 'Thanks, mate!'

'I think he fancies me.'

'I did wonder. By the way,' said Flora, 'nobody who knows me at all well calls me a lady.'

'What do they call you?'

'At my convenience.'

The man took a second to get the joke. As it dawned on him, he said, 'Bet they do. Sorry! Brain-dead. It's the drugs.'

'Scrambled?'

'Blended.'

'It gets me through the week,' said Flora.

'Me too. I haven't seen you here before.'

'I prefer to party at home these days.'

'Me too. You do realise it's the first step towards middle age?'

'I know, but I work all week. It's easier to do all that eating, sleeping, washing, living stuff if I stay indoors.'

The man pulled a face as though he were trying to remember something. 'Eating? And what was that other thing you mentioned?'

'Sleeping,' said Flora.

Still the man looked confused. 'Like on Rohypnol,' he said, using facial expressions Flora liked.

'That's the one.'

'Oh! Why didn't you say?'

'What's your name?' she asked.

'Mate.'

'You're not serious?'

'I'm not Mate, or Serious. I'm Paul.'

'You're a funny bugger, Paul.'

'What, funny titter, or funny kooky?'

'Titter and kooky will cover it.'

That'll probably be your drugs.'

'What do you mean?'

'They'll be making me seem more titter and kooky than I really am.'

'Are you not?'

'Less so, I imagine.'

Flora was surprised at his way of talking. Paul took a swig of his drink. He offered it to Flora, who did the same.

'Paul, I don't know if you're aware of this, but you're huge.'

'Yeah. I have a bit of weight problem.'

'I wouldn't call it a problem.'

'If you had to inject steroids, work-out most days, eat huge amounts causing you to shit constantly, you might think it a problem.'

'This may be a stupid question, especially here at Tragic, but, why?'

'Cos I'm gay, insecure, got hang-ups about my masculinity. Shall I go on?'

'I get the picture. You mean you're a normal person?'

'I'm not that normal. I don't work, or anything.'

'What do you do? How do you live?' The barman came back with Flora's drink.

'I get disability benefit. I had Aids for a while, was quite sick.'

'And now?'

'Not dead.'

'But still claiming?'

'You got it.'

'How do you spend your time?'

'I'm a writer-cum-artist-cum-drug-taking gay.'

Flora burst out laughing. 'God! You're different.'

'From who?'

Flora made a gesture with her hand, meaning everybody around them.

'You'd be surprised,' said Paul. 'I know lots of cum-sucking-bum-fucking-drug-taking-gays.'

'I bet you do, looking like that,' said Flora. 'Like flies round shit.'

'Pretty metaphor.'

'Sorry.'

'I do okay,' he said, a little coyly. 'Are you with friends?'

'I thought so, but I'm beginning to wonder.'

'Would you like to meet mine? They'd really get you.'

'That would be a nice change.'

'We're in the far corner. It might be best if you get hold of my belt loop.'

'Okay.'

Paul seemed to know everybody. He couldn't go a few feet without somebody kissing him, hugging him, at least nodding, or mouthing hello. As they entered the main dance area, a blotchy, red-faced man put an Ecstasy in Paul's mouth. Paul made a 'tastes-horrible face', bit the pill in half and popped it into Flora's mouth. Looking around, he gestured to a group of people, for a drink. One of them handed him a small bottle, nearly full. After taking a gulp, he appeared to keep the water in his mouth. He gestured for Flora to come closer. Although confused, she did, and realised he wanted her to put her mouth against his. She did this too. When their lips were touching, Paul squirted some of the water into her mouth. She accepted and swallowed her Ecstasy.

Paul thanked the water person, and the red-faced man and said, 'Ugh! What can you do? It would be rude to refuse.' As they got to the place where they were heading, he said, 'Can I tell you one of my poems?'

'Sure,' said Flora, shouting over the music. Paul cupped his hands around her ear, cutting out a surprising amount of background noise, and spoke clearly:

"Looking for meaning is something to do
And has something to do with
Expecting
Wanting a need
Blaming the air
Not accepting
Dissatisfaction with the day
Uncomfortable within it
Pampering a desire to be more
And in trying becoming less

It is familiar
And unfriendly
Cosy and restrictive
The hum of unblurred nothingness
Affecting a lot by its littleness
Its stationaryness
Its aggressive pining
Its indolent desperation
Its enthusiastic depression
Its lively and perpetual lethargy
Its sluggish and glue-like insistence
Its assuming human habit
Of being something to do."

Paul pulled back. Flora was silent.

'Is he telling you a poem?' said a woman's voice.

'He is, actually,' said Flora.

'Good?'

'Really good!'

'I'm Josie.'

'Josie!' said Paul. 'Flora, this is one of the friends who I said would get you. Josie, Flora. Flora, Josie.'

Flora was surprised by Josie's appearance. She looked as if she were in a different place from everybody else. She didn't seem hot, wasn't sweating. She did have some dress sense, beyond comfortable-enough-for-a-long-night-at-a-disco wear. She didn't seem cunted, or drunk, and she had control of her face. The strangest thing was she used it to smile, and it looked genuine, not chemical.

Flora was confused. 'What are you doing here?'

'Am I not welcome?'

'Of course you are, by me at least, but you seem out of place.'

'Thank you!'

'You're right to take it as a compliment.' She looked Josie up and down. Referring to her long black dress and Doctor Marten boots, Flora said, 'Are you not hot?'

'Yes, but I'm not about to strip off.'

'Sure! Still, you must be dying of heat.'

'No, she's too cool,' said Paul.

'Even *I'm* not that cool,' said Josie. 'It's probably just that I'm not on E.'

'How do you stand it here sober?'

Josie shuddered. 'Please! Do you have to use the s word?'

'Sorry! How do you stay so cool?'

'Speed-ball.'

'Oh!' said Flora, shocked, not letting on that she didn't know what it was. She knew it entailed shooting up, and possibly involved smack mixed with another drug.

'Hence,' said Josie, 'the long sleeves.' Flora smiled knowingly, feeling slightly out of her depth, and thought to change the subject before she was caught out.

'Did you really write that, Paul?'

'Last week.'

'You should be published.'

'I am.'

'You two aren't what I expected to find here.'

'In this place,' said Paul, 'it's best to keep your expectations low.'

'In life generally I always keep expectations low,' said Flora. 'Less disappointment.'

'What do you do?' said Paul.

'I design buildings, well only parts of them usually.'

'What do you mean?'

'I adapt areas of buildings for the disabled, old people, children. Anybody with special needs.'

'Fuck,' said Paul. 'That must be interesting.'

'Relatively. It's a bit formulaic.'

'My sister's an architect,' said Josie.

'Mine's a cow,' said Paul.

'Dairy or beef?' said Flora.

'A plain old cow-cow,' said Paul. 'Who did you say you were here with?'

'A friend of mine, called Joe.'

'Not Joe Holtzman?' said Paul.

'Yeah. Do you know him?'

'I was having you on. I saw him here. That's why I made the joke. Are you really a friend of his?'

'Yeah. He's great.'

'I think he's incredible,' said Paul.

'Paul's got a crush on him,' said Josie.

'Josie!' said Paul.

'Get over it,' said Josie. 'You wanted me to tell her. Can you introduce them Flora?'

'Of course. He'd like you, I'm sure. That's if I ever find him.'

'He went that way a minute ago,' said Paul, pointing upstairs.

'He went by here?' said Flora.

'Yeah. I didn't know you knew him. You were talking to Josie, and he was holding on to somebody's shoulders.'

'Who?'

'Don't know. Some man with a beard.'

'Sounds like George. He works with him. He edits Joe's commercials.'

'That Levi's one was brilliant,' said Paul.

'Everybody likes that,' said Flora.

'Do you?' said Josie.

'I think the albino was cute.'

'Clear this up for me,' said Paul. 'That fight scene had stand-ins, didn't it?'

'Of course, and animation.'

'Guessed as much, but you never know.'

'Listen,' said Josie, 'I'm bored of shouting. Do you want to go up to the café?'

'I have to sort out some shit with this dealer first,' said Paul. 'I'll follow you up.'

'Josie?' said Flora.

'Right behind you,' said Josie.

They headed off. As was common at Tragic, Josie took hold of Flora's hand so they wouldn't get separated.

25

The phone rang. Flora rolled over, and picked it up, whilst simultaneously looking at her bedroom clock. It read, eighteen thirty-six.

'Flora. It's Paul.'

'Who?' said Flora.

'Paul, from Tragic.' Flora was none the wiser.

'You don't know who I am, do you?'

'Sorry, Paul. I took downers to get to sleep.'

'It's nice to know I'm so memorable. No worry. Can I speak to Josie?'

'Josie,' said Flora, relocating her thoughts, and putting this one in the right place, somewhere that made sense. Then she rolled back into her original position and waved the phone above Josie's face.

'What?' said Josie, barely out of sleep.

'It's Paul,' said Flora, saying the name as though she didn't know who he was. A couple of times during sleep, she'd got up to pee, so was aware of Josie lying next to her, and why. Each time Flora got back into bed, she'd wrapped herself around Josie, as though she'd been doing it all her life.

Josie put the receiver to her ear. 'Hey little thing.'

For the next few minutes, Flora could only hear the tinny buzzing sound of Paul's voice through the receiver, and Josie's replies. 'Rotten... Yeah... The music's been the same for years... Yeah... Great...!

I don't know. I'll find out.' Still without opening her eyes properly, Josie rocked her head towards Flora. 'Any idea what time we'll be functioning?'

'None. I could get up now,' said Flora. 'Why?'

'He wants to know if I want to go see a friend of ours in Brighton.'

'Tell him you'll call him back.'

'Paul. Can I call you back? We're still asleep, I think... Sure... Do you mind going by yourself? Okay... I'm sorry. Give me a call when you get back.' Josie looked at Flora, and was awake enough to make a resigned face. 'Okay,' she continued to Paul. 'I'll speak to you later. Yeah. Love you, too.' She handed Flora the phone. 'Sorry!'

'It's no biggy. Sounds like you got yourself a regular family.'

'Closer.'

'Yeah, mine too. My friends, I mean. Do you think that's because we don't have close family, or we have particularly close friends?'

'Yes,' said Josie, leaning towards Flora and kissing her. 'Definitely!'

Kiss finished, Flora said, 'Breakfast?'

'What a fast it was! Juice would be good.'

'Does Bloody Mary sound better?'

'Like butter to the ears.'

'Sounds messy.'

'You should try it.'

'I get the feeling you're going to show me lots of new stuff.'

'If you want.'

Flora just looked Josie in the eye. They were only barely apart, so the look was intense. It meant a lot Flora had difficulty putting into words. Things about David, Don and every other man she'd ever come into contact with, or at least been intimate with. It felt so right in Josie's arms. Complete. Already it felt like the next phase in life. She pulled Josie towards her and kissed her. Josie complied, feeling gorgeous inside, warm, fluid and at ease. Something important had begun between them.

'Bloody Josie it is,' said Flora, getting out her side of the bed.

'Be careful what you wish for,' said Josie. 'Make that heavy on the Mary.'

'I know the ratio of Blood and Mary. There's the just-finished-a-hard-week-at-work ratio, the don't-fancy-anything-sweet-but-still-want-a-drink ratio, and my particular favourite, the got-drug-fucked-and-discovered-something-new ratio.'

'Please, don't call me something. And what's that ratio? Just to be sure.'

'One part Blood, two parts Mary.'

'Aren't you forgetting something?'

Flora thought for a moment, puzzled, shaking her head. Then she nodded. 'And a liberal splash of Worcester sauce.' Josie smiled and nodded calmly. 'How do you manage so much composure and elegance, this early?'

'I'm just trying really hard to impress you.'

'You're doing a good job. Let me get the bloody-taking-too-longs.'

Flora left, and in a couple of minutes returned with the drinks.

'Ah! The bloody-quicks.'

'I thought I'd left that joke in the kitchen.'

'That was unnecessary,' said Josie, more disappointed than hurt.

'Sorry. I forget to be nice sometimes.'

'Is it something you have to remember?'

'Shouldn't be, but probably is.'

'That's sad.'

'Maybe. Maybe it's just different.'

'Are you happy?'

'What's happy?'

'So, you're not,' said Josie. Flora shrugged. 'Let's see what we can do about that.'

26

'I brought some notes,' said Flora, pulling a folder from her briefcase.

'Miss Professional.'

'Why waste time?'

'That's what time's for.'

Flora raised her finger and breathed in, as if to start a lengthy explanation. Joe cut her off. 'What you got, then?'

'Just some writing.'

'Writing's good.'

'Actually, it's more words than writing.'

'Words are okay, too.'

'They're just ideas.'

'Yep! Those, too. Let me see.'

Flora pulled away. 'I'll read them to you.'

'Hey! What are you scared of?'

'Very little.'

'I believe that.'

'It's just that you might not be able to read my writing.'

'Okay!' said Joe, not quite believing Flora's explanation. He folded his arms and cocked his head to one side. 'Fire away.'

'Beyond fear.' She paused, watching for a response from Joe. He didn't give one. 'Beyond hate.' Again she looked.

'Yeah,' said Joe, meaning "carry on".

'Beyond pain.' She stopped.

'Nice! Is there more?'

Flora's confidence grew a little. 'Beyond self-doubt?'

Joe looked bewildered. 'Is there anything beyond self-doubt?'

'Yes.' She paused. 'Complete doubt.'

'This from a woman who fears nothing.'

'You're missing the point.'

'Sorry. I'm not with you.'

'Instead of doubting yourself, doubt everything else.' Joe didn't reply, only squinted. 'Why not?'

'I don't know.'

'Do you wish you hadn't asked me to work with you?'

'No,' said Joe. 'Quite the opposite.'

'You would tell me, wouldn't you?'

Joe nodded. 'Anything else on that paper?' He leant over to look. Flora pulled away, but it was too late. Her notes weren't illegible in the slightest, but very precise, and beautifully written. It looked as if it had taken her hours, more like design than text. Arrows led to boxes and circles. In these were groups of words, or simply letters, sometimes even numbers.

'Joe!' said Flora, annoyed.

'Don't be embarrassed. It looks like you've put a lot of work into it. I'm impressed.'

'It's just how I'm used to working.'

'Give me more.'

'I thought about your last exhibition, how it made me feel, what those feelings meant, how important they were.' She paused and looked away from her notes somewhere on the floor in front of her. 'About David's death, and how it became intrinsically linked to the exhibition, to us and possibly everyone who read about it.'

'Stop! Let me digest this.'

Flora paused for only a second. 'This all loops, convolutes, and goes I don't know where.'

'Are you talking about karma?'

'No. I think karma's about a belief in some sort of universal justice, and let's face it, what bollocks.'

'So?'

'So, let's talk, and see what happens visually. Hopefully, something will be expressed that we are incapable of saying in words.'

'Right on sister. You've done this before.'

'I've tried to communicate before. That's what we're doing here, isn't it?'

'I think some artists forget that.'

'They're not artists.'

'I agree.'

'It's part of the whole process. Live, sense, interpret, consider, articulate, and communicate.'

'For some people the process is feel, respond, express, full stop. The expression is more about catharsis than communicating.'

'And that's fine. Everything has its place. But I say, don't exhibit it. Just cathart, and throw it away. Otherwise they may as well show us their shit.'

'Sounds like my last exhibition.'

'I think we can safely say, that was everybody's shit, not just yours.'

'Thank you.'

'The way I see it, beyond can mean a couple of things. Either, whoever's saying it has left these things behind, or they've taken it to an extreme, another level.'

'I must admit, I quite like both.'

'Me, too. That's exactly where I was heading with this. Maybe going beyond is an extreme response, a reaction, or device.'

'Could be. It's subjective, isn't it?'

'Whoever's feeling the state of beyond is the one who decides. And they're hardly the best judge.'

'Where are we going with this?'

'Just wriggling in the shit.'

'I like the image, even if it has a negative slant to it.'

'No. Not this time. Even shit becomes nutrients . . .'

'For growth!'

'Now you're with me.'

'So you're saying, beyond all our shit, whether it's perceived or otherwise, there's growth?'

'There can be.'

'It's naïve to think that good always prevails.'

'But we do want to show some kind of progress, or if we're not careful we just end up moaning.'

'Which is okay, and it's more fun than selling your arse,' said Joe.

'Is that why we're doing this?'

'No,' said Joe. 'It's because we feel like it.'

'And that's a good enough reason for me.'

'Actually, I do it because I have to. It hurts not to.'

'Hurts?'

'Well, annoys me, irritates me, makes me feel there is something wrong, and I can fix it.'

'I know that feeling,' said Flora. 'I deal with it by writing, drawing, or having sex that interests me.'

'Really?'

'If really refers to the sex bit of that sentence, only sometimes.'

Joe started imagining what she meant by this, what she got up to generally, and how Don fitted into this picture.

'This may show too clearly what I was thinking, but I haven't seen Don for a while.'

'Really?'

'He hasn't called, or anything.'

'I wonder why,' said Flora vaguely, then with more enthusiasm, 'I'm dying for a coffee.'

'I'm the opposite, I live for it.' Joe fell for Flora's device to distract him, but more by his joke than the idea of having a coffee.

'Am I just looking for a distraction from work?'

'Distraction's okay.'

'Only from first thing in the morning, until last thing at night.'

'You mean, there are moments when you're not distracted?' said Flora in mock horror.

'Just before I fall asleep, that hazy, groggy, blurred state of consciousness. I just about cope with not being distracted then.'

'That sounds tormented,' said Flora. 'Are you unhappy?'

'Of course I'm unhappy. Who the fuck's happy?'

'I am.' She paused. 'Well, kind of.'

'Really?' said Joe.

'Yes, really. I smile sometimes.'

'On drugs?'

'No.'

'I don't understand.'

'It happens for no reason.'

'Weird.'

'I'm sorry!'

Flora and Joe talked for hours, made some notes, argued about colours they liked and disliked. Joe was quite bossy, but Flora didn't mind. She considered Joe was doing her a favour, by letting her be involved. Their thoughts wove in and out of each other, connecting, clashing, or sometimes spinning off only to arrive at a dead end. This was the first day of their collaboration, and it was much like their tenth and fortieth. The weather, their outfits and mood changed, but at the core was something consistent, even potent. They would meet up about three times a week. Joe postponed all video projects during this time, and Flora put all extraneous activities on hold. She didn't try to keep in touch with Don, feeling she'd had enough of him. It was convenient that he wasn't around, lying was that much easier. She started seeing Josie regularly, who conveniently filled the space Don left. Flora felt she was the happiest she'd been for a long time. Her love life was incredible, her career was taking an interesting turn, and her plan to get closer to Joe was working.

27

The Serpentine. Opening night. Joe had been sick twice. Flora had been to the gym, and maintained a sort of calm. She tried to help, and gave him some coke. They polished off a gram before leaving the house, and started on another shortly after entering the gallery.

Journalists waited in line to speak to Joe and Flora. A woman who was difficult to look at sat down in front of them.

'What makes you feel you are a suitable applicant for the job.'

The woman didn't get the joke. 'I'm with The Face.'

Joe smiled. 'What she means is, what makes you a more suitable applicant than the next person?'

'It's my job,' said the woman, looking confused.

'We were making a joke about this looking like an interview for a job.'

'Oh! You were being funny,' said the interviewer.

'Clearly not,' said Flora.

'Whichever,' said the woman.

Joe raised his eyebrows, surprised. He looked at Flora, who didn't look back, but smiled slightly, just enough to let him know she was aware he was looking. Then she bit her bottom lip, and squinted, as though trying to work out her opponent. Joe was on the verge of laughter.

'Right!' said The Face woman. 'Joseph Holtzman.' Joe nodded with a serious expression. 'This is your first collaboration. Why now?'

'It's her fault,' he said, leaning his head toward Flora.

'Some are saying that after your last exhibition, you've lost confidence.'

'That's right.'

Flora thought this was below the belt, and retaliated.

'In journalists.'

Joe continued to nod slowly. The interviewer was shocked.

'What happened at the last exhibition was extreme. It made me lose confidence in most things.'

'But, in your work?'

'I imagine so. It comes from me. How could it not be affected?'

'Are you less sure about your ideas?' said the woman.

'I feel more sure of this exhibition than any before.'

Flora turned to Joe, feeling as though he were giving her a compliment. The journalist picked up on this.

'Because of Miss Evans?'

Flora was offended by the way the interviewer said this. 'Journalists are behind the scenes for a reason,' she said.

'That is?'

'Cos they're not interesting enough to be in the scene.'

'That's a perspective.'

'And I guess that's why they tend to inject as much of their personality as they can into an interview about someone else. Someone more interesting, more sparkling.'

'Do you feel you fit into those categories?'

Flora hesitated. The cocaine only gave her so much confidence.

'She has something you'll only ever write about,' said Joe. He turned to Flora, and at the same time they said, 'Charisma.'

'Can I quote that?'

'You can do what you like with it.'

'I think I've got all I need.'

'Oh!' said Joe. ' Please don't forget to mention the website.'

'Right,' said the woman. 'Sure thing.' She collected her Dictaphone, scarf, and mints into her bag.

'You'll need the address.'

'Yes.'

'It's www.blahblahblah.com.'

'Of course it is.'

She stood, acknowledging the man waiting to take her place. He said hello to Flora and Joe, who were both deadly charming. The Face journalist refrained from showing a response. Addressing Flora, she said,

'You've got something white on your nose.'

As Flora went to wipe it, Joe shook his head. But not soon enough. Flora assumed that everyone must have been able to tell she'd been doing cocaine, and felt ridiculous. In reality, there was nothing on her nose. Joe looked at the journalist.

'Not really,' she said, and smiled.

Flora and Joe both burst out laughing.

'Well done, bitch,' said Flora.

'Thanks! I'm right in taking that as a compliment?' said the woman.

'You bet,' said Flora.

'Don't worry about the article,' said the woman as she started to leave. 'I'm on your side.'

28

Joe was in his living room, only it looked different. The walls were painted bright green, the floor carpeted in artificial grass, and the ceiling covered in long threads of silver tinsel.

He sat alone, with David's modelling portfolio closed on his lap. Tears were drying on his face. He stared into space. The doorbell rang. Automatically, Joe stood and moved towards it. This movement made a draught causing the tinsel above him to sway. Joe stood behind the door, and collected himself. After a few seconds he opened the door. It was Ryan.

'Ryan,' said Joe.

'Joe!' said Ryan sensing there was something wrong. He stepped into the hall, revealing somebody who'd been standing behind. 'This is the Dylan I told you about.'

Joe couldn't remember. His thoughts were still swirling with images of David. He tried to focus, to drag his attention to the present. 'Right! I mean, yeah. I think so.'

Dylan stepped in, and Joe reached out to shake his hand.

'I'm sweating,' said Dylan. 'It's wet.'

'Don't worry,' said Joe, and held out his hand, as if to imply that shaking Dylan's wet hand was what he intended to do. Afterwards, Joe resisted wiping his own hand on his jeans. Dylan noticed. He'd been dealing with this scenario for years, so had become aware of how people responded. He followed Ryan into the living room, feeling at ease, and welcome.

'Hey!' said Ryan. 'What's with the park feel?'

'How did you know it was a park? It's actually meant to be Hyde Park. It was Flora's idea.'

'I get it,' said Ryan. 'The Serpentine gallery.'

'Jesus! You understand the mind of Flora.'

'It's kind of obvious, isn't it?'

'Must be.'

'It's why I'm here.' Joe didn't respond. 'The exhibition.' He wasn't even listening.

Ryan looked concerned. 'You seem distracted,' he said, and walked Joe into the living room. Seeing David's portfolio, he turned, took hold of Joe, and gave him a warm hug.

'You missing David?'

Joe's eyes darted quickly away, his focus landing on some indiscriminate point on the far wall.

'Joe!' said Ryan, trying to get his attention, to bring him back from his reverie. Joe nodded erratically, like broken clockwork. His eyes filled with tears.

'You caught me at a bad time. I'm sorry.'

'Don't be daft. Looks like we caught you at exactly the right time.'

Joe smiled through his upset. 'You're a sweetheart Ryan.'

'Learned it all from you and David. Listen, you sit here and let me get you some tea or something. What will it be?'

'I guess I wouldn't mind a Coke,' said Joe.

'Dylan?' said Ryan.

'Yeah, a cuppa would be nice.'

'A Coke and a cuppa coming up.'

'Let me,' said Joe.

'No way,' said Ryan. 'I know where everything is. Unless you've changed it all.'

'Not structurally.'

As Ryan walked into the kitchen he could be heard saying 'Jesus!' Joe and Dylan were left feeling uncomfortable, Dylan because he was inexperienced, and Joe because he wasn't concentrating enough to address his thoughts to the situation. If he had been, he'd have realised that he was attracted to Dylan, and noticed that Dylan was attracted to him too.

Ryan eased the situation by returning with their drinks.

'Don't let me stop you chatting,' said Ryan.

'Sorry, I'm not on my best form,' said Joe.

'You're still better than most,' said Ryan. As Joe wasn't paying attention, Ryan looked at Dylan and gestured for him to talk to Joe. Dylan blushed and gulped at his tea. It was still too hot, so he spat it out.

'Nice!' said Ryan. 'Are you aware that Joe and I are counted as other people?'

'It doesn't matter about the floor. I think it's made from some kind of plastic, waterproof. And, just between you and me, I don't think it will last long. I don't think I like it. I'm more of an urban type myself. Rural's not really me.'

'I hardly think a synthetic, woman-made version of a city park is classed as rural,' said Ryan.

'Proves my point,' said Joe. 'I think it's positively wilderness.'

Dylan laughed, then continued to sip his still-too-hot-but-gave-him-something-to-do tea.

'When was the last time you let your hair down?' said Ryan.

'Don't you like it up?' said Joe.

'My point was . . .'

'I know exactly where that was heading.'

'Is that so bad?'

'Not so bad.'

'Oh, come on,' said Ryan. 'I want Dylan to see it.'

Joe made a series of expressions that communicated, no, maybe, then okay. He paused, his face motionless for a moment, then he squinted and said, 'Get my bitch on the phone.'

'I assume you're referring to Flora?'

'Of course. I don't think I could do it without some moral support.'

'What are we?' said Ryan, almost offended.

'You're encouragement, but she's support.'

'I get it. You mean, she'd score the drugs, be able to sort it out if you got in a fight, and make sure nobody bothered you.'

'Stuff of that nature,' said Joe.

'Couldn't you just tell them to leave you alone,' said Dylan.

'That's like telling them not to take drugs,' said Ryan.

'You must understand,' said Joe in a fatherly way, 'at Tragic there's a suspension of belief in the real world.'

'What Joe's trying to say,' said Ryan, 'is nobody gives a fuck.'

'On the contrary, they give lots of that,' said Joe.

'Joe, don't go all gay on me,' said Ryan.

Joe released some air from his mouth, his version of a half-hearted laugh. The nearest thing to a real one since Ryan arrived.

'That's more like it,' said Ryan. 'The bitch's number?'

'Six, six, six.'

'Seriously.'

'Well, that's what it says on her scalp.'

'Joe!'

'I was speaking to her before you came. You can just hit re-dial.' He laughed in the same way he had moments before. 'Rather, I was crying to her before you came.'

Ryan did as he was told, leaving the room to make the call.

Dylan edged his way slightly towards Joe, sipping continually as he did.

'So, you're studying the same as Ryan?'

'Yeah! I like it.'

'I'm sure it likes you.' Dylan looked confused.

'Sorry, I was just being stupid.'

'From what Ryan tells me, you'd have difficulty doing that.'

'Oh yeah. What else does he say?'

'That I'd like you.'

'Really!'

'What's not to like?'

'I see you've been taking the same class as Ryan...'

'It's a good course,' said Dylan nervously, cutting Joe off.

'In sweetness,' said Joe. As soon as he finished speaking, he wondered if it was inappropriate. He felt embarrassed. Dylan noticed, and started to bite his lip. This made Joe uncomfortable, and he started to straighten a pile of newspapers. Wanting something to do, Dylan put his cup on the floor. Not noticing he'd done this, Joe kicked it over. Dylan tried to mop it with a small piece of tissue from his pocket. It got soaked, immediately. Joe felt out of control, all limbs, with too many feet. By the time Ryan came back, Dylan and Joe were both blushing and acting awkward. Again Ryan rescued them.

'Can't leave you two alone for a minute. Okay, who said what?'

'Nobody, nothing much,' said Joe.

'Was that English?' said Ryan.

'I mean, we didn't say anything.'

'Maybe that was the problem,' said Ryan.

'Who are you? The communication police.'

'For now, yes. I just communicated with Flora. Sorry, your bitch...'

'What did she say?' said Joe.

'If you let me finish. She'll be here at three.'

'The rest?'

'She'll have a friend with her, some Josie character.'

'I feel you're missing something.'

'Yes, yes, yes! She'll have the stash.'

'Are you referring to drugs?' said Dylan.

'Yes and yes,' said Ryan.

'You're very yes-y all of a sudden,' said Joe.

'Yes,' said Ryan.

'I've never seen you like this before,' Dylan said to Ryan. 'Are you two always so silly?'

'Maybe,' said Ryan.

Joe spoke slowly, as though solving a mystery in his head, 'Josie?'

'That's right. Why? What are you thinking?'

'Nothing. Flora likes her.'

'That sounds like a euphemism, if ever I heard one,' said Ryan.

'You're right.'

'What! Flora a dyke?'

'So it seems.'

'Fuck! That one's full of surprises.'

'Um,' said Joe, starting to daydream. 'Yeah.'

'Hallo,' said Ryan. 'Calling all stations to Planet Joe.'

'Sorry. They want me to meet this friend of theirs.'

'Oh that's right, I forgot, Flora said to tell you she's meeting Paul at the club. Who's Paul?' said Ryan defensively.

'Just some geezer.'

'Since when have you used such slang?'

'Okay, some bloke.'

'I assume you're trying to impress Dylan, cause it ain't washing with me. Try guy, or boy.'

'They're both so Nineties,' said Joe.

'Yeah. It's retro already,' said Ryan.

'I'm sorry,' said Joe.

'Good boy,' said Ryan.

'I like that,' said Joe. 'Good that is, not boy.'

'You *are* a good boy.' Joe had a nice feeling in his gut. Ryan could tell he'd triggered something. 'I'll have to keep that. Got you all gushy.'

'It's allowed,' said Joe.

'Too loud.'

'Don't pick on me, Ryan.' Joe was still feeling sensitive.

Without warning, explanation, or knowing he was going to do it, Dylan put his hand on Joe's neck and rubbed it reassuringly. Joe wore a hooded sweatshirt, so Dylan wasn't concerned about his hand sweating. Ryan looked at Dylan as though something important had just happened. Joe gave in to Dylan's hand, and moaned.

'You could do with a massage,' said Dylan.

'Yes please,' said Joe.

Dylan laughed, out of embarrassment, but stepped in behind Joe and rubbed his neck.

'See, I knew you two would like each other.'

'I hope you're not referring to my masseuse!' said Joe as though disgusted. Dylan pressed hard into Joe's neck. 'Ouch, ouch, ouch!'

'Sorry, did I hurt you?' said Dylan sarcastically.

Joe relaxed again, becoming soft, pliable, responsive. 'Um!' he said and made a face as though he was eating chocolate.

'It's getting very touchy-feely,' said Ryan.

'Oh! I get the joke now,' said Joe. 'Touchy-feel-E.'

'What's the point in me being all sharp, quick, and witty, when you can't keep up. You taken yours already?'

'Not my Ecstasy. My anti-depressants.'

'Are you on them?' said Ryan.

'No. I'm mended.'

'Like that's all it would take.'

'You're hard on me.'

'I'm only messing,' said Ryan.

'I know, but . . .'

'There are loads of good movies out,' said Dylan. 'We could kill some time.'

'I'm up for that,' said Joe.

'Have you got a Time Out?' said Ryan.

'Sure. It's on the kitchen table.'

'I'll get it,' said Dylan. 'Anyway I want to see what the Jesus was about.' He went to the kitchen and stood in the doorway. 'Jesus!' he said in an exaggerated way. The whole of one wall was a montage of brightly coloured flower photographs, from magazines. Another wall was a montage of leaves, another insects, and the fourth labels from tins of food, baked beans, spaghetti, and soup.

'Very Warhol,' shouted Dylan. He grabbed the Time Out and returned to the others.

'Give me a break,' said Joe. 'Warhol hasn't the rights on labels.'

Ryan felt the need to defend Dylan. 'Yeah, but he did coin the idea.'

'I can't help it if they're so beautifully designed.'

'You can help using them as decoration.'

'Okay, okay!' said Joe. 'It wasn't my idea anyway. A kid Flora knew saw the house in some Sunday supplement, and asked if he could decorate a room. His idea sounded okay, a change at least. All I asked was no pet-food labels. If you must know, I see it as a parody of Warhol. And I'm sure he'd approve.'

'Only 'cos you're cute.'

'Whatever,' said Joe.

'I bet he'd love you,' said Ryan, following his fantasy to what he thought was its natural conclusion.

'Since when have you been so interested in Warhol?'

'There's been a series on tv,' said Dylan.

'More about the man behind the artist,' said Ryan.

'You mean the fag behind the man,' said Joe.

'Sexy image,' said Ryan.

'Calm down,' said Joe. 'You still haven't done it yet, have you?'

'I'm saving myself for Mister Right.'

'I didn't know you were . . .' Dylan paused. 'Gay.'

'I'm not...' Ryan paused. 'Gay. We're just messing.'

'But you are, Joe?' said Dylan.

'As often as I can be,' said Joe. 'Which lately isn't that much.'

'What do you mean, as often as you can be?' said Dylan.

'Don't ask,' said Ryan. 'He'll tell you. In detail.'

Dylan now understood what Joe meant. 'I wouldn't mind hearing,' he said sheepishly.

'Well!' said Joe.

'Spare me,' said Ryan. 'Please.'

'Till when?'

'Sometime later.'

'By that, do you mean just some other time, or not at all?'

'Anyway, I wrote this poem. It was an assignment. Can I read it to you?'

'Go for it.'

'It's in my bag.'

'Get it.'

'Okay. I don't have to be asked twice.' He rooted around in his bag. 'You might recognise your influence.'

'I'm flattered.'

'Only in its simplicity.'

'Cow!'

'I mean, it is like a children's poem, but with more adult content. You know, like Stargirl.' Then, to fill Dylan in, 'That's a story Joe wrote, and David read it to me when I was little.'

'I thought you said you don't have to be asked twice,' said Joe.

'It's coming,' said Ryan, fumbling with loose sheets of paper.

He went to the window, faced them, and began,

'A something exists
More see-through than mist
It has many names
But none are the same.'

After the first stanza he looked up at Dylan and Joe. Without waiting for a response he continued,

'Some call it plucky
A wish, or unlucky
An alien host
Or the Holy Ghost.'

This time he went straight on.

'In colour, it's said
There's violets, reds
But these we don't see
We simply believe

'It's the same with sound
There's lots more around
Than ones we can hear
Dogs bark when they're near.'

Joe smiled and casually looked at Dylan, who was already looking at him, but quickly looked away. Realising he'd been caught, he looked back. By this time, Joe had looked away, and barely noticed Dylan looking back at him. Meanwhile, Ryan continued, oblivious to their silent dialogue.

'So think in your head
Of something once said
Something that you felt
That made you feel melt

'This could be a place
A thing, or a race
With no feet or toes
From God only knows.'

Ryan decided to mime the action of God only knows. It made both Joe and Dylan snort with laughter. Ryan understood this as appreciation, so continued, with more confidence,

'It seems quite a shame
Not using a name
Let's just call it "It"
This name seems to fit

'"It's" for a reason
Although it's not clear
Maybe a season
Perhaps just a beer.'

'Hear! Hear!' said Joe.
'Sssh,' said Dylan and gave Joe a look of disapproval.

'Waiting and drifting
"It" noticed a tear
Turning and shifting
"It" sensed massive fear

'Behind a locked door
Where nobody saw
A man was confused
A little girl bruised.'

Ryan made a caricature of a sad face, almost as though he were mocking himself, his own poem.

'She'd black and blue eyes
And so full of whys
Her face very wet
Her blood and spit met

'"It" got both their minds
And did a flip-flop
And what did "It" find?
This made the pain stop

'Why? I do not know?
Bye! It's time to go
There's much to sort out
A lot to re-route.'

Ryan paused. 'Tell me if it gets too soft.'
'It's already too soft,' said Joe. 'But that's what I like about it. Go on, please.'

'An old man was next
Who thought he was hexed
He'd had quite enough
Of the living stuff

'He'd had a sweet life
With his long-gone wife
Although now not near
She was still so dear

'"It" made him recall
Things large and small
His silly black cat
Which he'd stroke and pat.'

Relaxed and confident by this point, Ryan spoke fluidly. No longer using exaggerated gestures, he seemed to intimate possible meanings. Joe thought Ryan's facial expressions were subtle, and surprisingly skilful, especially for his age.

'His worn-out blue coat
A trip in a boat
The smell of clean air
A kiss off dear Claire

'A smile then appeared
Where before he'd sneered
It warmed his sour soul
Exactly the goal.'

Ryan paused, and looked up just in time to catch Joe shaking his head. He stopped reading. 'It's embarrassing, isn't it?'

Joe and Dylan said in unison, 'No!'

'Why'd you shake your head?' said Ryan.

'I thought it was too cute. Too cute in a good way.'

Slightly reluctant to carry on, Ryan thought for a moment.

'Oh, come on,' said Joe. 'Please! I won't respond any more. I won't even think a response. I promise!'

'You're allowed to respond,' said Ryan. Then, as though timed to the second he said, 'As long as it's good.' Without waiting for an answer, he started his poem again.

'"Yeah, so what" you say
"Well great, big hooray
Shit's always around
Is this all you found?"'

'Blah, blah, blah!' he said trailing off. Then he said, 'I think I'll skip the next two verses. Even more blah, blah, blah.'

'Don't leave stuff out,' said Dylan.

'It's crap. I don't even know why I started it.'

'Can't we decide for ourselves?' said Joe.

'Why? I'm the one reading it,' said Ryan, a little annoyed.

'Don't stop,' said Joe. 'We want to hear it.' He looked at Dylan. 'Don't we?'

'We do.'

'Well, let me skip the boring bits. So then it ends with...

'Try swapping set thoughts
Old things you've been taught
Instead of being snide
Try going inside.'

'Schmaltz, or what? How would I know about these things? It's obvious I'm only guessing.'

'Just finish, or die,' said Joe, strained. Ryan did as he was told.

'We're powerful things
Affecting like kings
We can change so much
With no magic touch

'So what does this mean?
Should I share my dream?
Between me and you
I haven't a clue.'

Ryan lifted his head, and let the hand holding the poem fall by his side. It was clear he was finished.

'I haven't, either,' said Joe.

Dylan started to clap.

'Well?' said Ryan looking unsure.

'Good use of back-light,' said Joe.

'Is that all you can say?'

'No,' said Joe. 'I see what you mean about the Stargirl influence. It was cute, but the metre was a bit choppy.' Ryan looked disappointed. 'Although you saved it by reading it so well. You're a good actor.'

'His tutors think so,' said Dylan.

'I'd like to read it myself,' said Joe.

'You don't like it,' said Ryan.

'I didn't say that. I try not to have a like-dislike response to things like this. Anything somebody has put time into deserves more than an immediate reaction. Otherwise it might be based on what kind of day I've had, or who phoned me last.'

'Okay! I get your point. But how will I know if it's good or not?'

'Somebody else isn't necessarily the best judge. My advice would be to leave it sit for a couple of weeks, then read it again in a different mood at a different time of day and see if your response is any different.'

'Why is yours a reaction, and mine a response?'

'Yours is deeper. You know it, understand it, felt the need to create it.'

'Yeah! The need being, my tutor told me.'

'Yes, but you could have written about your mum, and you chose to write about God.'

'So that's clear, at least?'

'To me it made sense.'

'That's a good start,' said Ryan. 'You know how much I respect you.'

'I think it was cool,' said Dylan.

'Sorry,' said Joe. 'That's what I meant to say.'

'Are you taking the piss?'

'No. Whatever way I show approval, It's much the same.'

'It can't be just a simple yes or no with you Joe, can it?'

'I can't think of a single question, where a simple yes or no would be the appropriate answer.' Joe looked at his watch. 'So, anyway! We've got quite some time to kill. Anything at the cinema you fancy seeing?'

Ryan flicked through the pages, not really concentrating.

'Actually, I wouldn't mind a kip. I'm knackered.'

'Why don't you lie down,' said Joe. 'Your bed's where it always was. Dylan can keep me company.' He looked at Dylan. 'Unless you want to sleep, too.'

'I'm not tired,' said Dylan.

'Okay,' said Joe. 'I'll try to entertain Dylan for a few hours and you can sleep.'

'Is that okay?' said Ryan. Dylan nodded. 'You're in safe hands.'

Ryan ran up the stairs, four at a time.

'Long legs,' said Joe, listening to the footsteps. Dylan nodded his head again, and sighed.

'Why the sigh?' said Joe.

'Did I sigh?' Joe nodded. 'God knows what I was thinking.'

'Are you okay?'

'Do I seem not okay?'

'I don't know.' Joe laughed, a little exasperated. 'Do you feel not okay?'

Dylan was about to answer and Joe put his hand over his mouth. Joe's fingers felt lovely against Dylan's lips. The smell went straight from his nose to his balls. He thought of sex, abstract and unfocused. He breathed in deeply. Joe let his hand linger, pulling it away, sliding it over Dylan's lips. As Joe's hand left Dylan's mouth, his lips puckered slightly, as though kissing, reaching out, or wanting Joe's hand to stay. Joe thought it very sexy, held back and gorgeous.

Joe's face was very close to Dylan's.

'I felt your lips move.'

'I was just rubbing them together. They could do with some lip balm.'

'Here, use mine.' Joe got it out, and with one hand, uncapped it and applied it to Dylan's lips.

Dylan rubbed them together. Joe put the cap back on, still with one hand. Then he reached for Dylan's mouth and rubbed his lips with one of his fingers. Joe's finger was warm, thick, and slightly rough. His dick throbbed inside his jeans. Dylan saw it move. He focused on Joe's fly. Aware of this, Joe made it move again. Dylan didn't have much choice now. Driven by a craving he didn't understand, he knelt and took hold of Joe's fly. His conscious mind questioned his actions. He looked up at Joe, for approval, anything that meant he should go ahead. His more powerful unconscious didn't care to hesitate. It knew exactly what it wanted, so drove him on. Catching Joe's eye, Dylan saw approval. He leaned forward, closer; his lips puckered, and his mouth opened.

29

At two o'clock, Ryan woke and made his way downstairs. Again, he strode several steps at a time, but more slowly, with a just-woken-up-weight to them. As he entered the living room he yawned, scratched his neck, and vaguely registered a smell, but because he was still sleepy and unfocused, didn't recognise what it was.

Joe and Dylan sat at opposite ends of the bench, watching a video. Ryan thought it funny. They leant away from each other, like sulking lovers.

'He won't bite you,' said Ryan to Dylan.

'How do you know?' said Joe.

'I guess I don't. What are you watching?'

'Blue Velvet.'

'You mean, one of the few decent things David Lynch ever directed?' said Ryan.

'I agree,' said Joe.

'You obviously like it,' said Ryan to Dylan.

Dylan looked around for the first time. 'Yeah,' he said.

'I think it's perfect,' said Joe. 'The lighting, the colours, the casting, the acting, and stuff I can't begin to put my finger on.'

'Stuff you wouldn't want to put your finger on. It'd get covered in something.'

'Sssh!' said Dylan.

'Sorry!' said Ryan in a hushed voice.

Ryan sat in between Joe and Dylan. He lay down and stretched out, resting his head on Joe's lap and his feet on Dylan's.

'Comfortable?' said Joe.

'Why do I get the feet?' said Dylan.

'I don't suppose you could give them a little rub.'

'You suppose right.'

Although there was a lot happening on the video, Ryan zoned out, losing his focus on the screen. Physically, he was still aware of the colours, but mentally, he was much younger, off school with measles. During the day, programmes aired were just too young for somebody already at school, but they were familiar and friendly, a reminder of when he was even younger. Like when he had jaundice and could only eat crackers and drink sugary drinks. It always felt exciting to be at home when the others were doing sums and writing. Of course he'd have to catch up, but this was okay. He would be treated differently, special.

On the sofa, between Joe and Dylan, he felt a similar excitement. It might have been that it was late and he was waiting to go to a club in London. It might simply have been that he was staying at Joe's. He had no clear answer, and only the feeling of a question. He caught himself being somewhere else, which broke his memory, so refocused on the tv screen. A bunch of people were talking, their conversation stilted and unnatural. 'Anyone want a brew?' Ryan said, wanting a distraction.

'Coffee, black, two sugars,' said Joe.

'Tea, white, no sugar,' said Dylan.

In a whisper, Ryan said, 'I can see I'm in the way, so I'll just . . .' He stood up in a controlled manner, 'Very quietly . . .' and started to walk. 'Without bothering anybody . . .' Acting as though in slow motion, he headed towards the door. 'I'll just slip . . . away.'

'Go!' said Joe.

Dylan didn't respond to their playing. 'Oh, my God!' he said in response to something on the video. Ryan pulled a comical, resigned expression and left the room.

Without moving his head, Dylan looked sideways at Joe, who was already doing the same. They were only just able to hold back their smiles. When tea-making noises were finally heard, Joe and Dylan looked at each other properly. Joe winked. Dylan felt a sensation in his stomach. His hands started to sweat. Joe poked Dylan's foot with his own. Ryan walked in.

'We're out of tea.'

Joe pulled back his foot quickly enough so that all Ryan saw was what looked like the tail end of Joe stretching his leg. Again, Ryan registered something, but he didn't have enough information for his thoughts to make another sense.

'There's some in the cupboard over the cooker,' said Joe.

'Great!' said Ryan.

When he left the room again, Joe made a cartoon-sounding "phew" noise, and said, 'It is illegal still, isn't it?'

'I think so,' said Dylan. 'I'm only four,' he added with an overly coy expression.

'Really!' said Joe. 'I've broken my record.'

'What is your record?'

'I haven't got one.'

'What is the youngest person you slept with?'

'Well, I was baby-sitting this kid last week, and . . .'

As Joe spoke, Dylan made an "I'm shocked," then a "you're not being serious", and finally a "you nearly got me" expression.

'Jesus, you're gullible,' said Joe. 'But seriously, I guess twenty-five. I think David was the youngest person I ever slept with.' Joe paused. 'That was my boyfriend who died.'

'I know who David was,' said Dylan and looked at the screen, more uncomfortable than actually interested in the film at this point. Then trying to change the topic of conversation he said, 'So I'm your new record.'

'You know how it is with new records,' said Joe. 'You play them to death.' Referring to the film, he said, 'I'm over this.'

'Me as well,' said Dylan, quickly adding, 'Being played to death sounds kind of sexy.'

Ryan returned with a cup in each hand. 'Nice to see someone finally broke the ice.'

'In our own time,' said Joe.

'Sure,' said Ryan. 'I was only messing.'

'I know,' said Joe. 'But you're wrong about me not biting. I love nothing more than the fresh blood of a teenager.'

'Vampires wouldn't last long these days,' said Ryan. Dylan looked puzzled. 'Cos of HIV,' Ryan explained. Turning to Joe he said, 'I guess you'd be all right, though.' Again, Dylan looked puzzled. 'Cause he's already got it.' Dylan gasped. 'What's wrong?' said Ryan. Dylan's face went pale, his lips dry. He started to say something, but nothing came out. 'It's all right,' said Ryan. 'You can't catch it by watching the same film.'

Dylan looked deadly serious. 'Have you?' he said to Joe, who in reply simply nodded. 'How do you catch it?'

'What's with the sudden interest in HIV transmission?'

'Nothing!' Dylan could still barely speak, but managed to force out, 'Just... wondering.'

'Is there something you're not telling me?' said Ryan, feigning suspicion.

'No!'

'You can get it by fucking without a condom,' said Joe, trying to ease Dylan's fears. 'Some people say that you shouldn't swallow cum, others say you should avoid getting pre-cum in your mouth, too.' Joe's face winced involuntarily. 'Some even say you should suck with a condom.'

'Ugh!' said Ryan, pretending to retch. 'How kinky.'

'It's not a preference,' said Joe. 'But some believe a necessity.'

'What do you think?' said Dylan, almost stammering.

'I don't know for sure. It seems nobody does. All I am sure of is my own boundaries, I think. I try to balance quality of life with practicality.'

'How does that affect the people you have sex with?' said Dylan.

Ryan thought Dylan's question a little personal, considering he didn't know Joe very well. 'Dylan,' he said. 'You're starting to embarrass me.'

'I don't mind,' said Joe. 'Let me answer. I assume most people I have sex with know the basics about the risk of HIV transmission. Presumably, they have their own boundaries as to what they will and won't do, how much risk they are prepared to take, etc. Like with the rest of life, people make choices, how much to drink, or smoke, or how fast to drive, and how much it affects others.'

'I feel like I've just walked into a tv debate on safer sex,' said Ryan. 'Why are you so interested?' he added, looking at Dylan.

Joe reached for Dylan's head, tousled his hair, and said, 'I'll fill you in later.'

Ryan looked confused. 'Enough serious talk,' he said. 'What should I wear tonight?'

'Something waterproof,' said Joe.

'Sounds comfortable.'

'How about drag-queen proof, and . . .'

'I get the picture,' said Ryan, cutting him off.

'It doesn't matter what you wear,' said Joe. 'Everything suits youth.'

'You've got a point,' said Ryan, pretending to be arrogant.

'I asked you never to mention my point. You know I'm self-conscious about it.'

'I'm sorry!' said Ryan. 'I thought you were going to get it removed, anyway.'

'I was going to. I even went to a plastic surgeon, but when I got there he couldn't see the point.'

'Did you have it covered?'

'The surgeon said there was no point.'

'So, it wasn't real?'

'Yes.'

'Ah! I see your point.'

'Oh, you do?' said Joe, covering his face with his hands.

'Sorry. I mean, I don't.'

'I think we dragged the arse out of that joke,' said Joe.

'Yep! We killed it good.'

'That was a joke?' said Dylan.

'Oh! It talks,' said Ryan.

'I'm just trying to join in a bit.'

'Sorry,' said Joe. 'Were we leaving you out?'

'It's not a big deal.'

Joe looked at his watch. 'My God! We better get ready. It's heading towards three. Flora will be here.'

'I'll jump in the shower,' said Ryan. 'If that's okay.'

'Sure!' said Joe. 'That's if you don't mind me hopping down here until you've finished.'

'God you're so funny,' said Ryan.

'Do you think?' said Joe.

'No!' said Ryan. 'I was being funny.'

'Do you think?' said Dylan.

'I'm out of here,' said Ryan and went bounding up the stairs.

Dylan and Joe were left in silence, and acutely aware of it.

'Um,' said Dylan.

'Yeah?' said Joe.

'Nothing.'

'Doesn't look like nothing.'

'It's just that Aids stuff . . .'

'HIV. I don't have Aids.'

'Sorry.'

'No. I'm sorry. I guess I should have mentioned it.'

'Maybe you get sick of talking about it.'

'Actually, it's the opposite. It's become so familiar I don't really think of it, especially when I'm having my dick sucked.' Joe paused and smiled. 'I had other things on my mind.'

'Jesus! I don't know how you can be so casual about it.'

'Well, for the first ten years of the whole Aids thing, it was my every third or fourth thought. Then, when I became infected, it rose to about every second thought, but now with new medication, and people not dying as much, and what with David's death by something as arbitrary as a fire, I can't take Aids seriously any more. It's lost its sting.'

'I get you,' said Dylan, 'I think.' He was partly listening, but partly remembering the sex they'd had. At first this was because he was trying to work out how risky it had been, then his thoughts got jumbled, became influenced by his sex drive, his desire for Joe. He started picturing Joe fucking him. This made him stare at Joe's fly again. Joe watched Dylan staring at his crotch.

The doorbell rang and some high-pitched laughter could be heard through the front window.

'Saved by the bell,' said Joe. 'You get it. She'll be so confused.'

Without much thought, he did as he was told. Already he felt the urge to please Joe, to be a good boy. As he opened the door, the volume of the laughter rose. Flora's died suddenly, leaving Josie trying to hold hers in. Although she held her lips closed tightly, her body quivered as though still laughing.

'What have we here?' said Flora, a little surprised.

Playing the part to the full, Dylan simply smiled and raised one eyebrow. 'Can I help you?'

'Is Joe in?' said Flora.

'Joe?' said Dylan.

'Joseph Holtzman.'

'You must have the wrong house,' said Dylan.

Flora craned her neck hoping to recognise the hallway. As she did, Dylan pulled the door in tight, leaving only the slightest crack.

He also flipped the light off in the hall. Flora couldn't see anything that would give her a clue. 'This is twenty-two?' she said.

'Ah! This is twenty-two A and you probably want what's-his-face at twenty-two B, the gay geezer.'

'That sounds like him, but gay geezer is a funny way to describe him.'

'What should I say, fag?'

'You ignorant little bastard,' said Josie.

'Don't get me wrong. I don't have a problem with him being like that. My mum and dad are gay.'

'What!' said Flora, scrunching her nose and looking confused. At this point, she heard laughter coming from behind the door. A hand appeared above Dylan's head and pulled the door open.

'Well done, Dylan!' said Joe.

'You cow!' said Flora.

'Got you,' said Joe.

'Good timing,' said Josie. 'I was about to punch him.' As she spoke, her eyes, mouth, even the skin on her face seemed to smile. 'I'm guessing that you're Joe.'

'What an embarrassing introduction,' said Flora.

'You wouldn't have it any other way,' said Joe.

'I think you might be right,' said Josie.

'Who's the kid?' said Flora. 'I hope to God he's not your new boyfriend.'

'This is Dylan. He's down for the weekend with Ryan.'

'Ah, Ryan. Of course! Where is the sweetmeat?'

'He's having a shower,' said Dylan.

'What if he was my new boyfriend,' said Joe. 'What's wrong with that?'

'He's half your age,' said Flora.

'There's only fifteen years between us,' said Dylan. 'My dad's twenty years older than my mum.'

'Funny how it's never the other way round,' said Flora.

'Sometimes it is,' said Josie.

'Yeah, but people make such a fuss if it is.'

'That's true,' said Josie.

'You must be Josie,' said Joe. 'God! Flora. You lucked out with this one.'

'It's definitely me who lucked out,' said Josie.

'Pumpkin!' said Flora.

'Steady on, tiger,' said Josie. 'Not in public.'

'Get you two, being all coupley,' said Joe. 'Come in. Come in.'

Joe led them into the living room.

'Cute space,' said Josie.

'She already knows I did it,' said Flora.

'It's still cute.'

'Thank you,' said Joe. 'Or should Flora thank you. I think I'll take the credit, for having it in my house.'

'You mean putting up with it in your house,' said Flora.

'Actually, I think I might be ready for a change,' said Joe. 'Any ideas?'

'Me! Me! Me!' said Dylan excitedly.

'I was about to say Josie's quite handy with a brush,' said Flora. 'But with enthusiasm like that, how could you refuse?'

'I don't think I can,' said Joe, looking at Dylan. For seconds, their eyes became locked, very intense.

'Mercy me!' said Flora. 'There is something going on between you two, isn't there?'

Both Dylan and Joe couldn't help smiling. Flora looked at Josie and shrugged her shoulders. 'You gays. I mean, you guys.'

Ryan came running down the stairs holding the banister with one hand and his towel with the other. 'Hey, Flora!'

'Ryan!'

'Josie, right?'

'Correct,' said Josie and went to shake his hand. It was the hand holding the towel.

He went to shake, and his towel began to drop. He switched hands quickly, but not quick enough.

'Big boy,' said Josie. 'That trick works every time.'

Flora's eyes widened. Dylan blushed. Joe pushed back his cuticles.

Flora regained her thoughts quickly, and scanned everybody else. 'That got us all in a tizzy.'

Joe noticed her noticing. 'It's a gay thing, I mean a guy thing.'

'It must be,' said Flora. 'I didn't even notice his smooth muscular thighs, his blond pubic hair, and his thick, brown, uncircumcised boy-meat.'

'Grandma!' said Ryan.

'She's not?' said Dylan.

'No! She isn't,' said Flora, pretending to be more offended than she really was.

'What a bunch,' said Josie.

'Yeah. Meet the family,' said Flora. There was a brief pause whilst everyone laughed. 'How's that chick of yours?' she said to Ryan.

'I like to think of her as a fully-grown bird.'

'Free-range even,' said Flora. Ryan groaned. 'I'm sorry, I couldn't help it.'

'Spare us the un-jokes,' said Joe. 'And put your nice head on while you're there.'

'If I have to,' said Flora.

'In answer to your question,' said Ryan. 'Leila's good. Thankyou for asking. She's in Manchester. Had too much work to do this weekend.'

'Leila, work?' said Flora, looking confused.

'College work. For her Masters.'

'In?'

'Law.'

'Impressive. She's a dark horse,' said Flora.

'And you're not?'

'I bet she keeps your hands full.'

'Yes they do,' said Ryan smiling. Nobody laughed, but all of them couldn't help picturing Ryan holding Leila's breasts.

'So!' said Flora.

'Right!' said Joe.

'What are we waiting for?' said Flora and pulled a bag out of her pocket. She threw it to Dylan, who knocked it from one hand to the other before catching it properly. 'Chop, door-boy.' She paused, then, with music hall bawdiness, added, 'Or whatever Joe has you doing.'

'Flora!' said Ryan.

'You don't have to protect this one. He can handle it.'

Ryan looked at Dylan, who was smiling and nodding. 'I can handle her, I mean it.'

'See what I mean?' said Flora. 'You should have seen the act he put on at the front door.'

'What act?'

'It was nothing. Really,' said Dylan. Holding up the coke in one hand, he said, 'I don't know what you expect me to do with this. I could pretend, but I haven't a clue.'

'How sweet!' said Flora.

'I've seen it done in films. They use a credit card, but I don't even have one.'

'Okay! Don't overdo it.'

'Give it to me,' said Joe, and squeezed Dylan's neck affectionately.

Ryan noticed this. 'Have I missed something?'

Flora, suddenly realising that Ryan was unaware what was going on between Joe and Dylan said, 'I think you might have.'

She looked at Joe, who shrugged and pulled a smile that verged on self-satisfied.

'What have I walked into?' said Josie. 'The intrigue of it all. I feel like I'm in a scene from Dangerous Liaisons.'

'Will somebody tell me what's going on?' said Ryan.

Realising the need to cover for Dylan and Joe, Flora said, 'It's just some joke I made earlier.' She paused. 'It's not even funny.'

'Tell us again,' said Joe mischievously.

'I couldn't,' she said. Looking at Joe pointedly she added, 'It's far too tedious, Joe.' She placed extra emphasis on the word Joe, implying it was he that was tedious.

'Why do I feel like I'm the only one who doesn't know what's going on?' said Ryan.

'Welcome to life,' said Joe. 'I've had that feeling ever since I can remember.'

'I hear ya!' said Josie.

Within just a couple of minutes, Joe had five lines cut. He didn't wait on ceremony, but did his line first. 'Who's next?'

Everybody, apart from Dylan, was pretending not to notice the lines were cut. Joe handed Josie the straw he had used. She took it, bent, and did her line without saying a word. Josie then handed the straw to Flora, who thought to hand it to Ryan.

'Go on kid,' she said. 'It'll make a man of you.'

'It won't do that to me, will it?' said Josie.

'No, but it will put hair on your chest,' said Ryan.

'Josie with a hairy chest?' said Flora. 'Stop, you're giving me a hard-on.'

Ryan did his line and hesitantly offered the straw to Dylan.

'Do you want some?' said Joe.

'I don't know,' said Dylan.

'Joe will look after you,' said Flora. 'And if he doesn't, I will.'

Reassured by this, Dylan knelt on the floor beside the coke. He paused, then looked around at Joe, who simply watched. Dylan thought Joe looked warm. He felt he'd be safe. Joe would make sure of that. Dylan could think of nothing more incredible than going out with Joe, coming home with him, and falling asleep naked with him. Waking up next to him was almost too much to contemplate. At that moment, Dylan wanted Joe more than anything in the world. Joe nodded, smiling. Dylan leaned forward and snorted.

Flora started clapping. 'For a moment, I wondered if you'd back out.' Joe looked at her and shook his head. He didn't want her to tease Dylan. She changed her approach. 'It's not so bad, hey?'

Dylan smiled, quite proud of himself. 'Just one more line, please.

I'll do anything. I mean anything.'

'Good, we've got him hooked,' said Ryan. 'It won't be long now before he's on heroin. Then it's just slavery, paedophilia, and death.' He laughed with a dramatic evil voice.

'You're too good at that,' said Flora.

'I do take acting classes,' said Ryan.

'Oh yeah. I forgot. And that's how you know Dylan who we know, only too well, can act.'

✪

Six lines of coke, four vodkas, two speed-bombs, and half an Ecstasy later, they remembered they were meant to be going to Tragic. Once they did, it took them about three-quarters of an hour to get out the door. Luckily, a black cab was just across the road from the house.

'Are you waiting for somebody?' said Josie.

'No.'

'Your light was off,' said Joe as he got in. 'Is it broken?'

'No,' said the driver. 'I was just sorting out some stuff. Jump in.' This was the last thing the driver said during the journey. A couple of times Flora caught his eye in the rear-view mirror, but he looked away quickly. They joked, laughed, and talked rubbish all the way to Tragic. As usual, there were lots of people waiting in line, and, as usual, Joe charmed his way in.

30

Inside the club, they headed straight to the downstairs bar. They were already high enough to not mind the heat, the music, and people being too sweaty whilst too close. Shirtless men stared at them with eyes that seemed out of proportion with their faces. Josie ordered drinks. They all asked for alcohol, except Dylan. Chairs were collected and put around a table that had had an ashtray emptied out over it. Flora took off a shoe, and whilst keeping her bare foot on top of the other, scraped the cigarette butts onto the floor. None of them really cared whether the ashtray was there or not. In Tragic, caring about such things became redundant shortly after arriving. Within a few hours most melted off their chairs, their dignity mixing with the other filth on the floor. Few escaped Tragic's ability to do this. Actually, Josie managed to a certain extent. Sometimes she left looking as though she'd just arrived. This was due to choosing outfits that didn't crease, stain, lose their shape, or still looked stylish if they did. At least she always left looking dignified.

Although they sat in a conspicuous place, Paul pretended he hadn't seen them. He was hoping Josie would notice him, and call him over. He was nervous because he fancied Joe. The fact that he was famous didn't help. In the hope of catching Josie's eye Paul laughed loudly, and assuming he'd been heard, scanned the room. He thought he would have attracted her attention. He hadn't. Finally, swallowing his pride, he decided to walk past her, as though on his way to the toilet. The nearer he got to Joe, the more handsome he looked. Paul started to get nervous. Random images flashed through his mind. Joe at the gym, the grocery shop, and naked in the shower. Within the time it takes to move about two metres in Tragic when it's busy, Paul wondered many things about Joe. One thought seemed to surface more than any other. Fucking with Joe.

Ryan and Dylan both sat to Joe's right, in a separate little cluster. Paul wondered who they were. Joe appeared to be interested in them. Paul couldn't understand why. He thought them cute enough, but a bit young to be any fun in bed. One of them seemed to be making Josie laugh a lot. Maybe she was just being kind. When near enough to be heard, Paul said,

'Josie! You're here.'

'Paul! We've been here a while.' Josie gave him a hug. She never made kiss noises to the side of your face, squeezed you as though you might crack, or acted out affection. If she noticed you, and felt you worth acknowledging, she gave you her full attention. Paul always felt lucky that he was someone she liked. As she hugged him, he smelled her perfume. It was the same citrus-fresh smell she'd always worn. Even through the breath-soiled air of Tragic it was recognisable, familiar, and reassuring.

'Good to see you,' he said.

'Likewise,' she said. 'Paul, this is Joe. Joe, this is the man I told you about.'

Joe looked at Paul and said, 'Hey!' Paul didn't recognise the accompanying expression, but he trusted Josie, so wasn't too worried.

'Hey!' said Paul. He thought hey was a dumb thing for Joe to have said, and even more of a dumb response.

'This is Ryan and Dylan,' said Josie.

'That's not Ryan and Dylan,' said Ryan. 'It's Ryan, and Dylan.'

That's important, Paul thought, if you're straight. Neither of them looked gay. If they weren't, he wondered what their relationship was to Joe. He thought that they might be rent boys. Ryan looked like one. Dylan looked like he still lived at home, with a mum who loved him a little too much.

'Hey, Ryan,' said Paul. Then he turned in an exaggerated way and said, 'Hey, Dylan.' They all found this funny. Paul didn't know why he'd suddenly adopted the expression hey. He'd never used it before.

Josie watched Paul, to see how he responded to Joe. Paul didn't know what to make of him yet, he had little to go on.

'Hi,' said Flora.

'Yes, quite,' said Paul, grateful that he'd finally dropped hey. 'I'm sorry. There's so many of you to get through.' As soon as he'd said this, he felt awkward and quickly looked at Josie for reassurance, or at least a distraction.

'What have you taken?' said Josie, sensing his uneasiness.

'Ecstatic, or something. An old gypsy woman sold it to me. She said it would bring me luck.'

'Is that the same as get lucky?' said Flora.

'I hope so,' said Paul, and unintentionally caught Joe's eye. 'Sorry, that wasn't meant to be addressed to you, Joe. I just . . .' Words failed him suddenly.

'Maybe you should quit while you're ahead,' said Josie.

'You call this ahead? If I blamed it on the drugs, would I get away with it?'

'If you said you'd taken something really, really, really, really strong,' said Flora.

'Something that gives you thought-paralysis, and broken-mouth,' said Josie.

'Can I remind you that you're my friend, and you like me?' said Paul.

At this, Josie got hold of him, and sang as though petting a baby. 'My lovely damaged thing.' Then she sat him down in her chair and sat on his knee. 'So talk, you two,' she said to Paul, and Joe, who now sat side by side. 'No pressure.' She paused. 'In your own time.' She paused again. 'Whenever you're ready.' Then she sat looking at them both, arms folded, waiting.

'Your name's Snow?' said Paul, improvising. 'What's your favourite colour, and what's your birth sign?'

'Funny you should say that. My nickname at school was Snowy Joey.' He paused. 'Yellow. And Aquarius.'

'Yellow's mine, too,' said Paul.

'That's 'cos it's the best.'

'I know that,' said Paul. 'What's your blah, blah, blah.' He turned to Josie. 'Look, Mum, we're talking.' Then he pretended he'd been telling a joke, and said, 'That's how I came to have three ears and live in a giant shoe.'

'You ninny,' said Flora.

'Talk properly,' said Josie.

Joe and Paul both pretended to talk, Joe making senseless sentences, and Paul making up words.

'Okay!' said Josie. 'Do it your own way.' At this she swivelled on Paul's knees, and faced away from them. Slowly she looked back, pretending she was doing it secretly.

'You're peeping,' said Paul.

'I'm just keeping my little eye on you,' she said.

'That's my favourite one,' said Joe.

'I like the one on her elbow,' said Flora.

'Can I just say?' said Ryan. 'Is it my imagination, or are we not fucked-up enough?'

'He does have a point,' said Flora. Joe covered his face with his hands. Ryan laughed. He was the only one who got the joke. 'What's the plan?'

'Well, I have to pick up the kids tomorrow,' said Josie. 'So I can't stay up late.'

'You have kids?' said Dylan.

'Yeah, the goat kind,' said Flora.

Dylan wasn't keeping up with the conversation. He wasn't used to being high, and felt quite confused. Flora had given him half an E, partly for the fun of seeing what happened. Dylan said he felt great, strange, and horny. He gave a running commentary. The music was so loud, and his voice so quiet, he had to speak very close to everyone's ears. Paul thought it tickled, and consciously tried to do the same thing back. He could feel Dylan's hair brush against his face, could smell his skin, and feel his body heat against his own lips. Beyond this, Dylan didn't intentionally give anything more, but directed most things he said to Joe. At one point Joe turned to say something in response to Dylan and they bumped noses. They hovered, side to side, each trying to reach an ear to speak into. This ignited something in Dylan, and his face lunged forward. It didn't look like a particularly conscious decision, but they kissed. It attracted the attention of the whole group. Paul glanced around to see everybody's responses. Ryan looked shocked. Flora smiled, presumably finding it cute, possibly even sexy. Josie was looking back at Paul. She was trying to read what he was thinking. Generally, she found this quite easy. At this moment, she thought Paul was upset seeing Joe and Dylan kiss. In actuality, Paul felt contempt for Joe, thinking he was showing off, and jealousy for Dylan. Josie noticed he was feeling something unpleasant, so took hold of his hand and, close to his ear, said,

'Come to the toilet. Let's sort you out.' To Flora, she said, 'I'll just be a minute.' This meant half an hour, or more.

They stood, and made a believable exit, making it look as though it had nothing to do with Dylan and Joe kissing. Josie held Paul's hand all the way upstairs. Near the top, where the music wasn't so loud, Paul said, 'They should rename this place, Homo-genise.'

'Or Happ-E.'

'Or Trend, or just Shit!'

'Bitter?'

'Maybe,' said Paul as they walked into the toilets, which were surprisingly empty.

'Maybe, you're just too good for him,' said Josie, noticing a cubicle door beginning to open.

'Nice try, but a bit corny,' said Paul. Josie took hold of his hand and led him to the opening door. 'He seems okay, but what's with the fluff on his arm?' The person next in line assumed they must have been waiting, and didn't say anything as they went in front.

'Who, Dylan?' Josie wiped the seat with some toilet paper. 'I don't know the story there.' She handed Paul a wrap. 'Let's do a big line and see what we can do about the situation.' Josie had a wicked look in her eye. Paul noticed, and chopped two lines. 'What are you saving that for? My great-grandmother would turn her nose up at those.' He pushed more of the coke into the lines. Josie looked at him as though he'd done something wrong. 'All of it!'

'But we'll be flying.'

'Better than walking.'

'Sorry! We want flying don't we?'

'Go for it.'

Paul emptied the wrap, split the powder in two and said, 'I wish I'd brought my extra nostrils.'

'Lightweight,' said Josie.

'They're not even lines any more.'

'Um. Good.'

'At least let me do them in parts.'

'However you want, but you're not leaving here till you do them.' Paul bent over and did about a quarter of his pile up the one nostril and another quarter up the other. His nose was clear, so it landed somewhere between his sinuses and his throat. It made him cough. Luckily, Josie had brought her drink, so Paul took a swig to clear his throat. 'Have I not taught you anything over the years?'

'Probably lots.'

'Obviously nothing important. You can't even do your drugs properly.'

'Sorry Mum.' Josie bent forward. There was nothing left of her line when she came up. 'Impressive!'

'Some people are good with children. Some travel the world doing charity work. I do a mean line of Charlie. It takes all sorts.' Paul looked at the coke again, and thought twice about doing any more. He shuddered, bent, and snorted. Luckily, his nose had begun to block, so this time the coke settled in mucus. He stood up and rubbed his nose to massage it in. 'That's my boy! Out of here.'

'Let me pee first,' said Paul.

After a few minutes of standing with his dick out, talking, Josie said, 'Shall we call it a day?'

'Sounds good to me,' said Paul.

'So the plan is, I'll take Dylan to dance and you work on Joe.'

'Okay!'

On the way back to their seats, they saw arms stabbing the air, and faces on spin-cycle which looked as if they were asking questions, to which the answers usually were, 'You're at Tragic. You're drug-fucked as hell. And you look like shit.' The room at the foot of the stairs looked as if it were full of livestock. There were countless men, heavy with muscles, who, as if aware of their impending slaughter, were agitated, restless, and fretting. It reminded Paul of the gay beach in Miami, where everyone tries and succeeds in being an ideal, and in doing so, becomes both ridiculous and grotesque. For seconds, Paul wondered what these sweaty-Tragic-things were insulating themselves from with so many muscles and drugs. He guessed it might be the only thing he would find attractive about them.

Joe and the others hadn't moved, but the crowd had mutated. Branches went off in different directions, as people tagged on. Josie took hold of Flora's hand, and Dylan's, and without explaining led them off. Immediately, Paul grabbed Dylan's seat, next to Joe.

Paul didn't know where to begin, but was coke-confident enough not to care. Usually this worked fine. He generally found that if he showed enough confidence, most men gave in easily to what he wanted.

'I bring my kids here, too,' he said, referring to Dylan being led away bewildered.

'Really,' said Joe, uninterested.

'How would you like a big dick up your arse?' said Paul.

'It's charming of you to ask, but . . .'

'Sorry, did I get it wrong? A nice arse around your dick?'

'I like the concept.'

'Excellent.'

'But, I was thinking of it being someone else's.'

'How about that someone else, and me in the middle?'

'That's very generous of you, but I prefer one on one.'

'So ditch the kid.'

'Although I find your approach charming, I'm with somebody.'

'Sorry, I wasn't sure.'

'I'm going to get a drink. Do you want one?'

'Yeah. A vodka-Red Bull, large.' Joe got up. 'You don't know what you're missing.'

'So, a large vodka-Red Bull.'

Joe went off into the crowd, leaving Paul feeling annoyed. If it hadn't been for the coke, he would have felt rejected instead.

Josie had been watching and was quickly by Paul's side. 'No go?' she said.

'I think he's smitten with the kid.'

'Possibly.'

'Another time,' said Paul.

'How do you feel?'

'Coked-up to fuck.'

'Me too.'

Paul looked around the room and said, 'I feel like getting really, really cunted.'

'Sounds marvellous.'

'Do you know what I fancy?'

'Go on, surprise me.'

'Acid.'

'God!' said Josie. 'I haven't done acid for years.'

'That doesn't sound like a no.'

'You know me and drugs.'

'I know you both quite well, especially when you're together.'

'Do you want me to get?'

'Let's both go.'

At this they wandered off in search of acid. They found a dealer under the stairs. It was somebody who hoped to get Paul into bed, so although he'd only been asked for two, he gave them a small plastic bagful.

'Don't forget,' said the dealer. 'Later, if you think you're losing it, just give me a shout. I'll look after you. And I mean real good.' With this he gave Paul a wink, a kiss on the lips, and quickly returned to the growing queue of people waiting to get served.

On the way back to where they'd been sitting, they bumped into Ryan. They asked him if he liked acid. On seeing his enthusiastic response, they gave him two tabs. Acid was Ryan's favourite drug, and unlike Josie and Paul, who felt it was more fun when done a quarter of a tab at a time, Ryan didn't think twice about taking the whole tab in one go. Later, when it didn't seem to be working, he assumed it was very weak, and took the other. Like generations of clubbers before him, this was when the first one started to work, and it was strong. Realising what he'd done, he thought it wise to get home before the second kicked in. With some difficulty, he found Joe, told him what had happened, excused himself, swore he'd be fine, and said goodbye. It was all a bit arduous, so he was quite glad to have to leave. Joe and Dylan walked him to the door. Luckily, there was a black cab just sitting outside.

31

'Where to mate?'

'Hampstead please.'

'Right it is . . .Off we go.'

'Home to your missus, now you've had your fun.'

'No, not tonight.'

'I get you mate.'

Ryan wondered what it was the driver understood by what he'd said, and thought he seemed familiar.

'Good club?' said the driver.

'Yeah.'

'Interesting crowd.'

'What do you mean?' said Ryan.

'Lot of gays.'

Ryan thought this a funny thing to say, and laughed, 'Quite a lot.'

'Are you that way?'

'No.'

'Why'd you go to that club then?'

'My mates do.'

'Don't get me wrong. I've nuffing against them.'

'Me neither.'

'As long as they don't touch the kiddies, they can do what they want.'

Ryan felt as if he'd gone back in time. He didn't realise anybody really talked liked this. It suddenly clicked why this man seemed so familiar.

'You've picked me up before.'

'Don't fink so mate.'

'You did. It was from here. I was with a girl who smelt of sick.'

'No mate. I'd 'av remembered. I've a photogenic memory.'

Photographic thought Ryan, as a knee-jerk response. Then he noticed the driver looking at him in his rear-view, but assumed he was probably trying to see if he recognised him. This thought didn't last long. He was distracted by scenery outside the window. The air looked green, and the buildings had very crisp edges, yet seemed to glow also. He hadn't noticed before how beautiful the architecture was in London. The streets were empty, so the cab sped through them. Occasionally, traffic lights made them stop. This gave Ryan more of a chance to take in his surroundings. It was only whilst stationary that he could tell how much he was tripping. When moving, his brain was so busy trying to register everything that passed that it was occupied, and distracted.

'This is my last fare,' said the driver.

'How come you were outside Tragic?'

'Just dropped someone off. You were lucky.'

'I know, those mini cabs really rip you off.'

'Yeah, you're better off in a black cab.'

Nothing was said for a few seconds. Then Ryan said, 'Fuck!'

'What was that mate?'

Ryan hadn't realised he'd spoken. He thought he was just acknowledging a wave of acid as it affected him. It came on suddenly, and unexpectedly, confusing him. He was only just able to manage a response, 'Nothing.'

The driver, talking into his rear-view, said, 'Are you all right mate?'

Again, Ryan managed to muster, 'Sweet!' By now, his eyes rolled, and his lids flickered, half-shut. He leaned his head against the window.

'You should get to bed mate,' said the driver. 'Have you anyone at home to look after you?'

'No, but I'm cool.'

'You sure?'

'Yep!' Ryan was getting really sick of talking, and hoped the driver would stop.

He closed his eyes and started to trip. He could see the driver talking, could actually see the words. They came out as threatening, and dangerous. Leila fought him. Killed him, chopping off his head. They were in bed, feeling love. David was there too, and Joe with Dylan. David started crying. Joe didn't love him anymore. It was Ryan's job to deal with this, to love him instead. Leila was David. David was Leila, now both just one person. Sexual. Passionate. Loving. Breasts turned into arse cheeks, their dicks into syringes. Dylan also became a part of them. He merged with David and Leila. Ryan loved them, physically and mentally.

'Here we are mate,' said the driver.

Ryan opened his eyes. They were right outside the house.

'Shit!' He came to, a little more. 'That was quick.'

'You must have slept.'

'I don't even remember giving you the address.'

'You did mate, outside the club. Before you got in the cab.'

'I must be wasted.'

Ryan read the meter and tried to get his money out. He managed it eventually, and clumsily got out.

'Do you need any help, mate?'

'Don't think so,' said Ryan, leaning on the cab for balance.

'You okay getting to the house?'

'I'm sweet.' He stepped away from the cab, and concentrated on walking. The driver watched him stumble towards the front door. Again Ryan fumbled in his pockets. After going through each one in succession twice, he found it in the pocket he always kept it in, but wondered why he'd moved it. With some difficulty, he got the key in the door, the right way up, turned it, and fell in as it opened. He picked himself up clumsily, leaning against the walls for support. As he closed the door, he noticed that the cab hadn't left yet. What he found strange was that the driver wasn't in it. If Ryan wasn't so high, he might have taken a moment to look around, but he was distracted; thinking he was going to be sick. He headed straight up to the bathroom, wasn't sick, so stumbled into bed. Guessing that he wouldn't sleep, he took two Rohypnol from a sheet Joe had given him. He lay on his bed, without undressing. After ten minutes, but thinking it had been much longer, he took another Rohypnol. He was normally good at navigating his trips, but he'd had too much coke and speed, so his thoughts raced, going with one negative idea, then being replaced, or added to by another.

As the Rohypnol started to take effect, he began to relax, his tripping getting dreamy. He decided to get into bed properly, so started to take off his clothes, but because he was still lying down, he only managed to get his jeans half way down, with boxers in tow, then gave up. Naked from his waist to his knees, he lay, barely awake. He heard a noise downstairs. Maybe the others were home. But, why breaking glass? For a moment he was confused, then forgot what he was thinking. There was nothing to worry about. He was in his bed, warm, comfortable, and safe.